sense, this ... ... as in the hands they have often
been taken out and held to reanimal Shakespeare's own

NON SANZ DROICT.

William Shakespeare

The Tragedy of
MACBETH

Edited by Sylvan Barnet

The Signet Classic Shakespeare
GENERAL EDITOR: SYLVAN BARNET

Revised and Updated
Bibliography

Ⓒ

A SIGNET CLASSIC
NEW AMERICAN LIBRARY

TIMES MIRROR
New York and Scarborough, Ontario

SIGNET, SIGNET CLASSICS, MENTOR, PLUME, MERIDIAN AND NAL
BOOKS are published *in the United States* by
The New American Library, Inc.,
1633 Broadway, New York, New York 10019,
in Canada by The New American Library of Canada Limited
81 Mack Avenue, Scarborough Ontario M1I 1M8

· · 22 23 24 25 26 27

PRINTED IN THE UNITED STATES OF AMERICA

Contents

Shakespeare: Prefatory Remarks   *vii*

Introduction   *xxii*

The Tragedy of Macbeth   37

Textual Note   132

The Source of *Macbeth*   136

  Selections from Raphael Holinshed: *Chronicles of England, Scotland, and Ireland*   137

Commentaries

  Samuel Johnson: *Macbeth*   156

  A. C. Bradley: From *Shakespearean Tragedy*   166

  Elmer Edgar Stoll: Source and Motive in *Macbeth* and *Othello*   183

  Cleanth Brooks: The Naked Babe and the Cloak of Manliness   196

  Oscar James Campbell: From "Shakespeare and the 'New' Critics"   222

  Mary McCarthy: General Macbeth   229

Suggested References   241

Shakespeare: Prefatory Remarks

Between the record of his baptism in Stratford on 26 April 1564 and the record of his burial in Stratford on 25 April 1616, some forty documents name Shakespeare, and many others name his parents, his children, and his grandchildren. More facts are known about William Shakespeare than about any other playwright of the period except Ben Jonson. The facts should, however, be distinguished from the legends. The latter, inevitably more engaging and better known, tell us that the Stratford boy killed a calf in high style, poached deer and rabbits, and was forced to flee to London, where he held horses outside a playhouse. These traditions are only traditions; they may be true, but no evidence supports them, and it is well to stick to the facts.

Mary Arden, the dramatist's mother, was the daughter of a substantial landowner; about 1557 she married John Shakespeare, who was a glove-maker and trader in various farm commodities. In 1557 John Shakespeare was a member of the Council (the governing body of Stratford), in 1558 a constable of the borough, in 1561 one of the two town chamberlains, in 1565 an alderman (entitling him to the appellation "Mr."), in 1568 high bailiff—the town's highest political office, equivalent to mayor. After 1577, for an unknown reason he drops out of local politics. The birthday of William Shakespeare, the eldest son of this locally prominent man, is unrecorded; but the Stratford parish register records that the infant was baptized on 26 April 1564. (It is quite possible that he was born on 23 April, but this date has probably been assigned by tradition because it is the date on which, fifty-two years later, he died.) The attendance records of the Stratford grammar school of the period are not extant, but it is reasonable to assume that the son of a local official attended the school and received substantial training in Latin. The masters of the school from Shakespeare's seventh to fifteenth years held Oxford degrees; the Elizabethan curriculum excluded mathematics and the natural sciences but taught a good deal of Latin rhetoric, logic, and literature. On 27 November 1582 a marriage license was issued to Shakespeare and Anne Hathaway, eight years his senior. The couple had a child in May, 1583. Perhaps the marriage was necessary, but perhaps the couple had earlier engaged in a formal "troth plight" which would render their children legitimate even if no further ceremony were performed. In 1585 Anne Hathaway bore Shakespeare twins.

That Shakespeare was born is excellent; that he married and had children is pleasant; but that we know nothing about his departure from Stratford to London, or about the beginning of his theatrical career, is lamentable and must be admitted. We would gladly sacrifice details about his children's baptism for details about his earliest days on the stage. Perhaps the poaching episode is true (but it is first reported almost a century after Shakespeare's death), or perhaps he first left Stratford to be a schoolteacher, as another tradition holds; perhaps he was moved by

Such wind as scatters young men through the world,
To seek their fortunes further than at home
Where small experience grows.

In 1592, thanks to the cantankerousness of Robert Greene, a rival playwright and a pamphleteer, we have our first reference, a snarling one, to Shakespeare as an actor and playwright. Greene warns those of his own educated friends who wrote for the theater against an actor who has presumed to turn playwright:

There is an upstart crow, beautified with our feath-
ers, that with his *tiger's heart wrapped in a player's
hide* supposes he is as well able to bombast out a
blank verse as the best of you, and being an absolute
Johannes-factotum is in his own conceit the only
Shake-scene in a country.

The reference to the player, as well as the allusion to
Aesop's crow (who strutted in borrowed plumage, as an
actor struts in fine words not his own), makes it clear
that by this date Shakespeare had both acted and written. That Shakespeare is meant is indicated not only by
"Shake-scene" but by the parody of a line from one of
Shakespeare's plays, *3 Henry VI*: "O, tiger's heart
wrapped in a woman's hide." If Shakespeare in 1592
was prominent enough to be attacked by an envious
dramatist, he probably had served an apprenticeship in
the theater for at least a few years.

In any case, by 1592 Shakespeare had acted and
written, and there are a number of subsequent references to him as an actor: documents indicate that in
1598 he is a "principal comedian," in 1603 a "principal
tragedian," in 1608 he is one of the "men players." The
profession of actor was not for a gentleman, and it occasionally drew the scorn of university men who re-
sented writing speeches for persons less educated than
themselves, but it was respectable enough: players, if
prosperous, were in effect members of the bourgeoisie,
and there is nothing to suggest that Stratford considered
William Shakespeare less than a solid citizen. When, in
1596, the Shakespeares were granted a coat of arms,
the grant was made to Shakespeare's father, but probably
William Shakespeare (who the next year bought the
second-largest house in town) had arranged the matter
on his own behalf. In subsequent transactions he is occasionally styled a gentleman.

Although in 1593 and 1594 Shakespeare published
two narrative poems dedicated to the Earl of Southampton,
Venus and Adonis and *The Rape of Lucrece,* and may
well have written most or all of his sonnets in the mid-

dle nineties, Shakespeare's literary activity seems to have
been almost entirely devoted to the theater. (It may be
significant that the two narrative poems were written
in years when the plague closed the theaters for several
months.) In 1594 he was a charter member of a theatrical company called the Chamberlain's Men (which in
1603 changed its name to the King's Men); until he re-
tired to Stratford (about 1611, apparently), he was with
this remarkably stable company. From 1599 the company acted primarily at the Globe Theatre, in which
Shakespeare held a one-tenth interest. Other Elizabethan
dramatists are known to have acted, but no other is
known also to have been entitled to a share in the
profits of the playhouse.

   Shakespeare's first eight published plays did not have
his name on them, but this is not remarkable; the most
popular play of the sixteenth century, Thomas Kyd's *The
Spanish Tragedy,* went through many editions without
naming Kyd, and Kyd's authorship is known only because
a book on the profession of acting happens to quote
(and attribute to Kyd) some lines on the interest of
Roman emperors in the drama. What is remarkable is
that after 1598 Shakespeare's name commonly appears
on printed plays—some of which are not his. Another
indication of his popularity comes from Francis Meres,
author of *Palladis. Tamia: Wit's Treasury* (1598): in
this anthology of snippets accompanied by an essay on
literature, many playwrights are mentioned, but Shakespeare's name occurs more often than any other, and
Shakespeare is the only playwright whose plays are listed.

   From his acting, playwriting, and share in a theater,
Shakespeare seems to have made considerable money.
He put it to work, making substantial investments in
Stratford real estate. When he made his will (less than a
month before he died), he sought to leave his property
intact to his descendants. Of small bequests to relatives
and to friends (including three actors, Richard Burbage,
John Heminges, and Henry Condell), that to his wife of
the second-best bed has provoked the most comment;
perhaps it was the bed the couple had slept in, the best

being reserved for visitors. In any case, had Shakespeare not excepted it, the bed would have gone (with the rest of his household possessions) to his daughter and her husband. On 25 April 1616 he was buried within the chancel of the church at Stratford. An unattractive monument to his memory, placed on a wall near the grave, says he died on 23 April. Over the grave itself are the lines, perhaps by Shakespeare, that (more than his literary fame) have kept his bones undisturbed in the crowded burial ground where old bones were often dislodged to make way for new:

> Good friend, for Jesus' sake forbear
> To dig the dust enclosèd here.
> Blessed be the man that spares these stones
> And cursed be he that moves my bones.

Thirty-seven plays, as well as some nondramatic poems, are held to constitute the Shakespeare canon. The dates of composition of most of the works are highly uncertain, but there is often evidence of a *terminus a quo* (starting point) and/or a *terminus ad quem* (terminal point) that provides a framework for intelligent guessing. For example, *Richard II* cannot be earlier than 1595, the publication date of some material to which it is indebted; *The Merchant of Venice* cannot be later than 1598, the year Francis Meres mentioned it. Sometimes arguments for a date hang on an alleged topical allusion, such as the lines about the unseasonable weather in *A Midsummer Night's Dream*, II.i.81-117, but such an allusion (if indeed it is an illusion) can be variously interpreted, and in any case there is always the possibility that a topical allusion was inserted during a revision, years after the composition of a play. Dates are often attributed on the basis of style, and although conjectures about style usually rest on other conjectures, sooner or later one must rely on one's literary sense. There is no real proof, for example, that *Othello* is not as early as *Romeo and Juliet*, but one feels *Othello* is later, and because the first record of its performance is 1604, one is glad enough to set its composi-

tion at that date and not push it back into Shakespeare's
early years. The following chronology, then, is as much
indebted to informed guesswork and sensitivity as it is
to fact. The dates, necessarily imprecise, indicate something like a scholarly consensus.

PLAYS

1588–93	*The Comedy of Errors*
1588–94	*Love's Labor's Lost*
1590–91	*2 Henry VI*
1590–91	*3 Henry VI*
1591–92	*1 Henry VI*
1592–93	*Richard III*
1592–94	*Titus Andronicus*
1593–94	*The Taming of the Shrew*
1593–95	*The Two Gentlemen of Verona*
1594–96	*Romeo and Juliet*
1595	*Richard II*
1594–96	*A Midsummer Night's Dream*
1596–97	*King John*
1596–97	*The Merchant of Venice*
1597	*1 Henry IV*
1597–98	*2 Henry IV*
1598–1600	*Much Ado About Nothing*
1598–99	*Henry V*
1599	*Julius Caesar*
1599–1600	*As You Like It*
1599–1600	*Twelfth Night*
1600–01	*Hamlet*
1597–1601	*The Merry Wives of Windsor*
1601–02	*Troilus and Cressida*
1602–04	*All's Well That Ends Well*
1603–04	*Othello*
1604	*Measure for Measure*
1605–06	*King Lear*
1605–06	*Macbeth*
1606–07	*Antony and Cleopatra*
1605–08	*Timon of Athens*
1607–09	*Coriolanus*

1608-09	*Pericles*
1609-10	*Cymbeline*
1610-11	*The Winter's Tale*
1611	*The Tempest*
1612-13	*Henry VIII*

POEMS

1592	*Venus and Adonis*
1593-94	*The Rape of Lucrece*
1593-1600	*Sonnets*
1600-01	*The Phoenix and the Turtle* ·

Shakespeare's Theater

In Shakespeare's infancy, Elizabethan actors performed wherever they could—in great halls, at court, in the courtyards of inns. The innyards must have made rather unsatisfactory theaters: on some days they were unavailable because carters bringing goods to London used them as depots; when available, they had to be rented from the innkeeper; perhaps most important, London inns were subject to the Common Council of London, which was not well disposed toward theatricals. In 1574 the Common Council required that plays and playing places in London be licensed. It asserted that

> sundry great disorders and inconveniences have been found to ensue to this city by the inordinate haunting of great multitudes of people, specially youth, to plays, interludes, and shows, namely occasion of frays and quarrels, evil practices of incontinency in great inns having chambers and secret places adjoining to their open stages and galleries,

and ordered that innkeepers who wished licenses to hold performances put up a bond and make contributions to the poor.

The requirement that plays and innyard theaters be licensed, along with the other drawbacks of playing at inns, probably drove James Burbage (a carpenter-turned-actor) to rent in 1576 a plot of land northeast of the city walls and to build here—on property outside the jurisdiction of the city—England's first permanent construction designed for plays. He called it simply the Theatre. About all that is known of its construction is that it was wood. It soon had imitators, the most famous being the Globe (1599), built across the Thames (again outside the city's jurisdiction), out of timbers of the Theatre, which had been dismantled when Burbage's lease ran out.

There are three important sources of information about the structure of Elizabethan playhouses—drawings, a contract, and stage directions in plays. Of drawings, only the so-called De Witt drawing (c. 1596) of the Swan—really a friend's copy of De Witt's drawing—is of much significance. It shows a building of three tiers, with a stage jutting from a wall into the yard or center of the building. The tiers are roofed, and part of the stage is covered by a roof that projects from the rear and is supported at its front on two posts, but the groundlings, who paid a penny to stand in front of the stage, were exposed to the sky. (Performances in such a playhouse were held only in the daytime; artificial illumination was not used.) At the rear of the stage are two doors; above the stage is a gallery. The second major source of information, the contract for the Fortune, specifies that although the Globe is to be the model, the Fortune is to be square, eighty feet outside and fifty-five inside. The stage is to be forty-three feet broad, and is to extend into the middle of the yard (i.e., it is twenty-seven and a half feet deep). For patrons willing to pay more than the general admission charged of the groundlings, there were to be three galleries provided with seats. From the third chief source, stage directions, one learns that entrance to the stage was by doors, presumably spaced widely apart at the rear ("Enter one citizen at one door, and another at the other"), and that in addition to the platform stage there was occasionally some sort of curtained booth or alcove allowing for "discovery" scenes, and some sort of playing space "aloft" or "above" to represent (for example) the top of a city's walls or a room above the street. Doubtless each theater had its own peculiarities, but perhaps we can talk about a "typical" Elizabethan theater if we realize that no theater need exactly have fit the description, just as no father is the typical father with 3.7 children. This hypothetical theater is wooden, round or polygonal (in *Henry V* Shakespeare calls it a "wooden *O*"), capable of holding some eight hundred spectators standing in the yard around the projecting elevated stage and some fifteen hundred additional spectators seated in the three roofed galleries. The stage, protected by a "shadow" or "heavens" or roof, is entered by two doors; behind the doors is the "tiring house" (attiring house, i.e., dressing room), and above the doors is some sort of gallery that may sometimes hold spectators but that can be used (for example) as the bedroom from which Romeo—according to a stage direction in one text—"goeth down." Some evidence suggests that a throne can be lowered onto the platform stage, perhaps from the "shadow"; certainly characters can descend from the stage through a trap or traps into the cellar or "hell." Sometimes this space beneath the platform accommodates a sound-effects man or musician (in *Antony and Cleopatra* "music of the hautboys is under the stage") or an actor (in *Hamlet* the "Ghost cries under the stage"). Most characters simply walk on and off, but because there is no curtain in front of the platform, corpses will have to be carried off (Hamlet must lug Polonius' guts into the neighbor room), or will have to fall at the rear, where the curtain on the alcove or booth can be drawn to conceal them.

Such may have been the so-called "public theater." Another kind of theater, called the "private theater" because its much greater admission charge limited its audience to the wealthy or the prodigal, must be briefly mentioned. The private theater was basically a large room, entirely roofed and therefore artificially illuminated, with a stage at one end. In 1576 one such theater was established in Blackfriars, a Dominican priory in London that had been suppressed in 1538 and confiscated by the Crown and thus was not under the city's jurisdiction. All the actors in the Blackfriars theater were boys about eight to thirteen years old (in the public theaters similar boys played female parts; a boy Lady Macbeth played to a man Macbeth). This private theater had a precarious existence, and ceased operations in 1584. In 1596 James Burbage, who had already made theatrical history by building the Theater, began to construct a second Blackfriars theater. He died in 1597, and for several years this second Blackfriars theater was used by a troupe of boys, but in 1608 two of Burbage's sons and five other actors (including Shakespeare) became joint operators of the theater, using it in the winter when the open-air Globe was unsuitable. Perhaps such a smaller theater, roofed, artificially illuminated, and with a tradition of a courtly audience, exerted an influence on Shakespeare's late plays.

Performances in the private theaters may well have had intermissions during which music was played, but in the public theaters the action was probably uninterrupted, flowing from scene to scene almost without a break. Actors would enter, speak, exit, and others would immediately enter and establish (if necessary) the new locale by a few properties and by words and gestures. Here are some samples of Shakespeare's scene painting:

> This is Illyria, lady.

> Well, this is the Forest of Arden.

> This castle hath a pleasant seat; the air
> Nimbly and sweetly recommends itself
> Unto our gentle senses.

On the other hand, it is a mistake to conceive of the Elizabethan stage as bare. Although Shakespeare's

Chorus in *Henry V* calls the stage an "unworthy scaffold" and urges the spectators to "eke out our performance with your mind," there was considerable spectacle. The last act of *Macbeth,* for example, has five stage directions calling for "drum and colors," and another sort of appeal to the eye is indicated by the stage direction "Enter Macduff, with Macbeth's head." Some scenery and properties may have been substantial; doubtless a throne was used, and in one play of the period we encounter this direction: "Hector takes up a great piece of rock and casts at Ajax, who tears up a young tree by the roots and assails Hector." The matter is of some importance, and will be glanced at again in the next section.

The Texts of Shakespeare

Though eighteen of his plays were published during his lifetime, Shakespeare seems never to have supervised their publication. There is nothing unusual here, when a playwright sold a play to a theatrical company he surrendered his ownership of it. Normally a company would not publish the play, because to publish it meant to allow competitors to acquire the piece. Some plays, however, did get published: apparently treacherous actors sometimes pieced together a play for a publisher, sometimes a company in need of money sold a play, and sometimes a company allowed a play to be published that no longer drew audiences. That Shakespeare did not concern himself with publication, then, is scarcely remarkable; of his contemporaries only Ben Jonson carefully supervised the publication of his own plays. In 1623, seven years after Shakespeare's death, John Heminges and Henry Condell (two senior members of Shakespeare's company, who had performed with him for about twenty years) collected his plays—published and unpublished —into a large volume, commonly called the First Folio. (A folio is a volume consisting of sheets that have been folded once, each sheet thus making two leaves, or four pages. The eighteen plays published during Shakespeare's lifetime had been issued one play per volume in small books called quartos. Each sheet in a quarto has been folded twice, making four leaves, or eight pages.) The First Folio contains thirty-six plays; a thirty-seventh, *Pericles*, though not in the Folio is regarded as canonical. Heminges and Condell suggest in an address "To the great variety of readers" that the republished plays are presented in better form than in the quartos: "Before you were abused with diverse stolen and surreptitious copies, maimed and deformed by the frauds and stealths of injurious impostors that exposed them; even those, are now offered to your view cured and perfect of their limbs, and all the rest absolute in their numbers, as he [i.e., Shakespeare] conceived them."

Whoever was assigned to prepare the texts for publication in the First Folio seems to have taken his job seriously and yet not to have performed it with uniform care. The sources of the texts seem to have been, in general, good unpublished copies or the best published copies. The first play in the collection, *The Tempest*, is divided into acts and scenes, has unusually full stage directions and descriptions of spectacle, and concludes with a list of the characters, but the editor was not able (or willing) to present all of the succeeding texts so fully dressed. Later texts occasionally show signs of carelessness: in one scene of *Much Ado About Nothing* the names of actors, instead of characters, appear as speech prefixes, as they had in the quarto, which the Folio reprints; proofreading throughout the Folio is spotty and apparently was done without reference to the printer's copy; the pagination of *Hamlet* jumps from 156 to 257.

A modern editor of Shakespeare must first select his copy; no problem if the play exists only in the Folio, but a considerable problem if the relationship between a quarto and the Folio—or an early quarto and a later one—is unclear. When an editor has chosen what seems to him to be the most authoritative text or texts for his copy, he has not done with making decisions. First of all,

he must reckon with Elizabethan spelling. If he is not
producing a facsimile, he probably modernizes it, but
ought he to preserve the old form of words that apparently were pronounced quite unlike their modern
forms—"lanthorn," "alablaster"? If he preserves these
forms, is he really preserving Shakespeare's forms or perhaps those of a compositor in the printing house? What is
one to do when one finds "lanthorn" and "lantern" in adjacent lines? (The editors of this series in general, but not
invariably, assume that words should be spelled in their
modern form.) Elizabethan punctuation, too, presents
problems. For example in the First Folio, the only text for
the play, Macbeth rejects his wife's idea that he can wash
the blood from his hand:

> no: this my Hand will rather
> The multitudinous Seas incarnardine,
> Making the Greene one, Red.

Obviously an editor will remove the superfluous capitals,
and he will probably alter the spelling to "incarnadine,"
but will he leave the comma before "red," letting Macbeth speak of the sea as "the green one," or will he (like
most modern editors) remove the comma and thus have
Macbeth say that his hand will make the ocean *uni-
formly* red?

An editor will sometimes have to change more than
spelling or punctuation. Macbeth says to his wife:

> I dare do all that may become a man,
> Who dares no more, is none.

For two centuries editors have agreed that the second
line is unsatisfactory, and have emended "no" to "do":
"Who dares do more is none." But when in the same
play Ross says that fearful persons

> floate vpon a wilde and violent Sea
> Each way, and moue,

need "move" be emended to "none," as it often is, on the hunch that the compositor misread the manuscript? The editors of the Signet Classic Shakespeare have restrained themselves from making abundant emendations. In their minds they hear Dr. Johnson on the dangers of emending: "I have adopted the Roman sentiment, that it is more honorable to save a citizen than to kill an enemy." Some departures (in addition to spelling, punctuation, and lineation) from the copy text have of course been made, but the original readings are listed in a note following the play, so that the reader can evaluate them for himself.

The editors of the Signet Classic Shakespeare, following tradition, have added line numbers and in many cases act and scene divisions as well as indications of locale at the beginning of scenes. The Folio divided most of the plays into acts and some into scenes. Early eighteenth-century editors increased the divisions. These divisions, which provide a convenient way of referring to passages in the plays, have been retained, but when not in the text chosen as the basis for the Signet Classic text they are enclosed in square brackets [ ] to indicate that they are editorial additions. Similarly, although no play of Shakespeare's published during his lifetime was equipped with indications of locale at the heads of scene divisions, locales have here been added in square brackets for the convenience of the reader, who lacks the information afforded to spectators by costumes, properties, and gestures. The spectator can tell at a glance he is in the throne room, but without an editorial indication the reader may be puzzled for a while. It should be mentioned, incidentally, that there are a few authentic stage directions—perhaps Shakespeare's, perhaps a prompter's—that suggest locales: for example, "Enter Brutus in his orchard," and "They go up into the Senate house." It is hoped that the bracketed additions provide the reader with the sort of help provided in these two authentic directions, but it is equally hoped that the reader will remember that the stage was not loaded with scenery.

No editor during the course of his work can fail to recollect some words Heminges and Condell prefixed to the Folio:

> It had been a thing, we confess, worthy to have been wished, that the author himself had lived to have set forth and overseen his own writings. But since it hath been ordained otherwise, and he by death departed from that right, we pray you do not envy his friends the office of their care and pain to have collected and published them.

Nor can an editor, after he has done his best, forget Heminges and Condell's final words: "And so we leave you to other of his friends, whom if you need can be your guides. If you need them not, you can lead yourselves, and others. And such readers we wish him."

SYLVAN BARNET
Tufts University

Introduction

The date of *Macbeth*, like that of many of Shakespeare's plays, is not beyond all dispute, but there are
good reasons for believing it was written in 1605-06 and
was performed at Hampton Court in 1606 before James I
of England and his brother-in-law, Christian of Denmark.
The play, indeed, seems to have been written to please
James (and perhaps thus to further the fortunes of
Shakespeare's theatrical company, which in 1603 had
been named the King's Men). The evidence that Shakespeare sought to please James ranges from the highly
favorable portrait of Banquo, from whom the Stuarts
claimed descent (the pageant in IV.i of Banquo and the
eight kings seems to be a polite tribute to James, who
was the ninth Stuart monarch), to such a small detail
as the omission of a defeat of the Danes—this to avoid
embarrassing the visiting Danish king. But for a discussion of all such evidence, the reader must consult Henry
N. Paul's *The Royal Play of Macbeth*. Our concern here
will not be with the play Shakespeare wrote for the two
kings, but with the play he wrote for us.

Although *Macbeth* draws its material from Holinshed's
Chronicles, a historical compilation that provided Shakespeare with much of the material for the ten plays that
in the Folio of 1623 comprise the section labeled "Histories," *Macbeth* was entitled a tragedy and was printed
among the tragedies in the Folio. James may have looked

on the play as history, but it is not history. (Banquo, for example, was a convenient invention of a Scottish historian who in the early sixteenth century needed to give the Stuart line a proper beginning.) It is something that poets and literary critics customarily consider superior to history: a vision of life that has the concreteness of history and yet the wisdom of philosophy. Of course none of Shakespeare's history plays is satisfactory history; the exclusion of *Macbeth* from the "Histories" does not mean that the editors of the Folio recognized in it any unusual departure from fact. Perhaps *Macbeth* was excluded simply because its dramatis personae are Scottish, not English. But its presence among the "Tragedies" may mean that the editors saw a fundamental difference between *Macbeth* and, say, *Richard III,* which had earlier been published as a tragedy and which is called a tragedy even while it is placed among the "Histories." When one reads or sees *Richard III,* one cannot help feeling—even despite some familiarity with modern historical accounts that have demonstrated Shakespeare's distortions of fact —that one is experiencing a re-creation or re-presentation of what men did to other men during a segment of English history. When one reads or sees *Macbeth,* one cannot help feeling that one is experiencing a re-creation or re-presentation of what a man is, in the present, even in the timeless.

Suppose we take a definition of tragedy and apply it to *Macbeth.* We may find that the play helps to support the definition, and that when we apply this touchstone we see things in the play that we might otherwise have missed. (But we will also see that the definition shrinks the play, and that after it has served its purpose it must be discarded for another that may further illuminate the play.) Let us take as our first touchstone a line uttered in Cyril Tourneur's *The Revenger's Tragedy,* a play apparently written about the same time as *Macbeth*:

When the bàd bleed, then is the tragedy good.

In this view, tragedy shows the punishment of evildoers;

at its conclusion (to quote the Duke of Albany, in *King Lear*)

> All friends shall taste
> The wages of their virtue, and all foes
> The cup of their deservings.

What is there of this in *Macbeth*? If Tourneur's "bad" includes, as it must, a man who knowingly kills his benefactor, and who follows this murder with tyrannical assaults upon the lives of his countrymen (including women and children), then the formula has some relevance to *Macbeth*. For although most discussions of tragedy start from Aristotle's assumption that the best tragedy concerns a man who does a deed of horror in ignorance (Oedipus kills an old man who unknown to him is his father, Othello kills Desdemona in the mistaken belief that she is unchaste, Brutus makes errors of judgment that undercut his high-minded aspirations), Macbeth is not confused about the criminal nature of his deed. When he kills the king who is his guest and generous lord, he knows, as Oedipus, Othello, and Brutus do not, that he does a "horrid deed." Even before he does the deed he foresees the outcome, apparently sensing that in the nature of things something rather like Albany's view will come about through the workings of even-handed justice. In his first soliloquy he says:

> . . . we but teach
> Bloody instructions, which, being taught, return
> To plague th' inventor: this even-handed justice
> Commends th' ingredients of our poisoned chalice
> To our own lips.[1]

> (I.vii.8-12)

---

[1] By the way, although the idea that an evil act engenders its own punishment is scarcely novel, Shakespeare's use of it here is probably indebted to a passage in Holinshed's *Chronicles*: "For the prick of conscience, as it chanceth ever in tyrants and such as attain to any estate by unrighteous means, caused him ever to fear, lest he should be served of the same cup as he had ministered to his predecessors."

Nor does Macbeth lose his moral sense after his first crime. Midway in the play, when he has already suffered violent feelings of guilt, he determines to toughen himself in villainous practice; he has seen the ghost of one of his victims because (he thinks) he is still a fearful novice in crime and he has not yet inured himself by "hard use." A little later, when he fears he is losing his control, he determines that his course must be bloodier:

> From this moment
> The very firstlings of my heart shall be
> The firstlings of my hand. And even now,
> To crown my thoughts with acts, be it thought and
>   done:
> The castle of Macduff I will surprise;
> Seize upon Fife; give to th' edge o' th' sword
> His wife, his babes, and all unfortunate souls
> That trace him in his line. No boasting like a fool;
> This deed I'll do before this purpose cool.
>
> (IV.i.146-54)

Another way of seeing something of Macbeth's calculated villainy—something of the quality that puts him in Tourneur's classification of "the bad"—is to see what his opponents are like. Who are they? Chief of them is Malcolm, the heir to the throne—a man chaste, trustworthy, and patriotic—and they include men who are distressed to hear that Macbeth has made "each new morn/ New widows howl, new orphans cry." To these enemies of Macbeth, he is a butcher, a tyrant, a hell-kite, a hellhound. Malcolm and his allies, on the other hand, are the instruments of the powers above, and are God's soldiers. The concluding speech sharply contrasts the defeated tyrant (at whose fall, Dr. Johnson says, "every reader rejoices") and the rightful king:

> What's more to do,
> Which would be planted newly with the time—
> As calling home our exiled friends abroad
> That fled the snares of watchful tyranny,

Producing forth the cruel ministers
Of this dead butcher and his fiendlike queen,
Who, as 'tis thought, by self and violent hands
Took off her life—this, and what needful else
That calls upon us, by the grace of Grace
We will perform in measure, time, and place:
So thanks to all at once and to each one,
Whom we invite to see us crowned at Scone.

                                        (V.viii.64-75)

Macbeth has been allied with witches or fiends, but the
rightful ruler will work "by the grace of Grace." Macbeth
has been unable to "buckle his distempered cause/Within
the belt of rule," but the rightful ruler will perform his
actions "in measure, time, and place." Macbeth had heard
Duncan say to him "I have begun to plant thee, and
will labor/To make thee full of growing," yet he had
turned against the source of his growth, killed Duncan
(and so made of himself a rootless branch that must become desiccated); the rightful ruler's mind turns to plant-
ing newly with the time.

   It can be put this way: Macbeth's action is contrary to
nature, and he knows it. The mere thought of his deed
makes his body function unnaturally. The witches' solici-
tation, he says,

                 doth unfix my hair
And make my seated heart knock at my ribs,
Against the use of nature.

                                        (I.iii.135-37)

The wounds inflicted on Duncan look like "a breach in
nature," and the sun feels the effect of the murder:

                 By the clock 'tis day,
And yet dark night strangles the traveling lamp:
Is't night's predominance, or the day's shame,
That darkness does the face of earth entomb,
When living light should kiss it?

                                        (II.iv.6-10)

To which the Old Man replies: " 'Tis unnatural,/ Even like the deed that's done."

By turning against the source of his growth, then, Macbeth becomes infected:

> Who then shall blame
> His pestered senses to recoil and start,
> When all that is within him does condemn
> Itself for being there?
>
> (V.ii.22-25)

But of course this is not the whole story, and the Macbeth that has been thus far discussed is only a part of Shakespeare's Macbeth. At the outset of the play we meet not Macbeth but the Weird Sisters. The next time they assemble, the third one says, it will be to meet with Macbeth. The incantatory quality of their verse—the power of the rhyme, the alliteration, and the mysterious paradoxes—can be felt even in a single couplet:

> Fair is foul, and foul is fair.
> Hover through the fog and filthy air.
>
> (I.i.10-11)

We may insist, on reflection, that Macbeth is a free agent who need not have yielded to the witches' hints; certainly he harbors within him what they present to our eye. Yet can we feel sure that he has not been ensnared: the charm has been wound up, and if he is the tyrant, viewed another way he is the victim of infernal tyranny. "The instruments of darkness tell us truths,/Win us with honest trifles, to betray 's/In deepest consequence." The witches can control the winds, and we first see Macbeth on a "blasted heath." The very air he breathes, as it is in part made up of the witches who "melted as breath into the wind," is infected. This second view, of Macbeth as victim, though it must not be pressed (the noble Duncan finds the air sweet—but, in another way, he too is a victim), finds support in Shakespeare's other tragedies and even in his use of the word "tragedy" and its derivatives. He seems never to use it in a context that bears much resemblance to Tourneur's line, "When the bad bleed, then is the tragedy good." Always, or almost always, the word is linked with a violent death that evokes woe or is said to be woeful. Because he does not mention "tragedy" in *Macbeth,* an example must be drawn from another play. One of his earliest uses of the word will suffice. In *1 Henry VI,* Salisbury, an English Commander, has been killed by a hidden French gunner. Talbot, Salisbury's cohort, laments the sudden fall:

> Accursed tower! Accursed fatal hand
> That hath contrived this woeful tragedy.
> (I.iv)

The reference to the tower, and the word "fatal" ("destined," "fated") are important, for they suggest that tragedy sets its woeful happenings against a mysterious backdrop of inhuman and inscrutable forces.

The Weird Sisters in *Macbeth* are of course part of this inscrutable surrounding. In the Folio their name is spelled "weyard" or "weyward" (perhaps with a glance at "wayward"?) but the stage directions and speech prefixes call them witches. They have the traditional petty malice (and beards) of witches, and they acknowledge "masters," but they also have properties not associated with witches: they vanish like bubbles, and they speak authoritatively. In the fourth act they are closer to the Furies than to mischievous hags. No English play before *Macbeth* has such imposing witches, and if the Weird Sisters resemble witches in their ability to sail in a sieve and in their animal-killing and in their cookery and in their revenge on the sailor's wife, they nevertheless seem also to merit the title Macbeth gives them—"juggling fiends." Their name suggests the Fates (Old English *wyrd,* fate), and Holinshed conjectures that they may be "The goddesses of destiny," though of course Holinshed's view need not be Shakespeare's.

Is it, then, Macbeth's bad luck that the witches wait for him? Or is there something within himself that has at-

tracted them, and that makes him recognize his kinship
with them? Are they the dramatist's concrete embodi-
ments of a part of Macbeth? As soon as we ask these
questions we realize that debate is futile; we cannot reply
by pointing to Elizabethan treatises on demonology; we can
only repeat portions of the play; and the play does
not provide unequivocal answers.

Equivocation, in fact, is in part what the play is about.
The Porter (II.iii) soliloquizes about an equivocator,
but we do not have to wait for him to introduce the
theme of doubleness or ambiguity. The Weird Sisters,
in the first scene, will meet "when the battle's lost and
won," and for them "fair is foul, and foul is fair." A few
moments later Macbeth will enter, and his first line will
be

So foul and fair a day I have not seen.

One aspect of this pervasive doubleness is in the wordplay. The Porter has his quibbles, of course, but so do
Macbeth and Lady Macbeth. Second meanings, however,
lurk not only under words (e.g., *gild-guilt*); there are
second meanings under whole speeches and actions. This
is not surprising in a play in which the protagonist is advised to "look like th' innocent flower,/But be the
serpent under 't," and in which we hear "Away, and mock
the time with fairest show:/False face must hide what
the false heart doth know." Still, it was not inevitable that
Shakespeare should so brilliantly follow the innocent Duncan's observation that "There's no art/To find the
mind's construction in the face:/He was a gentleman
on whom I built/An absolute trust" with a stage direction, *"Enter Macbeth,"* i.e., enter another whose appearance will deceive Duncan.

It is time that we look more closely at Macbeth's double
nature, for if he is the "devilish Macbeth" that Malcolm
says he is, he is also something else.

Very early in the play—immediately after the odd
ritual of a dozen lines in which the Weird Sisters inform
us that they will meet with Macbeth, we get a report of

Macbeth's loyalty and courage. He is "brave Macbeth," "valiant cousin! Worthy gentleman," and "noble Macbeth," and by his deeds against rebels and foreign invaders he has earned these words. His first appearance on the stage does not quite confirm this report, but if anything it even more potently engages our sympathetic interest; he starts and seems "to fear/Things that do sound so fair." With hindsight we can say that he starts because he has already harbored criminal impulses that respond to the witches' words, but what is more important is that his apprehensiveness suggests both an apartness from others and a self-division that will make us see in him a good deal more than the blackguard. Twice in this first view of Macbeth we hear him described as "rapt," and his asides—confessing his uncertainties—complicate him and make him more than the hero described in the previous scene. There he had unseamed a rebel from the nave to the chops, had been an eagle, a cannon, and valor's minion. That is, when we first hear of Macbeth we hear of a man of noble and unambiguous action; when we first see Macbeth, we see a man of uncertainty. His first appearance puts him in the company of sympathetic tragic heroes such as Hamlet and Romeo. (Hamlet's first remark is an aside, and his next few speeches reveal he is not at one with his surroundings or himself. When we first see Romeo he is so abstracted that he is unaware of the time of day, and he endures "sad hours.") Conversely, Macbeth is far from the evil Richard III, whose history Shakespeare presented in the tragic shape of a rise and fall. Richard is unambiguously a villain. As early as the thirtieth line of the play he begins

> I am determined to prove a villain,
> And hate the idle pleasures of these days.
> Plots have I laid, inductions dangerous,
> By drunken prophecies, libels, and dreams,
> To set my brother Clarence and the King
> In deadly hate, the one against the other.
> And if King Edward be as true and just

As I am subtle, false, and treacherous . . .

This unmitigated villainy is not without its attractions, but contrast it with Macbeth's recoil at his own murderous thoughts:

> My thought, whose murder yet is but fantastical,
> Shakes so my single state of man that function
> Is smothered in surmise, and nothing is
> But what is not.
>
> (I.iii. 139-42)

It is not, then, that he commits crimes and at the end suffers; he suffers even before he commits his first criminal action, and because he is his own tormentor he scarcely needs the spectator's punishing eyes. Immediately after killing Duncan he is afflicted with doubts and has a premonition of the sleeplessness that will ensue. Lady Macbeth takes a simpler view: "Consider it not so deeply," "These deeds must not be thought/After these ways; so, it will make us mad," "A little water clears us of this deed:/How easy is it then!" (But if she here seems as black as the evil angel that prompts Mankind to illicit deeds in the old morality plays, she too reveals inner depths in the sleepwalking scene, when we see that like her husband she is troubled with thick-coming fancies that keep her from her rest.)

Macbeth early recognizes the unnaturalness of his thoughts, and, as the asides in the first act make clear, they estrange him from his fellows and even almost from himself. They

> make my seated heart knock at my ribs,
> Against the use of nature.
>
> (I.iii.136-37)

The soldier who fought along with his countrymen—who is described as a savior—becomes, by the last act, a man who knows that he has no friends (enemy troops, rather than troops of friends, surround him); his sol-

diers at the end—those who do not desert him—are mere
"constrainèd things/Whose hearts are absent too." His
course in blood has separated him not only from God
("wherefore could I not pronounce 'Amen'?"), and from
his subjects (he cannot banquet at ease with them), but
even from his wife. At the start of the play she is his
"dearest partner of greatness," and his "dearest love."
But midway in the play (though she is "dearest chuck")
he keeps from her the plot against Banquo, and at the
end he seems almost insensible to her death: "She should
have died hereafter." There are many ways of respond-
ing to the news of the death of a beloved one, and in this
play Shakespeare gives us three. It is instructive to
compare Macduff's response (IV.iii) and Old Siward's
(V.viii), very different yet not totally so, and to contrast
them to Macbeth's utterly dissimilar response.

What of Macbeth's own death? Its effect on us is complex. When his severed head is brought in, perhaps we
sense a parallel between Macbeth's career and that of the
treacherous Macdonwald, whose head Macbeth had justly
fixed upon the battlements, and a contrast between, first,
Macbeth and the Thane of Cawdor, who confessed his
treasons and yielded up his life "as 'twere a trifle," and,
second, between Macbeth and Young Siward, who died
as "God's soldier"; but perhaps too we feel that there is
something of the soldierly Macbeth in his final contest,
and, equally important, that his death is the release
(hence it is not wholly painful to him) of one who
knows he harvested what he sowed, and who is aweary
of the sun.

The speech Macbeth makes before he dies can here be
used to remind us that he holds our interest partly by
his language. It is not a matter of confusing the character
with the author, but simply a matter of recognizing that
one of the things that makes us interested in Macbeth
(and in all of the people embodied in the play, or, rather,
the people who embody the play) is memorable speech.
The point might be made by printing the lines he utters
on the nothingness of life just after he learns of Lady
Macbeth's death—lines so potent that although they fit

exactly into their place in the drama they have often been taken out and held to represent Shakespeare's own view—yet the role that Macbeth's language plays can be still better seen by quoting a dying speech that David Garrick composed for Macbeth in the eighteenth century. Even the reader who has read only as much of the play as has been quoted in this introduction must recognize that every word of Shakespeare's Macbeth will engage him as Garrick's does not. Garrick's Macbeth says:

> Hell drags me down. I sink,
> I sink. Oh! my soul is lost forever.
> Oh!   *Dies.*

The final speech of Shakespeare's Macbeth is an almost indescribable blend of corrupted pride, desperation, animal fury, and courage; it is not one of the meditative or descriptive passages that even out of context has a life of its own, but like all the other lines in the play it holds us rapt.

SYLVAN BARNET

The Tragedy of
MACBETH

Duncan, King of Scotland

Malcolm
Donalbain } his sons

Macbeth
Banquo
Macduff
Lennox
Ross } noblemen of Scotland
Menteith
Angus
Caithness

Fleance, son to Banquo

Siward, Earl of Northumberland, general of the
    English forces

Young Siward, his son

Seyton, an officer attending on Macbeth

Son to Macduff

An English Doctor

A Scottish Doctor

A Porter

An Old Man

Three Murderers

Lady Macbeth

Lady Macduff

A Gentlewoman attending on Lady Macbeth

Hecate

Witches

Apparitions

Lords, Officers, Soldiers, Attendants, and Mes-
    sengers

    Scene: Scotland; England]

The Tragedy of Macbeth

ACT I

Scene I. [*An open place.*]

Thunder and lightning. Enter Three Witches.

First Witch. When shall we three meet again?
In thunder, lightning, or in rain?

Second Witch. When the hurlyburly's done,
When the battle's lost and won.

Third Witch. That will be ere the set of sun.　　　　　　　*5*

First Witch. Where the place?

Second Witch.　　　　　　　Upon the heath.

Third Witch. There to meet with Macbeth.

First Witch. I come, Graymalkin.° ¹

Second Witch. Paddock° calls.

Third Witch.　　　　　　Anon!°

All. Fair is foul, and foul is fair.　　　　　　　　*10*

　　　Hover through the fog and filthy air.

　　　　　　　　　　　　　　　Exeunt.

---

¹ The degree sign (°) indicates a footnote, which is keyed to the text by
line number. Text references are printed in *italic* type; the annotation
follows in roman type.
I.i. 8 *Graymalkin* (the witch's attendant spirit, a gray cat)　9 *Paddock*
toad　9 *Anon* at once

Scene II.   [*A camp.*]

Alarum within.° *Enter King [Duncan], Mal-*
colm, Donalbain, Lennox, with Attendants, meet-
ing a bleeding Captain.

King. What bloody man is that? He can report,
   As seemeth by his plight, of the revolt
   The newest state.

Malcolm.   This is the sergeant°
   Who like a good and hardy soldier fought
5   'Gainst my captivity. Hail, brave friend!
   Say to the king the knowledge of the broil°
   As thou didst leave it.

Captain.   Doubtful it stood,
   As two spent swimmers, that do cling together
   And choke their art.° The merciless Macdonwald—
10   Worthy to be a rebel for to that
   The multiplying villainies of nature
   Do swarm upon him—from the Western Isles°
   Of kerns and gallowglasses° is supplied;
   And Fortune, on his damnèd quarrel° smiling,
15   Showed like a rebel's whore:° but all's too weak:
   For brave Macbeth—well he deserves that name—
   Disdaining Fortune, with his brandished steel,
   Which smoked with bloody execution,
   Like valor's minion° carved out his passage

I.ii.s.d. *Alarum within* trumpet call offstage   3 *sergeant* i.e., officer
(he is called, perhaps with no inconsistency in Shakespeare's day,
a captain in the s.d. and speech prefixes. *Sergeant* is trisyllabic)
6 *broil* quarrel   9 *choke their art* hamper each other's doings   12 *West-*
ern Isles Hebrides   13 *Of kerns and gallowglasses* with lightly armed
Irish foot soldiers and heavily armed ones   14 *damnèd quarrel* accursed
cause   15 *Showed like a rebel's whore* i.e., falsely appeared to favor
Macdonwald   19 *minion* (trisyllabic) favorite

Till he faced the slave;   20
Which nev'r shook hands, nor bade farewell to him,
Till he unseamed him from the nave to th' chops,°
And fixed his head upon our battlements.

King. O valiant cousin! Worthy gentleman!

Captain. As whence the sun 'gins his reflection°   25
Shipwracking storms and direful thunders break,
So from that spring whence comfort seemed to come
Discomfort swells. Mark, King of Scotland, mark:
No sooner justice had, with valor armed,
Compelled these skipping kerns to trust their heels   30
But the Norweyan lord, surveying vantage,°
With furbished arms and new supplies of men,
Began a fresh assault.

King.   Dismayed not this
Our captains, Macbeth and Banquo?

Captain.   Yes;
As sparrows eagles, or the hare the lion.   35
If I say sooth,° I must report they were
As cannons overcharged with double cracks;°
So they doubly redoubled strokes upon the foe.
Except° they meant to bathe in reeking wounds,
Or memorize another Golgotha,°   40
I cannot tell—
But I am faint; my gashes cry for help.

King. So well thy words become thee as thy wounds;
They smack of honor both. Go get him surgeons.

                   [*Exit Captain, attended.*]

       Enter Ross and Angus.
Who comes here?

---

22 *nave to th' chops* navel to the jaws   25 *reflection* (four syllables;
the ending—*ion* here and often elsewhere in the play— is disyllabic)
31 *surveying vantage* seeing an opportunity   36 *sooth* truth   37 *cracks*
explosives   39 *Except* unless   40 *memorize another Golgotha* make
the place as memorable as Golgotha, "the place of the skull"

45 *Malcolm.*   The worthy Thane° of Ross.

Lennox. What a haste looks through his eyes! So
        should he look
    That seems to° speak things strange.

Ross.   God save the king!

King. Whence cam'st thou, worthy Thane?

Ross.   From Fife, great King;
    Where the Norweyan banners flout the sky
50   And fan our people cold.
    Norway° himself, with terrible numbers,
    Assisted by that most disloyal traitor
    The Thane of Cawdor, began a dismal° conflict;
    Till that Bellona's bridegroom, lapped in proof,°
55   Confronted him with self-comparisons,°
    Point against point, rebellious arm 'gainst arm,
    Curbing his lavish° spirit: and, to conclude,
    The victory fell on us.

King.   Great happiness!

Ross.   That now
    Sweno, the Norways' king, craves composition;°
60   Nor would we deign him burial of his men
    Till he disbursèd, at Saint Colme's Inch,°
    Ten thousand dollars° to our general use.

King. No more that Thane of Cawdor shall deceive
    Our bosom interest:° go pronounce his present°
        death,
65   And with his former title greet Macbeth.

Ross. I'll see it done.

King. What he hath lost, noble Macbeth hath won.
                                    Exeunt.

45 *Thane* (a Scottish title of nobility)   47 *seems to* seems about to
51 *Norway* the King of Norway   53 *dismal* threatening   54 *Bellona's
. . . proof* the mate of the goddess of war, clad in tested (proved)
armor   55 *self-comparisons* counter-movements   57 *lavish* insolent
59 *composition* terms of peace   61 *Inch* island   63 *dollars* (Spanish and
Dutch currency)   64 *Our bosom interest* my (plural of royalty)
heart's trust   64 *present* immediate

I, iii MACBETH 41

Scene III.   [*A heath.*]

Thunder. Enter the Three Witches.

First Witch. Where hast thou been, sister?

Second Witch. Killing swine.

Third Witch. Sister, where thou?

First Witch. A sailor's wife had chestnuts in her lap,
And mounched, and mounched, and mounched.
    "Give me," quoth I.   5
"Aroint thee,° witch!" the rump-fed ronyon° cries.
Her husband's to Aleppo gone, master o' th' Tiger:
But in a sieve I'll thither sail,
And, like a rat without a tail,
I'll do, I'll do, and I'll do.   10

Second Witch. I'll give thee a wind.

First Witch. Th' art kind.

Third Witch. And I another.

First Witch. I myself have all the other;
And the very ports they blow,°   15
All the quarters that they know
I' th' shipman's card.°
I'll drain him dry as hay:
Sleep shall neither night nor day
Hang upon his penthouse lid;°   20
He shall live a man forbid:°
Weary sev'nights nine times nine
Shall he dwindle, peak,° and pine:

I.iii. ⁶ *Aroint thee* begone   ⁶ *rump-fed ronyon* fat-rumped scabby creature   ¹⁵ *ports they blow* harbors to which the winds blow (?)
¹⁷ *card* compass card   ²⁰ *penthouse lid* eyelid (the figure is of a lean-to)
²¹ *forbid* cursed   ²³ *peak* waste away

Though his bark cannot be lost,
25 Yet it shall be tempest-tossed.
Look what I have.

Second Witch. Show me, show me.

First Witch. Here I have a pilot's thumb,
Wracked as homeward he did come.

                    Drum within.

80 *Third Witch.* A drum, a drum!
Macbeth doth come.

All. The weïrd° sisters, hand in hand,
Posters° of the sea and land,
Thus do go about, about:
85 Thrice to thine, and thrice to mine,
And thrice again, to make up nine.
Peace! The charm's wound up.

            Enter Macbeth and Banquo.

Macbeth. So foul and fair a day I have not seen.

Banquo. How far is 't called to Forres? What are these
40 So withered, and so wild in their attire,
That look not like th' inhabitants o' th' earth,
And yet are on 't? Live you, or are you aught
That man may question?° You seem to understand
    me,
By each at once her choppy° finger laying
45 Upon her skinny lips. You should be women,
And yet your beards forbid me to interpret
That you are so.

Macbeth.   Speak, if you can: what are you?

First Witch. All hail, Macbeth! Hail to thee, Thane of
Glamis!

Second Witch. All hail, Macbeth! Hail to thee, Thane of
Cawdor!

82 *weïrd* destiny-serving (?)   83 *Posters* swift travelers   43 *question* talk
to   44 *choppy* chapped

Third Witch. All hail, Macbeth, that shalt be King
    hereafter!   50

Banquo. Good sir, why do you start, and seem to fear
    Things that do sound so fair? I' th' name of truth,
    Are ye fantastical,° or that indeed
    Which outwardly ye show? My noble partner
    You greet with present grace° and great prediction   55
    Of noble having° and of royal hope,
    That he seems rapt withal:° to me you speak not.
    If you can look into the seeds of time,
    And say which grain will grow and which will not,
    Speak then to me, who neither beg nor fear   60
    Your favors nor your hate.

First Witch. Hail!

Second Witch. Hail!

Third Witch. Hail!

First Witch. Lesser than Macbeth, and greater.   65

Second Witch. Not so happy,° yet much happier.

Third Witch. Thou shalt get° kings, though thou be
    none.
    So all hail, Macbeth and Banquo!

First Witch. Banquo and Macbeth, all hail!

Macbeth. Stay, you imperfect° speakers, tell me more: 70
    By Sinel's° death I know I am Thane of Glamis;
    But how of Cawdor? The Thane of Cawdor lives,
    A prosperous gentleman; and to be King
    Stands not within the prospect of belief,
    No more than to be Cawdor. Say from whence   75
    You owe° this strange intelligence?° Or why
    Upon this blasted heath you stop our way

---

53 *fantastical* imaginary   55 *grace* honor   56 *having* possession   57 *rapt
withal* entranced by it   66 *happy* fortunate   67 *get* beget   70 *imperfect*
incomplete   71 *Sinel* (Macbeth's father)   76 *owe* own, have   76 *intelligence* information

With such prophetic greeting? Speak, I charge
    you.

                                    Witches vanish.

Banquo. The earth hath bubbles as the water has,
80   And these are of them. Whither are they vanished?

Macbeth. Into the air, and what seemed corporal°
    melted
    As breath into the wind. Would they had stayed!

Banquo. Were such things here as we do speak about?
    Or have we eaten on the insane° root
85   That takes the reason prisoner?

Macbeth. Your children shall be kings.

Banquo.   You shall be King.

Macbeth. And Thane of Cawdor too. Went it not so?
Banquo. To th' selfsame tune and words. Who's here?

            Enter Ross and Angus.

Ross. The King hath happily received, Macbeth,
90   The news of thy success; and when he reads°
    Thy personal venture in the rebels' fight,
    His wonders and his praises do contend
    Which should be thine or his.° Silenced with that,
    In viewing o'er the rest o' th' selfsame day,
95   He finds thee in the stout Norweyan ranks,
    Nothing afeard of what thyself didst make,
    Strange images of death. As thick as tale
    Came post with post,° and every one did bear
    Thy praises in his kingdom's great defense,
    And poured them down before him.

100 *Angus.*   We are sent
    To give thee, from our royal master, thanks;

81 *corporal* corporeal 84 *insane* insanity-producing 90 *reads* considers
92–93 *His* wonders . . . *his* i.e., Duncan's speechless admiration, appropriate to him, contends with his desire to praise you (?) 97–98 *As
thick . . . post* as fast as could be counted came messenger after messenger

Only to herald thee into his sight,
\ Not pay thee.

Ross. And for an earnest° of a greater honor,
He bade me, from him, call thee Thane of Cawdor;   *105*
In which addition,° hail, most worthy Thane!
For it is thine.

Banquo.   What, can the devil speak true?

Macbeth. The Thane of Cawdor lives: why do you dress
     me
In borrowed robes?

Angus.   Who was the thane lives yet,
But under heavy judgment bears that life   *110*
Which he deserves to lose. Whether he was com-
     bined°
With those of Norway, or did line° the rebel
With hidden help and vantage,° or that with both
He labored in his country's wrack,° I know not;
But treasons capital, confessed and proved,   *115*
Have overthrown him.

Macbeth.   [*Aside*] Glamis, and Thane of Cawdor:
The greatest is behind.° [*To Ross and Angus*] Thanks
     for your pains.
[*Aside to Banquo*] Do you not hope your children
     shall be kings,
When those that gave the Thane of Cawdor to me
Promised no less to them?

Banquo. [*Aside to Macbeth*] That, trusted home,° *120*
Might yet enkindle you unto the crown,
Besides the Thane of Cawdor. But 'tis strange:
And oftentimes, to win us to our harm,
The instruments of darkness tell us truths,
Win us with honest trifles, to betray 's   *125*

---

104 *earnest* pledge   106 *addition* title   111 *combined* allied   112 *line* support   113 *vantage* opportunity   114 *wrack* ruin   117 *behind* i.e., to follow   120 *home* all the way

In deepest consequence.°
Cousins,° a word, I pray you.

Macbeth.   [*Aside*] Two truths are told,
As happy prologues to the swelling° act
Of the imperial theme.—I thank you, gentlemen.—
130 [*Aside*] This supernatural soliciting°
Cannot be ill, cannot be good. If ill,
Why hath it given me earnest of success,
Commencing in a truth? I am Thane of Cawdor:
If good, why do I yield to that suggestion
135 Whose horrid image doth unfix my hair
And make my seated° heart knock at my ribs,
Against the use of nature?° Present fears
Are less than horrible imaginings.
My thought, whose murder yet is but fantastical,°
140 Shakes so my single° state of man that function
Is smothered in surmise, and nothing is
But what is not.

Banquo.   Look, how our partner's rapt.

Macbeth. [*Aside*] If chance will have me King, why,
    chance may crown me,
Without my stir.

Banquo.   New honors come upon him,
Like our strange° garments, cleave not to their
145   mold
But with the aid of use.

Macbeth.   [*Aside*] Come what come may,
Time and the hour runs through the roughest day.

Banquo. Worthy Macbeth, we stay upon your leisure.°

Macbeth. Give me your favor.° My dull brain was
    wrought

126 *In deepest consequence* in the most significant sequel 127 *Cousins*
i.e., fellow noblemen 128 *swelling* stately 130 *soliciting* inviting
136 *seated* fixed 137 *Against the use of nature* contrary to my natural
way 139 *fantastical* imaginary 140 *single* unaided, weak (or "entire"?)
145 *strange* new 148 *stay upon your leisure* await your convenience
149 *favor* pardon

With things forgotten. Kind gentlemen, your pains   150
Are registered where every day I turn
The leaf to read them. Let us toward the King.
[*Aside to Banquo*] Think upon what hath
    chanced, and at more time,
The interim having weighed it,° let us speak
Our free hearts° each to other.

Banquo.   Very gladly.   155

Macbeth. Till then, enough. Come, friends.

                                    Exeunt.

Scene IV.   [*Forres. The palace.*]

Flourish.° Enter King [Duncan], Lennox,
    Malcolm, Donalbain, and Attendants.

King. Is execution done on Cawdor? Are not
    Those in commission° yet returned?

Malcolm.   My liege,
    They are not yet come back. But I have spoke
    With one that saw him die, who did report
    That very frankly he confessed his treasons,   5
    Implored your Highness' pardon and set forth
    A deep repentance: nothing in his life
    Became him like the leaving it. He died
    As one that had been studied° in his death,
    To throw away the dearest thing he owed°   10
    As 'twere a careless° trifle.

---

154 *The interim having weighed it* i.e., when we have had time to
think 155 *Our free hearts* our minds freely I.iv.s.d. *Flourish* fanfare
2 *in commission* i.e., commissioned to oversee the execution 9 *studied*
rehearsed 10 *owed* owned 11 *careless* uncared-for

King.   There's no art
To find the mind's construction in the face:
He was a gentleman on whom I built
An absolute trust.

    Enter Macbeth, Banquo, Ross, and Angus.

                  O worthiest cousin!
15 The sin of my ingratitude even now
Was heavy on me: thou art so far before,
That swiftest wing of recompense is slow
To overtake thee. Would thou hadst less deserved,
That the proportion° both of thanks and payment
20 Might have been mine! Only I have left to say,
More is thy due than more than all can pay.

Macbeth. The service and the loyalty I owe,
In doing it, pays itself.° Your Highness' part
Is to receive our duties: and our duties
25 Are to your throne and state children and servants;
Which do but what they should, by doing every
    thing
Safe toward° your love and honor.

King.   Welcome hither.
I have begun to plant thee, and will labor
To make thee full of growing. Noble Banquo,
30 That hast no less deserved, nor must be known
No less to have done so, let me enfold thee
And hold thee to my heart.

Banquo.   There if I grow,
The harvest is your own.

King.   My plenteous joys,
Wanton° in fullness, seek to hide themselves
35 In drops of sorrow. Sons, kinsmen, thanes,
And you whose places are the nearest, know,
We will establish our estate° upon
Our eldest, Malcolm, whom we name hereafter

---

19 *proportion* preponderance   23 *pays itself* is its own reward   27 *Safe toward* safeguarding (?)   34 *Wanton* unrestrained   37 *establish our estate* settle the succession

       The Prince of Cumberland: which honor must
       Not unaccompanied invest him only,   40
       But signs of nobleness, like stars, shall shine
       On all deservers. From hence to Inverness,
       And bind us further to you.

Macbeth. The rest is labor, which is not used for you.°
       I'll be myself the harbinger, and make joyful   45
       The hearing of my wife with your approach;
       So, humbly take my leave.

King.   My worthy Cawdor!

Macbeth. [*Aside*] The Prince of Cumberland! That
       is a step
       On which I must fall down, or else o'erleap,
       For in my way it lies. Stars, hide your fires;   50
       Let not light see my black and deep desires:
       The eye wink at the hand;° yet let that be
       Which the eye fears, when it is done, to see.

                                                    Exit.

King. True, worthy Banquo; he is full so valiant,
       And in his commendations° I am fed;   55
       It is a banquet to me. Let's after him,
       Whose care is gone before to bid us welcome.
       It is a peerless kinsman.   *Flourish. Exeunt.*

       Scene V.   [*Inverness. Macbeth's castle.*]

       Enter Macbeth's wife, alone, with a letter.

Lady Macbeth. [*Reads*] "They met me in the day
       of success; and I have learned by the perfect'st

---

44 *The rest . . . you* i.e., repose is laborious when not employed for
you   52 *wink at the hand* i.e., be blind to the hand's deed   55 *his commendations* commendations of him

report they have more in them than mortal knowledge. When I burned in desire to question them
further, they made themselves air, into which they
vanished. Whiles I stood rapt in the wonder of it,
came missives° from the King, who all-hailed me
'Thane of Cawdor'; by which title, before, these
weïrd sisters saluted me, and referred me to the
coming on of time, with 'Hail, King that shalt
be!' This have I thought good to deliver thee,° my
dearest partner of greatness, that thou mightst not
lose the dues of rejoicing, by being ignorant of
what greatness is promised thee. Lay it to thy heart,
and farewell."

Glamis thou art, and Cawdor, and shalt be
What thou art promised. Yet do I fear thy nature;
It is too full o' th' milk of human kindness°
To catch the nearest way. Thou wouldst be great,
Art not without ambition, but without
The illness° should attend it. What thou wouldst
      highly,
That wouldst thou holily; wouldst not play false,
And yet wouldst wrongly win. Thou'dst have,
      great Glamis,
That which cries "Thus thou must do" if thou have
      it;
And that which rather thou dost fear to do
Than wishest should be undone. Hie thee hither,
That I may pour my spirits in thine ear,
And chastise with the valor of my tongue
All that impedes thee from the golden round°
Which fate and metaphysical° aid doth seem
To have thee crowned withal.°

Enter Messenger.

I.v. 7 *missives* messengers 11 *deliver thee* report to you 18 *milk of
human kindness* i.e., gentle quality of human nature 21 *illness* wickedness 29 *round* crown 30 *metaphysical* supernatural 31 *withal* with

What is your tidings?

Messenger. The King comes here tonight.

Lady Macbeth.   Thou'rt mad to say it!
    Is not thy master with him, who, were 't so,
    Would have informed for preparation?

Messenger. So please you, it is true. Our thane is
        coming.   35
    One of my fellows had the speed of him,°
    Who, almost dead for breath, had scarcely more
    Than would make up his message.

Lady Macbeth.   Give him tending;
    He brings great news.   *Exit Messenger.*
                    The raven himself is hoarse
    That croaks the fatal entrance of Duncan   40
    Under my battlements. Come, you spirits
    That tend on mortal° thoughts, unsex me here,
    And fill me, from the crown to the toe, top-full
    Of direst cruelty! Make thick my blood,
    Stop up th' access and passage to remorse,°   45
    That no compunctious visitings of nature°
    Shake my fell° purpose, nor keep peace between
    Th' effect° and it! Come to my woman's breasts,
    And take my milk for° gall, you murd'ring ministers,°
    Wherever in your sightless° substances   50
    You wait on° nature's mischief! Come, thick night,
    And pall° thee in the dunnest° smoke of hell,
    That my keen knife see not the wound it makes,
    Nor heaven peep through the blanket of the dark,
    To cry "Hold, hold!"

                Enter Macbeth.

                Great Glamis! Worthy Cawdor!   55
    Greater than both, by the all-hail hereafter!°

---

36 *had the speed of him* outdistanced him 42 *mortal* deadly 45 *re-morse* compassion 46 *compunctious visitings of nature* natural feelings of compassion 47 *fell* savage 48 *effect* fulfillment 49 *for* in exchange for 49 *ministers* agents 50 *sightless* invisible 51 *wait on* assist 52 *pall* enshroud 52 *dunnest* darkest 56 *all-hail hereafter* the third all-hail (?) the all-hail of the future(?)

Thy letters have transported me beyond
This ignorant° present, and I feel now
The future in the instant.°

Macbeth.   My dearest love,
Duncan comes here tonight.

60 *Lady Macbeth.*   And when goes hence?

Macbeth. Tomorrow, as he purposes.

Lady Macbeth.   O, never
Shall sun that morrow see!
Your face, my Thane, is as a book where men
May read strange matters. To beguile the time,°
65 Look like the time; bear welcome in your eye,
Your hand, your tongue: look like th' innocent
    flower,
But be the serpent under 't. He that's coming
Must be provided for: and you shall put
This night's great business into my dispatch;°
70 Which shall to all our nights and days to come
Give solely sovereign sway and masterdom.

Macbeth. We will speak further.

Lady Macbeth.   Only look up clear.°
To alter favor ever is to fear.°
Leave all the rest to me.   *Exeunt.*

---

58 *ignorant* unknowing   59 *instant* present   64 *To beguile the time* i.e.,
to deceive people of the day   69 *dispatch* management   72 *look up clear*
appear undisturbed   73 *To alter . . . fear* to show a disturbed face is
dangerous

Scene VI.   [*Before Macbeth's castle.*]

Hautboys° and torches. Enter King [Duncan],
Malcolm, Donalbain, Banquo, Lennox, Macduff,
Ross, Angus, and Attendants.

King. This castle hath a pleasant seat;° the air
Nimbly and sweetly recommends itself
Unto our gentle° senses.

Banquo.   This guest of summer,
The temple-haunting martlet,° does approve°
By his loved mansionry° that the heaven's breath   *5*
Smells wooingly here. No jutty,° frieze,
Buttress, nor coign of vantage,° but this bird
Hath made his pendent bed and procreant° cradle.
Where they most breed and haunt,° I have observed
The air is delicate.

Enter Lady [Macbeth].

King.   See, see, our honored hostess!   *10*
The love that follows us sometime is our trouble,
Which still we thank as love.° Herein I teach you
How you shall bid God 'ield° us for your pains
And thank us for your trouble.

Lady Macbeth.   All our service
In every point twice done, and then done double,   *15*
Were poor and single business° to contend
Against those honors deep and broad wherewith

I.vi.s.d. *Hautboys* oboes 1 *seat* site 3 *gentle* soothed 4 *temple-haunt-*
ing martlet martin (swift) nesting in churches 4 *approve* prove
5 *mansionry* nests 6 *jutty* projection 7 *coign of vantage* advantageous
corner 8 *procreant* breeding 9 *haunt* visit 11-12 *The love . . . love*
the love offered me sometimes inconveniences me, but still I value it
as love 13 *'ield* reward 16 *single business* feeble service

Your Majesty loads our house: for those of old,
And the late dignities heaped up to them,
We rest your hermits.°

20 *King.*   Where's the Thane of Cawdor?
We coursed° him at the heels, and had a purpose
To be his purveyor:° but he rides well,
And his great love, sharp as his spur, hath holp°
    him
To his home before us. Fair and noble hostess,
We are your guest tonight.

25 *Lady Macbeth.*   Your servants ever
Have theirs, themselves, and what is theirs, in
    compt,°
To make their audit at your Highness' pleasure,
Still° to return your own.

King.   Give me your hand.
Conduct me to mine host: we love him highly,
30 And shall continue our graces towards him.
By your leave, hostess.   *Exeunt.*

Scene VII.   *[Macbeth's castle.]*

*Hautboys. Torches. Enter a Sewer,° and diverse
    Servants with dishes and service over the stage.
    Then enter Macbeth.*

Macbeth. If it were done° when 'tis done, then 'twere
    well
It were done quickly. If th' assassination

20 *your hermits* dependents bound to pray for you   21 *coursed* pursued
22 *purveyor* advance-supply officer   23 *holp* helped   26 *Have theirs . . .
compt* have their dependents, themselves, and their possessions in trust
28 *Still* always   I.vii.s.d. *Sewer* chief butler   1 *done* over and done
with

Could trammel up° the consequence, and catch,
With his surcease,° success;° that but this blow
Might be the be-all and the end-all—here,   5
But here, upon this bank and shoal of time,
We'd jump° the life to come. But in these cases
We still° have judgment here; that we but teach
Bloody instructions, which, being taught, return
To plague th' inventor: this even-handed° justice   10
Commends° th' ingredients of our poisoned chalice
To our own lips. He's here in double trust:
First, as I am his kinsman and his subject,
Strong both against the deed; then, as his host,
Who should against his murderer shut the door,   15
Not bear the knife myself. Besides, this Duncan
Hath borne his faculties° so meek, hath been
So clear° in his great office, that his virtues
Will plead like angels trumpet-tongued against
The deep damnation of his taking-off;   20
And pity, like a naked newborn babe,
Striding° the blast, or heaven's cherubin horsed
Upon the sightless couriers° of the air,
Shall blow the horrid deed in every eye,
That° tears shall drown the wind. I have no spur   25
To prick the sides of my intent, but only
Vaulting ambition, which o'erleaps itself
And falls on th' other——

                    Enter Lady [Macbeth].

                              How now! What news?

Lady Macbeth. He has almost supped. Why have you
    left the chamber?

---

³ *trammel up* catch in a net ⁴ *his surcease* Duncan's death(?) the
consequence's cessation(?) ⁴ *success* what follows ⁷ *jump* risk ⁸ *still*
always ¹⁰ *even-handed* impartial ¹¹ *Commends* offers ¹⁷ *faculties*
powers ¹⁸ *clear* spotless ²² *Striding* bestriding ²³ *sightless couriers*
invisible coursers (i.e., the winds) ²⁵ *That* so that

Macbeth. Hath he asked for me?

30   *Lady Macbeth.*   Know you not he has?

    Macbeth. We will proceed no further in this business:
      He hath honored me of late, and I have bought°
      Golden opinions from all sorts of people,
      Which would be worn now in their newest gloss,
      Not cast aside so soon.

35   *Lady Macbeth.*   Was the hope drunk
      Wherein you dressed yourself? Hath it slept since?
      And wakes it now, to look so green° and pale
      At what it did so freely? From this time
      Such I account thy love. Art thou afeard
40   To be the same in thine own act and valor
      As thou art in desire? Wouldst thou have that
      Which thou esteem'st the ornament of life,
      And live a coward in thine own esteem,
      Letting "I dare not" wait upon° "I would,"
      Like the poor cat° i' th' adage?

45   *Macbeth.*   Prithee, peace!
      I dare do all that may become a man;
      Who dares do more is none.

    Lady Macbeth.   What beast was 't then
      That made you break° this enterprise to me?
      When you durst do it, then you were a man;
50   And to be more than what you were, you would
      Be so much more the man. Nor time nor place
      Did then adhere,° and yet you would make both.
      They have made themselves, and that their° fitness
        now
      Does unmake you. I have given suck, and know
55   How tender 'tis to love the babe that milks me:
      I would, while it was smiling in my face,
      Have plucked my nipple from his boneless gums,

---

32 *bought* acquired   37 *green* sickly   44 *wait upon* follow   45 *cat* (who wants fish but fears to wet its paws)   48 *break* broach   52 *adhere* suit 53 *that their* their very

And dashed the brains out, had I so sworn as you
Have done to this.

Macbeth.   If we should fail?

Lady Macbeth.   We fail?
But° screw your courage to the sticking-place,°   60
And we'll not fail. When Duncan is asleep—
Whereto the rather shall his day's hard journey
Soundly invite him—his two chamberlains
Will I with wine and wassail° so convince,°
That memory, the warder° of the brain,   65
Shall be a fume, and the receipt of reason
A limbeck only:° when in swinish sleep
Their drenchèd natures lies° as in a death,
What cannot you and I perform upon
Th' unguarded Duncan, what not put upon   70
His spongy° officers, who shall bear the guilt
Of our great quell?°

Macbeth.   Bring forth men-children only;
For thy undaunted mettle° should compose
Nothing but males. Will it not be received,
When we have marked with blood those sleepy two   75
Of his own chamber, and used their very daggers,
That they have done 't?

Lady Macbeth.   Who dares receive it other,°
As we shall make our griefs and clamor roar
Upon his death?

Macbeth.   I am settled, and bend up
Each corporal agent to this terrible feat.   80
Away, and mock the time° with fairest show:
False face must hide what the false heart doth know.

                                        Exeunt.

60 *But* only   60 *sticking place* notch (holding the bowstring of a taut
crossbow)   64 *wassail* carousing   64 *convince* overpower   65 *warder*
guard   66-67 *receipt . . . only* i.e., the receptacle (*receipt*), which
should collect the distillate of thought—reason—will be a mere vessel
(*limbeck*) of undistilled liquids   68 *lies* lie   71 *spongy* sodden   72 *quell*
killing   73 *mettle* substance   77 *other* otherwise   81 *mock the time* beguile the world

ACT II

Enter Banquo, and Fleance, with a torch before him.

Banquo. How goes the night, boy?

Fleance. The moon is down; I have not heard the
clock.

Banquo. And she goes down at twelve.

Fleance.   I take't, 'tis later, sir.

Banquo. Hold, take my sword. There's husbandry° in
heaven.
5   Their candles are all out. Take thee that too.
A heavy summons° lies like lead upon me,
And yet I would not sleep. Merciful powers,
Restrain in me the cursèd thoughts that nature
Gives way to in repose!

Enter Macbeth, and a Servant with a torch.

                          Give me my sword!
10   Who's there?

Macbeth. A friend.

Banquo. What, sir, not yet at rest? The King's a-bed:
He hath been in unusual pleasure, and
Sent forth great largess to your offices:°
15   This diamond he greets your wife withal,
By the name of most kind hostess; and shut up°
In measureless content.

II.i. 4 *husbandry* frugality 6 *summons* call (to sleep) 14 *largess to
your offices* gifts to your servants' quarters 16 *shut up* concluded

Macbeth.   Being unprepared,
　Our will became the servant to defect,°
　Which else should free have wrought.

Banquo.   All's well.
　I dreamt last night of the three weïrd sisters: 20
　To you they have showed some truth.

Macbeth.   I think not of them.
　Yet, when we can entreat an hour to serve,
　We would spend it in some words upon that
　　business,
　If you would grant the time.

Banquo.   At your kind'st leisure.

Macbeth. If you shall cleave to my consent, when
　'tis,°   25
　It shall make honor for you.

Banquo.   So° I lose none
　In seeking to augment it, but still keep
　My bosom franchised° and allegiance clear,°
　I shall be counseled.

Macbeth.   Good repose the while!

Banquo. Thanks, sir. The like to you!   80

　　　　　　　　Exit Banquo [with Fleance].

Macbeth. Go bid thy mistress, when my drink is ready,
　She strike upon the bell. Get thee to bed.

　　　　　　　　　　Exit [Servant].

　Is this a dagger which I see before me,
　The handle toward my hand? Come, let me clutch
　　thee.
　I have thee not, and yet I see thee still.   85
　Art thou not, fatal vision, sensible°
　To feeling as to sight, or art thou but
　A dagger of the mind, a false creation,

---

18 *Our . . . defect* our good will was hampered by our deficient preparations   25 *cleave . . . 'tis* join my cause, when the time comes
26 *So* provided that   28 *franchised* free (from guilt)   28 *clear* spotless
36 *sensible* perceptible

Proceeding from the heat-oppressèd brain?
40 I see thee yet, in form as palpable
As this which now I draw.
Thou marshal'st me the way that I was going;
And such an instrument I was to use.
Mine eyes are made the fools o' th' other senses,
45 Or else worth all the rest. I see thee still;
And on thy blade and dudgeon° gouts° of blood,
Which was not so before. There's no such thing.
It is the bloody business which informs°
Thus to mine eyes. Now o'er the one half-world
50 Nature seems dead, and wicked dreams abuse°
The curtained sleep; witchcraft celebrates
Pale Hecate's offerings;° and withered murder,
Alarumed° by his sentinel, the wolf,
Whose howl's his watch, thus with his stealthy pace,
55 With Tarquin's° ravishing strides, towards his design
Moves like a ghost. Thou sure and firm-set earth,
Hear not my steps, which way they walk, for fear
Thy very stones prate of my whereabout,
And take the present horror from the time,
Which now suits with it.° Whiles I threat, he
60   lives:
Words to the heat of deeds too cold breath gives.

A bell rings.

I go, and it is done: the bell invites me.
Hear it not, Duncan, for it is a knell
That summons thee to heaven, or to hell.

Exit.

46 *dudgeon* wooden hilt 46 *gouts* large drops 48 *informs* gives shape
(?) 50 *abuse* deceive 52 *Hecate's offerings* offerings to Hecate (goddess of sorcery) 53 *Alarumed* called to action 55 *Tarquin* (Roman
tyrant who ravished Lucrece) 59-60*take . . . it* remove (by noise) the
horrible silence attendant on this moment and suitable to it (?)

Scene II.   [*Macbeth's Castle.*]

Enter Lady [Macbeth].

Lady Macbeth. That which hath made them drunk hath
 made me bold;
 What hath quenched them hath given me fire. Hark!
  Peace!
 It was the owl that shrieked, the fatal bellman,
 Which gives the stern'st good-night.° He is about it.
 The doors are open, and the surfeited grooms   *5*
 Do mock their charge with snores. I have drugged
  their possets,°
 That death and nature° do contend about them,
 Whether they live or die.

Macbeth.   [*Within*] Who's there? What, ho?

Lady Macbeth. Alack, I am afraid they have awaked
 And 'tis not done! Th' attempt and not the deed *10*
 Confounds° us. Hark! I laid their daggers ready;
 He could not miss 'em. Had he not resembled
 My father as he slept, I had done 't.

Enter Macbeth.

            My husband!

Macbeth. I have done the deed. Didst thou not hear a
 noise?

Lady Macbeth. I heard the owl scream and the crickets
 cry.   *15*
 Did not you speak?

Macbeth.   When?

II.ii.3-4 *bellman . . . good-night* i.e., the owl's call, portending death,
is like the town crier's call to a condemned man 6 *possets* (bedtime
drinks) 7 *nature* natural vitality 11 *Confounds* ruins

Lady Macbeth.   Now.

Macbeth.   As I descended?

Lady Macbeth. Ay.

Macbeth. Hark!
  Who lies i' th' second chamber?

Lady Macbeth.   Donalbain.

20 *Macbeth.* This is a sorry° sight.

Lady Macbeth. A foolish thought, to say a sorry sight.

Macbeth. There's one did laugh in 's sleep, and one
  cried "Murder!"
  That they did wake each other. I stood and heard
  them.
  But they did say their prayers, and addressed them
  Again to sleep.

25 *Lady Macbeth.*   There are two lodged together.

Macbeth. One cried "God bless us!" and "Amen" the
  other,
  As they had seen me with these hangman's° hands:
  List'ning their fear, I could not say "Amen,"
  When they did say "God bless us!"

Lady Macbeth.   Consider it not so deeply.

Macbeth. But wherefore could not I pronounce
30 "Amen"?
  I had most need of blessing, and "Amen"
  Stuck in my throat.

Lady Macbeth.   These deeds must not be thought
  After these ways; so, it will make us mad.

Macbeth. Methought I heard a voice cry "Sleep no
  more!
85 Macbeth does murder sleep"—the innocent sleep,
  Sleep that knits up the raveled sleave° of care,

---

20 *sorry* miserable   27 *hangman's* executioner's (i.e., bloody)   36 *knits up the raveled sleave* straightens out the tangled skein

The death of each day's life, sore labor's bath,
Balm of hurt minds, great nature's second course,°
Chief nourisher in life's feast——

Lady Macbeth.   What do you mean?

Macbeth. Still it cried "Sleep no more!" to all the
    house: 40
  "Glamis hath murdered sleep, and therefore
    Cawdor
  Shall sleep no more: Macbeth shall sleep no more."

Lady Macbeth. Who was it that thus cried? Why,
    worthy Thane,
  You do unbend° your noble strength, to think
  So brainsickly of things. Go get some water,   45
  And wash this filthy witness° from your hand.
  Why did you bring these daggers from the place?
  They must lie there: go carry them, and smear
  The sleepy grooms with blood.

Macbeth.   I'll go no more.
  I am afraid to think what I have done;   50
  Look on 't again I dare not.

Lady Macbeth.   Infirm of purpose!
  Give me the daggers. The sleeping and the dead
  Are but as pictures. 'Tis the eye of childhood
  That fears a painted° devil. If he do bleed,
  I'll gild° the faces of the grooms withal,   55
  For it must seem their guilt.

                    Exit. Knock within.

Macbeth.   Whence is that knocking?
  How is 't with me, when every noise appalls me?
  What hands are here? Ha! They pluck out mine
    eyes!
  Will all great Neptune's ocean wash this blood
  Clean from my hand? No; this my hand will rather   60

---

38 *second course* i.e., sleep (the less substantial first course is food)
44 *unbend* relax 46 *witness* evidence 54 *painted* depicted 55 *gild* paint

The multitudinous seas incarnadine,°
Making the green one red.°

Enter Lady [Macbeth].

Lady Macbeth. My hands are of your color, but I
    shame
    To wear a heart so white. (*Knock.*) I hear a
    knocking
65   At the south entry. Retire we to our chamber.
    A little water clears us of this deed:
    How easy is it then! Your constancy
    Hath left you unattended.° (*Knock.*) Hark! more
    knocking.
    Get on your nightgown,° lest occasion call us
70   And show us to be watchers.° Be not lost
    So poorly° in your thoughts.

Macbeth. To know my deed, 'twere best not know
    myself. (*Knock.*)
    Wake Duncan with thy knocking! I would thou
    couldst!   *Exeunt.*

Scene III.   [*Macbeth's Castle.*]

Enter a Porter. Knocking within.

Porter. Here's a knocking indeed! If a man were
    porter of hell gate, he should have old° turning the
    key. (*Knock.*) Knock, knock, knock! Who's there,

---

61 *incarnadine* redden 62 *the green one red* (perhaps "the green one"
means "the ocean," but perhaps "one" here means "totally," "uniform-
ly") 67-68 *Your . . . unattended* your firmness has deserted you
69 *nightgown* dressing-gown 70 *watchers* i.e., up late 71 *poorly* weakly
II.iii. 2 *should have old* would certainly have plenty of

i' th' name of Beelzebub? Here's a farmer, that
hanged himself on th' expectation of plenty.° Come   5
in time! Have napkins enow° about you; here you'll
sweat for 't. (*Knock.*) Knock, knock! Who's there,
in th' other devil's name? Faith, here's an equivocator,° that could swear in both the scales against
either scale; who committed treason enough for   10
God's sake, yet could not equivocate to heaven. O,
come in, equivocator. (*Knock.*) Knock, knock,
knock! Who's there? Faith, here's an English tailor
come hither for stealing out of a French hose:°
come in, tailor. Here you may roast your goose.°   15
(*Knock.*) Knock, knock; never at quiet! What are
you? But this place is too cold for hell. I'll devil-
porter it no further. I had thought to have let in
some of all professions that go the primrose way
to th' everlasting bonfire. (*Knock.*) Anon, anon!   20
[*Opens an entrance.*] I pray you, remember the
porter.

Enter Macduff and Lennox.

Macduff. Was it so late, friend, ere you went to bed,
That you do lie so late?

Porter. Faith, sir, we were carousing till the second   25
cock:° and drink, sir, is a great provoker of three
things.

Macduff. What three things does drink especially pro-
voke?

Porter. Marry, sir, nose-painting, sleep, and urine.   30
Lechery, sir, it provokes and unprovokes; it provokes the desire, but it takes away the performance: therefore much drink may be said to be an
equivocator with lechery: it makes him and it mars

---

⁴⁻⁵ *farmer . . . plenty* (the farmer hoarded so he could later sell high,
but when it looked as though there would be a crop surplus he hanged
himself)   ⁶ *enow* enough   ⁸⁻⁹ *equivocator* i.e., Jesuit (who allegedly
employed deceptive speech to further God's ends)   ¹⁴ *French hose* tight-
fitting hose   ¹⁵ *goose* pressing iron   ²⁵⁻²⁶ *second cock* (about 3 a.m.)

35   him; it sets him on and it takes him off; it per-
        suades him and disheartens him; makes him stand
        to and not stand to; in conclusion, equivocates
        him in a sleep, and giving him the lie, leaves him.

Macduff. I believe drink gave thee the lie° last night.

40 *Porter.* That it did, sir, i' the very throat on me: but
        I requited him for his lie, and, I think, being too
        strong for him, though he took up my legs some-
        time, yet I make a shift to cast° him.

Macduff. Is thy master stirring?

                    Enter Macbeth.

45   Our knocking has awaked him; here he comes.

Lennox. Good morrow, noble sir.

Macbeth.   Good morrow, both.

Macduff. Is the king stirring, worthy Thane?

Macbeth.   Not yet.

Macduff. He did command me to call timely° on him:
        I have almost slipped° the hour.

Macbeth.   I'll bring you to him.

50 *Macduff.* I know this is a joyful trouble to you;
        But yet 'tis one.

Macbeth. The labor we delight in physics pain.°
        This is the door.

Macduff.   I'll make so bold to call,
        For 'tis my limited service.°

                              Exit Macduff.

Lennox. Goes the king hence today?

55 *Macbeth.*   He does: he did appoint so.

<hr />

39 *gave thee the lie* called you a liar (with a pun on "stretched you
out")   43 *cast* (with a pun on "cast," meaning "vomit")   48 *timely*
early   49 *slipped* let slip   52 *The labor . . . pain* labor that gives us
pleasure cures discomfort   54 *limited service* appointed duty

Lennox. The night has been unruly. Where we lay,
  Our chimneys were blown down, and, as they say,
  Lamentings heard i' th' air, strange screams of
    death,
  And prophesying with accents terrible
  Of dire combustion° and confused events   60
  ·New hatched to th' woeful time: the obscure bird°
  Clamored the livelong night. Some say, the earth
  Was feverous and did shake.

Macbeth.   'Twas a rough night.

Lennox. My young remembrance cannot parallel
  A fellow to it.   65

Enter Macduff.

Macduff. O horror, horror, horror! Tongue nor heart
  Cannot conceive nor name thee.

Macbeth and Lennox.   What's the matter?

Macduff. Confusion° now hath made his masterpiece.
  Most sacrilegious murder hath broke ope
  The Lord's anointed temple, and stole thence   70
  The life o' th' building.

Macbeth.   What is 't you say? The life?

Lennox. Mean you his Majesty?

Macduff. Approach the chamber, and destroy your
    sight
  With a new Gorgon:° do not bid me speak;
  See, and then speak yourselves. Awake, awake!   75

Exeunt Macbeth and Lennox.

  Ring the alarum bell. Murder and Treason!
  Banquo and Donalbain! Malcolm! Awake!
  Shake off this downy sleep, death's counterfeit,°
  And look on death itself! Up, up, and see
  The great doom's image!° Malcolm! Banquo!   80

---

⁶⁰ *combustion* tumult   ⁶¹ *obscure bird* bird of darkness, i.e., the owl
⁶⁸ *Confusion* destruction   ⁷⁴ *Gorgon* (creature capable of turning be-
holders to stone)   ⁷⁸ *counterfeit* imitation   ⁸⁰ *great doom's image* likeness of Judgment Day

As from your graves rise up, and walk like sprites,°
To countenance° this horror. Ring the bell.

   Bell rings. Enter Lady [*Macbeth*].

Lady Macbeth. What's the business,
 That such a hideous trumpet calls to parley
 The sleepers of the house? Speak, speak!

85 *Macduff.*   O gentle lady,
 'Tis not for you to hear what I can speak:
 The repetition,° in a woman's ear,
 Would murder as it fell.

     Enter Banquo.

        O Banquo, Banquo!
 Our royal master's murdered.

Lady Macbeth.   Woe, alas!
 What, in our house?

90 *Banquo.*   Too cruel anywhere.
 Dear Duff, I prithee, contradict thyself,
 And say it is not so.

    Enter Macbeth, Lennox, and Ross.

Macbeth. Had I but died an hour before this chance,
 I had lived a blessèd time; for from this instant
95 There's nothing serious in mortality:°
 All is but toys.° Renown and grace is dead,
 The wine of life is drawn, and the mere lees°
 Is left this vault° to brag of.

   Enter Malcolm and Donalbain.

Donalbain. What is amiss?

Macbeth.   You are, and do not know 't.
100 The spring, the head, the fountain of your blood
 Is stopped; the very source of it is stopped.

Macduff. Your royal father's murdered.

---

81 *sprites* spirits   82 *countenance* be in keeping with   87 *repetition* report   95 *serious in mortality* worthwhile in mortal life   96 *toys* trifles 97 *lees* dregs   98 *vault* (1) wine vault (2) earth, with the sky as roof (?)

Malcolm   O, by whom?

Lennox. Those of his chamber, as it seemed, had
    done 't:
  Their hands and faces were all badged° with blood;
  So were their daggers, which unwiped we found   *105*
  Upon their pillows. They stared, and were
    distracted.
  No man's life was to be trusted with them.

Macbeth. O, yet I do repent me of my fury,
  That I did kill them.

Macduff.   Wherefore did you so?

Macbeth. Who can be wise, amazed,° temp'rate and
    furious,   *110*
  Loyal and neutral, in a moment? No man.
  The expedition° of my violent love
  Outrun the pauser, reason. Here lay Duncan,
  His silver skin laced with his golden blood,
  And his gashed stabs looked like a breach in nature *115*
  For ruin's wasteful entrance: there, the murderers,
  Steeped in the colors of their trade, their daggers
  Unmannerly breeched with gore.° Who could
    refrain,°
  That had a heart to love, and in that heart
  Courage to make 's love known?

Lady Macbeth.   Help me hence, ho! *120*

Macduff. Look to° the lady.

Malcolm. [*Aside to Donalbain*] Why do we hold
    our tongues,
  That most may claim this argument for ours?°

Donalbain. [*Aside to Malcolm*] What should be
    spoken here,
  Where our fate, hid in an auger-hole,°

---

104 *badged* marked   110 *amazed* bewildered   112 *expedition* h a s t e
118 *Unmannerly breeched with gore* covered with unseemly breeches of
blood   118 *refrain* check oneself   121 *Look to* look after   123 *That
most . . . ours?* who are the most concerned with this topic   124 *auger-hole* i.e., unsuspected place

125   May rush, and seize us? Let's away:
        Our tears are not yet brewed.

Malcolm. [*Aside to Donalbain*] Nor our strong
            sorrow
        Upon the foot of motion.°
Banquo.   Look to the lady.

                    [*Lady Macbeth is carried out.*]

        And when we have our naked frailties hid,°
        That suffer in exposure, let us meet
130   And question° this most bloody piece of work,
        To know it further. Fears and scruples° shake us.
        In the great hand of God I stand, and thence
        Against the undivulged pretense° I fight
        Of treasonous malice.

Macduff.   And so do I.

All.   So all.

135 Macbeth. Let's briefly° put on manly readiness,
        And meet i' th' hall together.

All.   Well contented.

            Exeunt [*all but Malcolm and Donalbain*].

Malcolm. What will you do? Let's not consort with
            them.
        To show an unfelt sorrow is an office°
        Which the false man does easy. I'll to England.

140 Donalbain. To Ireland, I; our separated fortune
        Shall keep us both the safer. Where we are
        There's daggers in men's smiles; the near in blood,
        The nearer bloody.

Malcolm.   This murderous shaft that's shot
        Hath not yet lighted, and our safest way

---

¹²⁶⁻²⁷ *Our tears . . . motion* i.e., we have not yet had time for tears
nor to express our sorrows in action (?) ¹²⁸ *naked frailties hid* poor
bodies clothed ¹³⁰ *question* discuss ¹³¹*scruples* suspicions ¹³³ *un-
divulged pretense* hidden purpose ¹³⁵ *briefly* quickly ¹³⁸ *office* function

Is to avoid the aim. Therefore to horse;   *145*
And let us not be dainty of° leave-taking,
But shift away. There's warrant° in that theft
Which steals itself° when there's no mercy left.

                                        Exeunt.

Scene IV.   [*Outside Macbeth's castle.*]

Enter Ross with an Old Man.

Old Man. Threescore and ten I can remember well:
Within the volume of which time I have seen
Hours dreadful and things strange, but this sore°
    night
Hath trifled former knowings.°

Ross.   Ha, good father,
Thou seest the heavens, as troubled with man's act,   *5*
Threatens his bloody stage. By th' clock 'tis day,
And yet dark night strangles the traveling lamp:°
Is 't night's predominance,° or the day's shame,
That darkness does the face of earth entomb,
When living light should kiss it?

Old Man.   'Tis unnatural,   *10*
Even like the deed that's done. On Tuesday last
A falcon, tow'ring in her pride of place,°
Was by a mousing° owl hawked at and killed.

Ross. And Duncan's horses—a thing most strange
    and certain—
Beauteous and swift, the minions° of their race,   *15*

---

146 *dainty of* fussy about   147 *warrant* justification   148 *steals itself*
steals oneself away   II.iv.   3 *sore* grievous   4 *trifled former knowings*
made trifles of former experiences   7 *traveling lamp* i.e., the sun   8 *pre-*
dominance astrological supremacy   12 *tow'ring . . . place* soaring at
her summit   13 *mousing* i.e., normally mouse-eating   15 *minions* darlings

Turned wild in nature, broke their stalls, flung out,°
Contending 'gainst obedience, as they would make
War with mankind.

Old Man.   'Tis said they eat° each other.

Ross. They did so, to th' amazement of mine eyes,
That looked upon 't.

Enter Macduff.

20   Here comes the good Macduff.
How goes the world, sir, now?

Macduff.   Why, see you not?

Ross. Is 't known who did this more than bloody deed?

Macduff. Those that Macbeth hath slain.

Ross.   Alas, the day!
What good could they pretend?°

Macduff.   They were suborned:°
25   Malcolm and Donalbain, the king's two sons,
Are stol'n away and fled, which puts upon them
Suspicion of the deed.

Ross.   'Gainst nature still.
Thriftless° ambition, that will ravin up°
Thine own life's means! Then 'tis most like
30   The sovereignty will fall upon Macbeth.

Macduff. He is already named,° and gone to Scone
To be invested.°

Ross.   Where is Duncan's body?

Macduff. Carried to Colmekill,
The sacred storehouse of his predecessors
And guardian of their bones.

35   *Ross.*   Will you to Scone?

Macduff. No, cousin, I'll to Fife.

---

16 *flung out* lunged wildly   18 *eat* ate   24 *pretend* hope for   24 *suborned* bribed   28 *Thriftless* wasteful   28 *ravin up* greedily devour   31 *named* elected   32 *invested* installed as king

Ross.   Well, I will thither.

Macduff. Well, may you see things well done there.
     Adieu,
Lest our old robes sit easier than our new!

Ross. Farewell, father.

Old Man. God's benison° go with you, and with those   40
That would make good of bad, and friends of foes!

                       Exeunt omnes.

40 *benison* blessing

ACT III

Scene I. [*Forres. The palace.*]

Enter Banquo.

Banquo. Thou hast it now: King, Cawdor, Glamis, all,
As the weïrd women promised, and I fear
Thou play'dst most foully for 't. Yet it was said
It should not stand° in thy posterity,
5   But that myself should be the root and father
Of many kings. If there come truth from them—
As upon thee, Macbeth, their speeches shine—
Why, by the verities on thee made good,
May they not be my oracles as well
10 And set me up in hope? But hush, no more!

Sennet° sounded. Enter Macbeth as King, Lady
[*Macbeth*], *Lennox, Ross, Lords, and Attendants*

Macbeth. Here's our chief guest.

Lady Macbeth.   If he had been forgotten,
It had been as a gap in our great feast,
And all-thing° unbecoming.

Macbeth. Tonight we hold a solemn° supper, sir,
And I'll request your presence.

15 *Banquo.*   Let your Highness
Command upon me, to the which my duties

III.i 4 *stand* continue   s.d. *Sennet* trumpet call   13 *all-thing* altogether
14 *solemn* ceremonious

74

    Are with a most indissoluble tie
    For ever knit.

Macbeth. Ride you this afternoon?

Banquo.   Ay, my good lord.

Macbeth. We should have else desired your good advice   20
    (Which still° hath been both grave and
      prosperous°)
    In this day's council; but we'll take tomorrow.
    Is 't far you ride?

Banquo. As far, my lord, as will fill up the time
    'Twixt this and supper. Go not my horse the
      better,°   25
    I must become a borrower of the night
    For a dark hour or twain.

Macbeth.   Fail not our feast.

Banquo. My lord, I will not.

Macbeth. We hear our bloody cousins are bestowed°
    In England and in Ireland, not confessing   30
    Their cruel parricide, filling their hearers
    With strange invention.° But of that tomorrow,
    When therewithal we shall have cause of state
    Craving us jointly.° Hie you to horse. Adieu,
    Till you return at night. Goes Fleance with you?   35

Banquo. Ay, my good lord: our time does call upon 's.

Macbeth. I wish your horses swift and sure of foot,
    And so I do commend you to their backs.
    Farewell.   *Exit Banquo.*
    Let every man be master of his time   40
    Till seven at night. To make society
    The sweeter welcome, we will keep ourself

---

21 *still* always   21 *grave and prosperous* weighty and profitable   25 *Go
. . . better* unless my horse goes better than I expect   29 *are bestowed*
have taken refuge   32 *invention* lies   33-34 *cause . . . jointly* matters of
state demanding our joint attention

Till supper-time alone. While° then, God be with
   you!

    Exeunt Lords [and all but Macbeth and a Servant].

45   Sirrah,° a word with you: attend° those men
Our pleasure?

Attendant. They are, my lord, without° the palace
   gate.

Macbeth. Bring them before us.   *Exit Servant.*
To be thus is nothing, but° to be safely thus—
Our fears in° Banquo stick deep,
50   And in his royalty of nature reigns that
Which would° be feared. 'Tis much he dares;
And, to° that dauntless temper° of his mind,
He hath a wisdom that doth guide his valor
To act in safety. There is none but he
55   Whose being I do fear: and under him
My genius is rebuked,° as it is said
Mark Antony's was by Cæsar. He chid the sisters,
When first they put the name of King upon me,
And bade them speak to him; then prophetlike
60   They hailed him father to a line of kings.
Upon my head they placed a fruitless crown
And put a barren scepter in my gripe,°
Thence to be wrenched with an unlineal hand,
No son of mine succeeding. If 't be so,
65   For Banquo's issue have I filed° my mind;
For them the gracious Duncan have I murdered;
Put rancors° in the vessel of my peace
Only for them, and mine eternal jewel°
Given to the common enemy of man,°
70   To make them kings, the seeds of Banquo kings!

---

43 *While* until 44 *Sirrah* (common address to an inferior) 44 *attend*
await 46 *without* outside 48 *but* unless 49 *in* about 51 *would* must
52 *to* added to 52 *temper* quality 56 *genius is rebuked* guardian spirit
is cowed 62 *gripe* grasp 65 *filed* defiled 67 *rancors* bitter enmities
68 *eternal jewel* i.e., soul 69 *common enemy of man* i.e., the Devil

Rather than so, come, fate, into the list,°
And champion me to th' utterance!° Who's there?

Enter Servant and Two Murderers.

Now go to the door, and stay there till we call.

Exit Servant.

Was it not yesterday we spoke together?

Murderers. It was, so please your Highness.

Macbeth   Well then, now   75
Have you considered of my speeches? Know
That it was he in the times past, which held you
So under fortune,° which you thought had been
Our innocent self: this I made good to you
In our last conference; passed in probation° with
    you,   80
How you were born in hand,° how crossed;° the
    instruments,°
Who wrought with them, and all things else that
    might
To half a soul° and to a notion° crazed
Say "Thus did Banquo."

First Murderer.   You made it known to us.

Macbeth. I did so; and went further, which is now   85
Our point of second meeting. Do you find
Your patience so predominant in your nature,
That you can let this go? Are you so gospeled,°
To pray for this good man and for his issue,
Whose heavy hand hath bowed you to the grave   90
And beggared yours for ever?

First Murderer.   We are men, my liege.

Macbeth. Ay, in the catalogue ye go for° men;

71 *list* lists   72 *champion me to th' utterance* fight against me to the
death   77-78 *held . . . fortune* kept you from good fortune (?)   80 *passed
in probation* reviewed the proofs   81 *borne in hand* deceived   81 *crossed*
thwarted   81 *instruments* tools   83 *half a soul* a halfwit   83 *notion* mind
88 *gospeled* i.e., made meek by the gospel   92 *go for* pass as

As hounds and greyhounds, mongrels, spaniels,
    curs,
Shoughs, water-rugs° and demi-wolves, are clept°
95 All by the name of dogs: the valued file°
Distinguishes the swift, the slow, the subtle,
The housekeeper,° the hunter, every one
According to the gift which bounteous nature
Hath in him closed,° whereby he does receive
100 Particular addition, from the bill°
That writes them all alike: and so of men.
Now if you have a station in the file,
Not i' th' worst rank of manhood, say 't,
And I will put that business in your bosoms
105 Whose execution takes your enemy off,
Grapples you to the heart and love of us,
Who wear our health but sickly in his life,°
Which in his death were perfect.

Second Murderer.   I am one, my liege,
Whom the vile blows and buffets of the world
110 Hath so incensed that I am reckless what
I do to spite the world.

First Murderer.   And I another
So weary with disasters, tugged with fortune,
That I would set° my life on any chance,
To mend it or be rid on 't.

Macbeth.   Both of you
Know Banquo was your enemy.

115 *Both Murderers.*   True, my lord.

Macbeth. So is he mine, and in such bloody distance°
That every minute of his being thrusts
Against my near'st of life:° and though I could

---

94 *Shoughs, water-rugs* shaggy dogs, long-haired water dogs 94 *clept*
called 95 *valued file* classification by valuable traits 97 *housekeeper*
watchdog 99 *closed* enclosed 100 *Particular addition, from the bill*
special distinction in opposition to the list 107 *wear . . . life* have
only imperfect health while he lives 113 *set* risk 116 *distance* quarrel
118 *near'st of life* most vital spot

With barefaced power sweep him from my sight
And bid my will avouch° it, yet I must not,   *120*
For° certain friends that are both his and mine,
Whose loves I may not drop, but wail his fall°
Who I myself struck down: and thence it is
That I to your assistance do make love,
Masking the business from the common eye   *125*
For sundry weighty reasons.

Second Murderer.   We shall, my lord,
Perform what you command us.

First Murderer.   Though our lives——

Macbeth. Your spirits shine through you. Within this
          hour at most
I will advise you where to plant yourselves,
Acquaint you with the perfect spy° o' th' time,   *130*
The moment on 't;° for 't must be done tonight,
And something° from the palace; always thought°
That I require a clearness:° and with him—
To leave no rubs° nor botches in the work—
Fleance his son, that keeps him company,   *135*
Whose absence is no less material to me
Than is his father's, must embrace the fate
Of that dark hour. Resolve yourselves apart:°
I'll come to you anon.

Murderers.   We are resolved, my lord.

Macbeth. I'll call upon you straight.° Abide within.   *140*
It is concluded: Banquo, thy soul's flight,
If it find heaven, must find it out tonight.   *Exeunt.*

---

120 *avouch* justify   121 *For* because of   122 *wail his fall* bewail his death
130 *perfect spy* exact information (?) (*spy* literally means "observation";
apparently Macbeth already has the Third Murderer in mind)   131 *on 't*
of it   132 *something* some distance   132 *thought* remembered   133 *clearness* freedom from suspicion   134 *rubs* flaws   138 *Resolve yourselves
apart* decide by yourself   140 *straight* immediately

Scene II.   [*The palace*.]

Enter Macbeth's Lady and a Servant.

Lady Macbeth. Is Banquo gone from court?

Servant. Ay, madam, but returns again tonight.

Lady Macbeth. Say to the King, I would attend his
  leisure
For a few words.

Servant.   Madam, I will.   *Exit.*

Lady Macbeth.   Nought's had, all's spent,
5   Where our desire is got without content:
'Tis safer to be that which we destroy
Than by destruction dwell in doubtful joy.

Enter Macbeth.

How now, my lord! Why do you keep alone,
Of sorriest° fancies your companions making,
Using those thoughts which should indeed have
10   died
With them they think on? Things without° all
  remedy
Should be without regard: what's done is done.

Macbeth. We have scorched° the snake, not killed it:
She'll close° and be herself, whilst our poor malice°
15   Remains in danger of her former tooth.
But let the frame of things disjoint,° both the
  worlds° suffer,
Ere we will eat our meal in fear, and sleep
In the affliction of these terrible dreams

III.ii.   9 *sorriest* most despicable   11 *without* beyond   13 *scorched*
slashed, scored   14 *close* heal   14 *poor malice* feeble enmity   16 *frame
of things disjoint* universe collapse   16 *both the worlds* heaven and
earth (?)

That shake us nightly: better be with the dead,
Whom we, to gain our peace, have sent to peace,   *20*
Than on the torture° of the mind to lie
In restless ecstasy.° Duncan is in his grave;
After life's fitful fever he sleeps well.
Treason has done his° worst: nor steel, nor poison,
Malice domestic,° foreign levy, nothing,   *25*
Can touch him further.

Lady Macbeth.   Come on.
Gentle my lord, sleek° o'er your rugged° looks;
Be bright and jovial among your guests tonight.

Macbeth. So shall I, love; and so, I pray, be you:
Let your remembrance apply to Banquo;°   *30*
Present him eminence,° both with eye and tongue:
Unsafe the while, that we must lave°
Our honors in these flattering streams
And make our faces vizards° to our hearts,
Disguising what they are.

Lady Macbeth.   You must leave this.   *35*

Macbeth. O, full of scorpions is my mind, dear wife!
Thou know'st that Banquo, and his Fleance, lives.

Lady Macbeth. But in them nature's copy's° not eterne.

Macbeth. There's comfort yet; they are assailable.
Then be thou jocund. Ere the bat hath flown   *40*
His cloistered flight, ere to black Hecate's summons
The shard-borne° beetle with his drowsy hums
Hath rung night's yawning peal, there shall be done
A deed of dreadful note.

Lady Macbeth.   What's to be done?

21 *torture* i.e., rack 22 *ecstasy* frenzy 24 *his* its 25 *Malice domestic*
civil war 27 *sleek* smooth 27 *rugged* furrowed 30 *Let . . . Banquo*
focus your thoughts on Banquo 31 *Present him eminence* honor him
32 *Unsafe . . . lave* i.e., you and I are unsafe because we must dip
34 *vizards* masks 38 *nature's copy* nature's lease (?) imitation (i.e., a
son) made by nature (?) 42 *shard-borne* borne on scaly wings (?)
dung-bred (?)

Macbeth. Be innocent of the knowledge, dearest
45   chuck,°
            Till thou applaud the deed. Come, seeling° night,
            Scarf up° the tender eye of pitiful day,
            And with thy bloody and invisible hand
            Cancel and tear to pieces that great bond°
50   Which keeps me pale! Light thickens, and the crow
            Makes wing to th' rooky° wood.
            Good things of day begin to droop and drowse,
            Whiles night's black agents to their preys do rouse.
            Thou marvel'st at my words: but hold thee still;
55   Things bad begun make strong themselves by ill:
            So, prithee, go with me.   *Exeunt.*

Scene III.   [*Near the palace.*]

Enter Three Murderers.

First Murderer. But who did bid thee join with us?

Third Murderer.   Macbeth.

Second Murderer. He needs not our mistrust; since he
            delivers
            Our offices and what we have to do
            To the direction just.°

First Murderer.   Then stand with us.
5   The west yet glimmers with some streaks of day.
            Now spurs the lated° traveler apace
            To gain the timely inn, and near approaches
            The subject of our watch.

45 *chuck* chick (a term of endearment)   46 *seeling* eye-closing   47 *Scarf up* blindfold   49 *bond* i.e., between Banquo and fate (?) Banquo's lease on life (?) Macbeth's link to humanity (?)   51 *rooky* full of rooks III.iii.   2-4 *He needs . . . just* we need not mistrust him (i.e., the Third Murderer) since he describes our duties according to our exact directions   6 *lated* belated

Third Murderer.   Hark! I hear horses.

Banquo. (*Within*) Give us a light there, ho!

Second Murderer.   Then 'tis he. The rest
  That are within the note of expectation°   10
  Already are i' th' court.

First Murderer.   His horses go about.

Third Murderer. Almost a mile: but he does usually—
  So all men do—from hence to th' palace gate
  Make it their walk.

     Enter Banquo and Fleance, with a torch.

Second Murderer. A light, a light!

Third Murderer.   'Tis he.

First Murderer.   Stand to 't.   15

Banquo. It will be rain tonight.

First Murderer.   Let it come down.

     [*They set upon Banquo.*]

Banquo. O, treachery! Fly, good Fleance, fly, fly, fly!

                [*Exit Fleance.*]

  Thou mayst revenge. O slave! [*Dies.*]

Third Murderer. Who did strike out the light?

First Murderer.   Was 't not the way?°

Third Murderer. There's but one down; the son is fled.   20

Second Murderer. We have lost best half of our affair.

First Murderer. Well, let's away and say how much is
    done.   *Exeunt.*

10 *within the note of expectation* on the list of expected guests 19 *way*
i.e., thing to do

Scene IV.   [*The palace.*]

Banquet prepared. Enter Macbeth, Lady [Mac-
beth], Ross, Lennox, Lords, and Attendants.

Macbeth. You know your own degrees;° sit down:
  At first and last, the hearty welcome.

Lords. Thanks to your Majesty.

Macbeth. Ourself will mingle with society°
5   And play the humble host.
  Our hostess keeps her state,° but in best time
  We will require° her welcome.

Lady Macbeth. Pronounce it for me, sir, to all our
      friends,
  For my heart speaks they are welcome.

Enter First Murderer.

Macbeth. See, they encounter° thee with their hearts'
10   thanks.
  Both sides are even: here I'll sit i' th' midst:
  Be large in mirth; anon we'll drink a measure°
  The table round. [*Goes to Murderer*] There's
      blood upon thy face.

Murderer. 'Tis Banquo's then.

15 *Macbeth.* 'Tis better thee without than he within.°
  Is he dispatched?

Murderer. My lord, his throat is cut; that I did for
      him.

Macbeth. Thou art the best o' th' cutthroats.

III.iv.   ¹ *degrees* ranks   ⁴ *society* the company   ⁶ *keeps her state* remains seated in her chair of state   ⁷ *require* request   ¹⁰ *encounter* meet
¹² *measure* goblet   ¹⁵ *thee without than he within* outside you than
inside him

Yet he's good that did the like for Fleance;
If thou didst it, thou art the nonpareil.   20

Murderer. Most royal sir, Fleance is 'scaped.

Macbeth. [*Aside*] Then comes my fit again: I had
      else been perfect,
Whole as the marble, founded° as the rock,
As broad and general as the casing° air:
But now I am cabined, cribbed,° confined, bound in   25
To saucy° doubts and fears.——But Banquo's safe?

Murderer. Ay, my good lord: safe in a ditch he bides,
With twenty trenchèd° gashes on his head,
The least a death to nature.

Macbeth.   Thanks for that.
[*Aside*] There the grown serpent lies; the worm°
      that's fled   30
Hath nature that in time will venom breed,
No teeth for th' present. Get thee gone. Tomorrow
We'll hear ourselves° again.   *Exit Murderer.*

Lady Macbeth.   My royal lord,
You do not give the cheer.° The feast is sold
That is not often vouched, while 'tis a-making,   35
'Tis given with welcome. To feed were best at
      home;°
From thence, the sauce to meat° is ceremony;
Meeting were bare without it.

          *Enter the Ghost of Banquo, and sits in
                Macbeth's place.*

Macbeth.   Sweet remembrancer!°
Now good digestion wait on appetite,
And health on both!

---

²³*founded* firmly based   ²⁴ *broad . . . casing* unconfined as the surrounding   ²⁵ *cribbed* penned up   ²⁶ *saucy* insolent   ²⁸ *trenchèd* trench-
like   ³⁰ *worm* serpent   ³³ *hear ourselves* talk it over   ³⁴ *the cheer* a
sense of cordiality   ³⁴⁻³⁶ *The feast . . . home* i.e., the feast seems sold
(not given) during which the host fails to welcome the guests. Mere eat-
ing is best done at home   ³⁷ *meat* food   ³⁸ *remembrancer* reminder

⁴⁰ *Lennox.*　　　　　　　May 't please your Highness sit.

Macbeth. Here had we now our country's honor
　　roofed,°
　　Were the graced person of our Banquo present—
　　Who may I rather challenge for unkindness
　　Than pity for mischance!°

Ross.　　　　　　　　　　His absence, sir,
　　Lays blame upon his promise. Please 't your
⁴⁵　　Highness
　　To grace us with your royal company?

Macbeth. The table's full.

Lennox.　　　　　　Here is a place reserved, sir.

Macbeth. Where?

Lennox. Here, my good lord. What is 't that moves
　　your Highness?

Macbeth. Which of you have done this?

⁵⁰ *Lords.*　　　　　　　　What, my good lord?

Macbeth. Thou canst not say I did it. Never shake
　　Thy gory locks at me.

Ross. Gentlemen, rise, his Highness is not well.

Lady Macbeth. Sit, worthy friends. My lord is often
　　thus,
⁵⁵　　And hath been from his youth. Pray you, keep seat.
　　The fit is momentary; upon a thought°
　　He will again be well. If much you note him,
　　You shall offend him and extend his passion.°
　　Feed, and regard him not.—Are you a man?

⁶⁰ *Macbeth.* Ay, and a bold one, that dare look on that
　　Which might appall the devil.

Lady Macbeth.　　　　　　O proper stuff!
　　This is the very painting of your fear.
　　This is the air-drawn dagger which, you said,

---

⁴¹ *our country's honor roofed* our nobility under one roof　⁴³⁻⁴⁴ *Who
. . . mischance* whom I hope I may reprove because he is unkind rather
than pity because he has encountered an accident　⁵⁶ *upon a thought*
as quick as thought　⁵⁸ *extend his passion* lengthen his fit

Led you to Duncan. O, these flaws° and starts,
Impostors to° true fear, would well become   65
A woman's story at a winter's fire,
Authorized° by her grandam. Shame itself!
Why do you make such faces? When all's done,
You look but on a stool.

Macbeth.   Prithee, see there!
Behold! Look! Lo! How say you?   70
Why, what care I? If thou canst nod, speak too.
If charnel houses° and our graves must send
Those that we bury back, our monuments
Shall be the maws of kites.°   [*Exit Ghost.*]

Lady Macbeth.   What, quite unmanned in folly?

Macbeth. If I stand here, I saw him.

Lady Macbeth.   Fie, for shame!   75

Macbeth. Blood hath been shed ere now, i' th' olden
          time,
Ere humane statute purged the gentle weal;°
Ay, and since too, murders have been performed
Too terrible for the ear. The times has been
That, when the brains were out, the man would die,   80
And there an end; but now they rise again,
With twenty mortal murders on their crowns,°
And push us from our stools. This is more strange
Than such a murder is.

Lady Macbeth.   My worthy lord,
Your noble friends do lack you.

Macbeth.   I do forget.   85
Do not muse at me, my most worthy friends;
I have a strange infirmity, which is nothing
To those that know me. Come, love and health to
          all!

64 *flaws* gusts, outbursts   65 *to* compared with   67 *Authorized* vouched
for   72 *charnel houses* vaults containing bones   73-74 *our . . . kites*
our tombs shall be the bellies of rapacious birds   77 *purged the gentle
weal* i.e., cleansed the state and made it gentle   82 *mortal murders on
their crowns* deadly wounds on their heads

Then I'll sit down. Give me some wine, fill full.

Enter Ghost.

90   I drink to th' general joy o' th' whole table,
        And to our dear friend Banquo, whom we miss;
        Would he were here! To all and him we thirst,°
        And all to all.°

Lords.   Our duties, and the pledge.

Macbeth. Avaunt! and quit my sight! Let the earth hide
        thee!
95   Thy bones are marrowless, thy blood is cold;
        Thou hast no speculation° in those eyes
        Which thou dost glare with.

Lady Macbeth.   Think of this, good peers,
        But as a thing of custom; 'tis no other.
        Only it spoils the pleasure of the time.

100 *Macbeth.* What man dare, I dare.
        Approach thou like the rugged Russian bear,
        The armed rhinoceros, or th' Hyrcan° tiger;
        Take any shape but that, and my firm nerves°
        Shall never tremble. Or be alive again,
105   And dare me to the desert° with thy sword.
        If trembling I inhabit then, protest me
        The baby of a girl.° Hence, horrible shadow!
        Unreal mock'ry, hence!   [*Exit Ghost.*]
                        Why, so: being gone,
        I am a man again. Pray you, sit still.

Lady Macbeth. You have displaced the mirth, broke the
110   good meeting,
        With most admired° disorder.

Macbeth.   Can such things be,
        And overcome us° like a summer's cloud,

---

92 *thirst* desire to drink   93 *all to all* everything to everybody (?) let
everybody drink to everybody (?)   96 *speculation* sight   102 *Hyrcan* of
Hyrcania (near the Caspian Sea)   103 *nerves* sinews   105 *the desert* a
lonely place   106-07 *If . . . girl* if then I tremble, proclaim me a baby
girl   111 *admired* amazing   112 *overcome us* come over us

Without our special wonder? You make me strange
Even to the disposition that I owe,°
When now I think you can behold such sights,   *115*
And keep the natural ruby of your cheeks,
When mine is blanched with fear.

Ross.   What sights, my lord?

Lady Macbeth. I pray you, speak not: he grows worse
   and worse;
   Question enrages him: at once, good night.
   Stand not upon the order of your going,°   *120*
   But go at once.

Lennox.   Good night; and better health
   Attend his Majesty!

Lady Macbeth.   A kind good night to all!

                              Exeunt Lords.

Macbeth. It will have blood, they say: blood will have
   blood.
   Stones have been known to move and trees to
   speak;
   Augures and understood relations° have   *125*
   By maggot-pies and choughs and rooks brought
   forth°
   The secret'st man of blood. What is the night?°

Lady Macbeth. Almost at odds° with morning, which is
   which.

Macbeth. How say'st thou, that Macduff denies his
   person
   At our great bidding?

Lady Macbeth.   Did you send to him, sir?   *130*

Macbeth. I hear it by the way,° but I will send:

---

¹¹³⁻¹⁴ *You . . . owe* i.e., you make me wonder what my nature is
¹²⁰ *Stand . . . going* do not insist on departing in your order of rank
¹²⁵ *Augures and understood relations* auguries and comprehended reports   ¹²⁶ *By . . . forth* by magpies, choughs, and rooks (telltale
birds) revealed   ¹²⁷ *What is the night* what time of night is it
¹²⁸ *at odds* striving   ¹³¹ *by the way* incidentally

There's not a one of them but in his house
I keep a servant fee'd.° I will tomorrow,
And betimes° I will, to the weïrd sisters:
135   More shall they speak, for now I am bent° to know
By the worst means the worst. For mine own good
All causes° shall give way. I am in blood
Stepped in so far that, should I wade no more,
Returning were as tedious as go o'er.
140   Strange things I have in head that will to hand,
Which must be acted ere they may be scanned.°

Lady Macbeth. You lack the season of all natures,°
    sleep.

Macbeth. Come, we'll to sleep. My strange and self-
    abuse°
Is the initiate fear that wants hard use.°
145   We are yet but young in deed.   *Exeunt.*

Scene V.   [*A Witches' haunt.*]

*Thunder. Enter the Three Witches, meeting
Hecate.*

First Witch. Why, how now, Hecate! you look
    angerly.

Hecate. Have I not reason, beldams° as you are,
    Saucy and overbold? How did you dare
    To trade and traffic with Macbeth
5   In riddles and affairs of death;

---

133 *fee'd* i.e., paid to spy   134 *betimes* quickly   135 *bent* determined
137 *causes* considerations   141 *may be scanned* can be examined
142 *season of all natures* seasoning (preservative) of all living creatures
143 *My strange and self-abuse* my strange delusion   144 *initiate . . .
use* beginner's fear that lacks hardening practice   III.v. 2 *beldams* hags

And I, the mistress of your charms,
The close contriver° of all harms,
Was never called to bear my part,
Or show the glory of our art?
And, which is worse, all you have done   10
Hath been but for a wayward son,
Spiteful and wrathful; who, as others do,
Loves for his own ends, not for you.
But make amends now: get you gone,
And at the pit of Acheron°   15
Meet me i' th' morning: thither he
Will come to know his destiny.
Your vessels and your spells provide,
Your charms and everything beside.
I am for th' air; this night I'll spend   20
Unto a dismal and a fatal end:
Great business must be wrought ere noon.
Upon the corner of the moon
There hangs a vap'rous drop profound;°
I'll catch it ere it come to ground: 25
And that distilled by magic sleights°
Shall raise such artificial sprites°
As by the strength of their illusion
Shall draw him on to his confusion.°
He shall spurn fate, scorn death, and bear   30
His hopes 'bove wisdom, grace, and fear:
And you all know security°
Is mortals' chiefest enemy.

Music and a song.

Hark! I am called; my little spirit, see,
Sits in a foggy cloud and stays for me. [*Exit.*] 35
    Sing within, "Come away, come away," &c.

First Witch. Come, let's make haste; she'll soon be
        back again.   *Exeunt.*

---

⁷ *close contriver* secret inventor ¹⁵ *Acheron* (river of Hades) ²⁴ *profound* heavy ²⁶ *sleights* arts ²⁷ *artificial sprites* spirits created by magic arts (?) artful (cunning) spirits (?) ²⁹ *confusion* ruin ³² *security* overconfidence

Scene VI.   [*The palace.*]

Enter Lennox and another Lord.

Lennox. My former speeches have but hit your
          thoughts,°
     Which can interpret farther. Only I say
     Things have been strangely borne.° The gracious
          Duncan
     Was pitied of Macbeth: marry, he was dead.
5   And the right-valiant Banquo walked too late;
     Whom, you may say, if 't please you, Fleance
          killed,
     For Fleance fled. Men must not walk too late.
     Who cannot want the thought,° how monstrous
     It was for Malcolm and for Donalbain
10   To kill their gracious father? Damnèd fact!°
     How it did grieve Macbeth! Did he not straight,
     In pious rage, the two delinquents tear,
     That were the slaves of drink and thralls° of sleep?
     Was not that nobly done? Ay, and wisely too;
15   For 'twould have angered any heart alive
     To hear the men deny 't. So that I say
     He has borne° all things well: and I do think
     That, had he Duncan's sons under his key—
     As, an 't° please heaven, he shall not—they should
          find
20   What 'twere to kill a father. So should Fleance.
     But, peace! for from broad words,° and 'cause he
          failed
     His presence at the tyrant's feast, I hear,

III.vi. 1 *My . . . thoughts* i.e., my recent words have only coincided
with what you have in your mind   3 *borne* managed   8 *cannot want
the thought* can fail to think   10 *fact* evil deed   13 *thralls* slaves
17 *borne* managed   19 *an 't* if it   21 *for from broad words* because of
frank talk

Macduff lives in disgrace. Sir, can you tell
Where he bestows himself?

Lord.   The son of Duncan,
From whom this tyrant holds the due of birth,°   25
Lives in the English court, and is received
Of the most pious Edward° with such grace
That the malevolence of fortune nothing
Takes from his high respect.° Thither Macduff
Is gone to pray the holy King, upon his aid°   30
To wake Northumberland° and warlike Siward;
That by the help of these, with Him above
To ratify the work, we may again
Give to our tables meat, sleep to our nights,
Free from our feasts and banquets bloody knives,   35
Do faithful homage and receive free° honors:
All which we pine for now. And this report
Hath so exasperate the King that he
Prepares for some attempt of war.

Lennox.   Sent he to Macduff?

Lord. He did: and with an absolute "Sir, not I,"   4
The cloudy° messenger turns me his back,
And hums, as who should say "You'll rue the time
That clogs° me with this answer."

Lennox.   And that well might
Advise him to a caution, t' hold what distance
His wisdom can provide. Some holy angel   45
Fly to the court of England and unfold
His message ere he come, that a swift blessing
May soon return to this our suffering country
Under a hand accursed!

Lord.   I'll send my prayers with him.

                                        Exeunt.

---

25 *due of birth* birthright   27 *Edward* Edward the Confessor (reigned
1042–1066)   28-29 *nothing . . . respect* does not diminish the high respect in which he is held   30 *upon his aid* to aid him (Malcolm)
31 *To wake Northumberland* i.e., to arouse the people in an English
county near Scotland   36 *free* freely granted   41 *cloudy* disturbed
43 *clogs* burdens

ACT IV

Scene I. [*A Witches' haunt.*]

Thunder. Enter the Three Witches.

First Witch. Thrice the brinded° cat hath mewed.

Second Witch. Thrice and once the hedge-pig°
whined.

Third Witch. Harpier° cries. 'Tis time, 'tis time.

First Witch. Round about the caldron go:
5   In the poisoned entrails throw.
    Toad, that under cold stone
    Days and nights has thirty-one
    Swelt'red venom sleeping got,°
    Boil thou first i' th' charmèd pot.

10 *All.* Double, double, toil and trouble;
    Fire burn and caldron bubble.

Second Witch. Fillet° of a fenny° snake,
    In the caldron boil and bake;
    Eye of newt and toe of frog,
15   Wool of bat and tongue of dog,
    Adder's fork° and blindworm's° sting,
    Lizard's leg and howlet's° wing,

IV.i. 1 *brinded* brindled   2 *hedge-pig* hedgehog   3 *Harpier* (an attendant spirit, like Graymalkin and Paddock in I.i)   8 *Swelt'red venom sleeping got* venom sweated out while sleeping   12 *Fillet* slice   12 *fenny* from a swamp   16 *fork* forked tongue   16 *blindworm* (a legless lizard) 17 *howlet* owlet

94

For a charm of pow'rful trouble,
Like a hell-broth boil and bubble.

All. Double, double, toil and trouble;   20
Fire burn and caldron bubble.

Third Witch. Scale of dragon, tooth of wolf,
Witch's mummy,° maw and gulf°
Of the ravined° salt-sea shark,
Root of hemlock digged i' th' dark,   25
Liver of blaspheming Jew,
Gall of goat, and slips of yew
Slivered in the moon's eclipse,
Nose of Turk and Tartar's lips,
Finger of birth-strangled babe   30
Ditch-delivered by a drab,°
Make the gruel thick and slab:°
Add thereto a tiger's chaudron,°
For th' ingredience of our caldron.

All. Double, double, toil and trouble;   35
Fire burn and caldron bubble.

Second Witch. Cool it with a baboon's blood,
Then the charm is firm and good.

      Enter Hecate and the other Three Witches.

Hecate. O, well done! I commend your pains;
And every one shall share i' th' gains: 40
And now about the caldron sing,
Like elves and fairies in a ring,
Enchanting all that you put in.

      Music and a song: "Black Spirits," &c.

      [*Exeunt Hecate and the other Three Witches.*]

Second Witch. By the pricking of my thumbs,
Something wicked this way comes: 45
      Open, locks,
      Whoever knocks!

---

23 *Witch's mummy* mummified flesh of a witch 23 *maw and gulf*
stomach and gullet 24 *ravined* ravenous 31 *Ditch-delivered by a drab*
born in a ditch of a harlot 32 *slab* viscous 33 *chaudron* entrails

Enter Macbeth.

Macbeth. How now, you secret, black, and midnight
    hags!
    What is 't you do?

All.   A deed without a name.

50 **Macbeth.** I conjure you, by that which you profess,
    Howe'er you come to know it, answer me:
    Though you untie the winds and let them fight
    Against the churches; though the yesty° waves
    Confound° and swallow navigation up;
    Though bladed corn be lodged° and trees blown
55   down;
    Though castles topple on their warders' heads;
    Though palaces and pyramids do slope°
    Their heads to their foundations; though the treas-
    ure
    Of nature's germens° tumble all together,
60   Even till destruction sicken,° answer me
    To what I ask you.

First Witch.   Speak.

Second Witch.   Demand.

Third Witch.   We'll answer.

First Witch. Say, if th' hadst rather hear it from our
    mouths,
    Or from our masters?

Macbeth.   Call 'em, let me see 'em.

First Witch. Pour in sow's blood, that hath eaten
65   Her nine farrow;° grease that's sweaten°
    From the murderer's gibbet throw
    Into the flame.

All.   Come, high or low,
    Thyself and office° deftly show!

---

53 *yesty* foamy   54 *Confound* destroy   55 *bladed corn be lodged* grain
in the ear be beaten down   57 *slope* bend   59 *nature's germens* seeds
of all life   60 *sicken* i.e., sicken at its own work   65 *farrow* young pigs
65 *sweaten* sweated   68 *office* function

Thunder. First Apparition: an Armed Head.

Macbeth. Tell me, thou unknown power——

First Witch.   He knows thy thought:
  Hear his speech, but say thou nought.   70

First Apparition. Macbeth! Macbeth! Macbeth! Beware
  Macduff!
  Beware the Thane of Fife. Dismiss me: enough.

                        He descends.

Macbeth. Whate'er thou art, for thy good caution
  thanks:
  Thou hast harped° my fear aright. But one word
  more——

First Witch. He will not be commanded. Here's another,   75
  More potent than the first.

    Thunder. Second Apparition: a Bloody Child.

Second Apparition. Macbeth! Macbeth! Macbeth!

Macbeth. Had I three ears, I'd hear thee.

Second Apparition. Be bloody, bold, and resolute!
  Laugh to scorn
  The pow'r of man, for none of woman born   80
  Shall harm Macbeth.   *Descends.*

Macbeth. Then live, Macduff: what need I fear of
  thee?
  But yet I'll make assurance double sure,
  And take a bond of fate.° Thou shalt not live;
  That I may tell pale-hearted fear it lies,   85
  And sleep in spite of thunder.

    Thunder. Third Apparition: a Child Crowned,
         with a tree in his hand.

---

74 *harped* hit upon, struck the note of 84 *take a bond of fate* get a
guarantee from fate (i.e., he will kill Macduff and thus will compel
fate to keep its word)

                                        What is this,
That rises like the issue° of a king,
And wears upon his baby-brow the round
And top of sovereignty?°

All.   Listen, but speak not to 't.

Third Apparition. Be lion-mettled, proud, and take
90   no care
Who chafes, who frets, or where conspirers are:
Macbeth shall never vanquished be until
Great Birnam Wood to high Dunsinane Hill
Shall come against him.   *Descends.*

Macbeth.   That will never be.
95 Who can impress° the forest, bid the tree
Unfix his earth-bound root? Sweet bodements,°
       good!
Rebellious dead,° rise never, till the Wood
Of Birnam rise, and our high-placed Macbeth
Shall live the lease of nature,° pay his breath
100 To time and mortal custom.° Yet my heart
Throbs to know one thing. Tell me, if your art
Can tell so much: shall Banquo's issue ever
Reign in this kingdom?

All.   Seek to know no more.

Macbeth. I will be satisfied.° Deny me this,
105 And an eternal curse fall on you! Let me know.
Why sinks that caldron? And what noise° is this?

                        Hautboys.

First Witch. Show!

Second Witch. Show!

Third Witch. Show!

---

87 *issue* offspring 88-89 *round/And top of sovereignty* i.e., crown
95 *impress* conscript 96 *bodements* prophecies 97 *Rebellious dead*
(perhaps a reference to Banquo; but perhaps a misprint for "rebellion's
head") 99 *lease of nature* natural lifespan 100 *mortal custom* natural
death 104 *satisfied* i.e., fully informed 106 *noise* music

All. Show his eyes, and grieve his heart;   *110*
   Come like shadows, so depart!

   A show of eight Kings and Banquo, last [King]
        with a glass° in his hand.

Macbeth. Thou art too like the spirit of Banquo.
   Down!
   Thy crown does sear mine eyelids. And thy hair,
   Thou other gold-bound brow, is like the first.
   A third is like the former. Filthy hags!   *115*
   Why do you show me this? A fourth! Start,° eyes!
   What, will the line stretch out to th' crack of
      doom?°
   Another yet! A seventh! I'll see no more.
   And yet the eighth appears, who bears a glass
   Which shows me many more; and some I see   *120*
   That twofold balls and treble scepters° carry:
   Horrible sight! Now I see 'tis true;
   For the blood-boltered° Banquo smiles upon me,
   And points at them for his. What, is this so?

First Witch. Ay, sir, all this is so. But why   *125*
   Stands Macbeth thus amazedly?
   Come, sisters, cheer we up his sprites,°
   And show the best of our delights:
   I'll charm the air to give a sound,   *130*
   While you perform your antic round,°
   That this great king may kindly say
   Our duties did his welcome pay.

   Music. The Witches dance, and vanish.

Macbeth. Where are they? Gone? Let this pernicious
   hour
   Stand aye accursèd in the calendar!
   Come in, without there!

III.s.d. *glass* mirror   116 *Start* i.e., from the sockets   117 *crack of doom*
blast (of a trumpet?) at doomsday   121 *twofold balls and treble*
scepters (coronation emblems)   123 *blood-boltered* matted with blood
127 *sprites* spirits   130 *antic round* grotesque circular dance

Enter Lennox.

135 *Lennox.*   What's your Grace's will?

Macbeth. Saw you the weïrd sisters?

Lennox.   No, my lord.

Macbeth. Came they not by you?

Lennox.   No indeed, my lord.

Macbeth. Infected be the air whereon they ride,
      And damned all those that trust them! I did hear
140   The galloping of horse.° Who was 't came by?

Lennox. 'Tis two or three, my lord, that bring you
      word
      Macduff is fled to England.

Macbeth.   Fled to England?

Lennox. Ay, my good lord.

Macbeth. [*Aside*] Time, thou anticipat'st° my
      dread exploits.
145   The flighty purpose never is o'ertook
      Unless the deed go with it.° From this moment
      The very firstlings of my heart° shall be
      The firstlings of my hand. And even now,
      To crown my thoughts with acts, be it thought and
      done:
150   The castle of Macduff I will surprise;°
      Seize upon Fife; give to th' edge o' th' sword
      His wife, his babes, and all unfortunate souls
      That trace him in his line.° No boasting like a fool;
      This deed I'll do before this purpose cool:
155   But no more sights!—Where are these gentlemen?
      Come, bring me where they are.   *Exeunt.*

---

140 *horse* horses (or "horsemen")   144 *anticipat'st* foretold   145-46 *The flighty . . . it* the fleeting plan is never fulfilled unless an action accompanies it   147 *firstlings of my heart* i.e., first thoughts, impulses   150 *surprise* attack suddenly   153 *trace him in his line* are of his lineage

Scene II.   [*Macduff's castle.*]

Enter Macduff's wife, her Son, and Ross.

Lady Macduff. What had he done, to make him fly the
    land?

Ross. You must have patience, madam.

Lady Macduff.   He had none:
    His flight was madness. When our actions do not,
    Our fears do make us traitors.

Ross.   You know not
    Whether it was his wisdom or his fear.   *5*

Lady Macduff. Wisdom! To leave his wife, to leave his
    babes,
    His mansion and his titles,° in a place
    From whence himself does fly? He loves us not;
    He wants the natural touch:° for the poor wren,
    The most diminutive of birds, will fight,   *10*
    Her young ones in her nest, against the owl.
    All is the fear and nothing is the love;
    As little is the wisdom, where the flight
    So runs against all reason.

Ross.   My dearest coz,°
    I pray you, school° yourself. But, for your husband, *15*
    He is noble, wise, judicious, and best knows
    The fits o' th' season.° I dare not speak much
      further:
    But cruel are the times, when we are traitors
    And do not know ourselves; when we hold rumor
    From what we fear,° yet know not what we fear,   *20*

IV.ii. ⁷ *titles* possessions ⁹ *wants the natural touch* i.e., lacks natural
affection for his wife and children ¹⁴ *coz* cousin ¹⁵ *school* control
¹⁷ *fits o' th' season* disorders of the time ¹⁹⁻²⁰ *hold rumor/From what
we fear* believe rumors because we fear

But float upon a wild and violent sea
Each way and move. I take my leave of you.
Shall not be long but I'll be here again.
Things at the worst will cease,° or else climb up-
　　ward
25　To what they were before. My pretty cousin,
Blessing upon you!

Lady Macduff. Fathered he is, and yet he's fatherless.

Ross. I am so much a fool, should I stay longer,
It would be my disgrace° and your discomfort.
I take my leave at once.　　　　*Exit Ross.*

30　*Lady Macduff.*　　　　Sirrah,° your father's dead:
And what will you do now? How will you live?

Son. As birds do, mother.

Lady Macduff.　　　　What, with worms and flies?

Son. With what I get, I mean; and so do they.

Lady Macduff. Poor bird! thou'dst never fear the net
　nor lime,°
35　The pitfall nor the gin.°

Son. Why should I, mother? Poor birds they are not
　set for.
My father is not dead, for all your saying.

Lady Macduff. Yes, he is dead: how wilt thou do for a
　father?

Son. Nay, how will you do for a husband?

Lady Macduff. Why, I can buy me twenty at any
40　market.

Son. Then you'll buy 'em to sell° again.

Lady Macduff. Thou speak'st with all thy wit, and yet,
　i' faith,
With wit enough for thee.°

---

24 *cease* i.e., cease worsening　29 *It would be my disgrace* i.e., I would
weep　30 *Sirrah* (here an affectionate address to a child)　34 *lime* bird-
lime (smeared on branches to catch birds)　35 *gin* trap　41 *sell* betray
43 *for thee* i.e., for a child

Son. Was my father a traitor, mother?

Lady Macduff. Ay, that he was.   *45*

Son. What is a traitor?

Lady Macduff. Why, one that swears and lies.°

Son. And be all traitors that do so?

Lady Macduff. Every one that does so is a traitor, and must be hanged.

Son. And must they all be hanged that swear and lie? *50*

Lady Macduff. Every one.

Son. Who must hang them?

Lady Macduff. Why, the honest men.

Son. Then the liars and swearers are fools; for there are liars and swearers enow° to beat the honest *55* men and hang up them.

Lady Macduff. Now, God help thee, poor monkey! But how wilt thou do for a father?

Son. If he were dead, you'd weep for him. If you would not, it were a good sign that I should quickly *60* have a new father.

Lady Macduff. Poor prattler, how thou talk'st!

Enter a Messenger.

Messenger. Bless you, fair dame! I am not to you known,
  Though in your state of honor I am perfect.°
  I doubt° some danger does approach you nearly: *65*
  If you will take a homely° man's advice,
  Be not found here; hence, with your little ones.
  To fright you thus, methinks I am too savage;
  To do worse to you were fell° cruelty,
  Which is too nigh your person. Heaven preserve you! *70*

---

⁴⁷ *swears and lies* i.e., takes an oath and breaks it ⁵⁵ *enow* enough ⁶⁴ *in . . . perfect* I am fully informed of your honorable rank ⁶⁵ *doubt* fear ⁶⁶ *homely* plain ⁶⁹ *fell* fierce

I dare abide no longer.   *Exit Messenger.*

Lady Macduff.   Whither should I fly?
I have done no harm. But I remember now
I am in this earthly world, where to do harm
Is often laudable, to do good sometime
75 Accounted dangerous folly. Why then, alas,
Do I put up that womanly defense,
To say I have done no harm?—What are these faces?

Enter Murderers.

Murderer. Where is your husband?

Lady Macduff. I hope, in no place so unsanctified
Where such as thou mayst find him.

80 *Murderer.*   He's a traitor.

Son. Thou li'st, thou shag-eared° villain!

Murderer.   What, you egg!

[*Stabbing him.*]

Young fry° of treachery!

Son.   He has killed me, mother:
Run away, I pray you!

[*Dies.*]
Exit [*Lady Macduff*], *crying "Murder!"* [*followed by Murderers*].

Scene III.   [*England. Before the King's palace.*]

Enter Malcolm and Macduff.

Malcolm. Let us seek out some desolate shade, and
there
Weep our sad bosoms empty.

81 *shag-eared* hairy-eared (?), with shaggy hair hanging over the ears
(?) 82 *fry* spawn

Macduff.   Let us rather
Hold fast the mortal° sword, and like good men
Bestride our down-fall'n birthdom.° Each new
    morn
New widows howl, new orphans cry, new sorrows   *5*
Strike heaven on the face, that° it resounds
As if it felt with Scotland and yelled out
Like syllable of dolor.°

Malcolm.   What I believe, I'll wail;
What know, believe; and what I can redress,
As I shall find the time to friend,° I will.   *10*
What you have spoke, it may be so perchance.
This tyrant, whose sole° name blisters our tongues,
Was once thought honest:° you have loved him
    well;
He hath not touched you yet. I am young; but
    something
You may deserve of him through me;° and wisdom°   *15*
To offer up a weak, poor, innocent lamb
T' appease an angry god.

Macduff. I am not treacherous.

Malcolm.   But Macbeth is.
A good and virtuous nature may recoil
In° an imperial charge. But I shall crave your
    pardon;   *20*
That which you are, my thoughts cannot
    transpose:°
Angels are bright still, though the brightest° fell:
Though all things foul would wear° the brows of
    grace,
Yet grace must still look so.°

IV.iii. 3 *mortal* deadly   4 *Bestride our down-fall'n birthdom* protectively
stand over our native land   6 *that* so that   8 *Like syllable of dolor*
similar sound of grief   40 *to friend* friendly, propitious   12 *sole* very
13 *honest* good   15 *deserve of him through me* i.e., earn by betraying
me to Macbeth   15 *wisdom* it may be wise   19-20 *recoil/In* give way
under   21 *transpose* transform   22 *the brightest* i.e., Lucifer   23 *would
wear* desire to wear   24 *so* i.e., like itself

Macduff.   I have lost my hopes.

Malcolm. Perchance even there where I did find my
25   doubts.
         Why in that rawness° left you wife and child,
         Those precious motives, those strong knots of
              love,
         Without leave-taking? I pray you,
         Let not my jealousies° be your dishonors,
30   But mine own safeties. You may be rightly just°
         Whatever I shall think.

Macduff.   Bleed, bleed, poor country:
         Great tyranny, lay thou thy basis° sure,
         For goodness dare not check° thee: wear thou thy
              wrongs;
         The title is affeered.° Fare thee well, lord:
35   I would not be the villain that thou think'st
         For the whole space that's in the tyrant's grasp
         And the rich East to boot.

Malcolm.   Be not offended:
         I speak not as in absolute fear of you.
         I think our country sinks beneath the yoke;
40   It weeps, it bleeds, and each new day a gash
         Is added to her wounds. I think withal°
         There would be hands uplifted in my right;°
         And here from gracious England° have I offer
         Of goodly thousands: but, for° all this,
45   When I shall tread upon the tyrant's head,
         Or wear it on my sword, yet my poor country
         Shall have more vices than it had before,
         More suffer, and more sundry ways than ever,
         By him that shall succeed.

Macduff.   What should he be?

50   *Malcolm.* It is myself I mean, in whom I know

---

26 *rawness* unprotected condition   29 *jealousies* suspicions   30 *rightly just*
perfectly honorable   32 *basis* foundation   33 *check* restrain   34 *affeered*
legally confirmed   41 *withal* moreover   42 *in my right* on behalf of my
claim   43 *England* i.e., the King of England   44 *for* despite

All the particulars° of vice so grafted°
That, when they shall be opened,° black Macbeth
Will seem as pure as snow, and the poor state
Esteem him as a lamb, being compared
With my confineless harms.°

Macduff.   Not in the legions   55
Of horrid hell can come a devil more damned
In evils to top Macbeth.

Malcolm.   I grant him bloody,
Luxurious,° avaricious, false, deceitful,
Sudden,° malicious, smacking of every sin
That has a name: but there's no bottom, none,   60
In my voluptuousness:° your wives, your daughters,
Your matrons and your maids, could not fill up
The cistern of my lust, and my desire
All continent° impediments would o'erbear,
That did oppose my will. Better Macbeth   65
Than such an one to reign.

Macduff.   Boundless intemperance
In nature° is a tyranny; it hath been
Th' untimely emptying of the happy throne,
And fall of many kings. But fear not yet
To take upon you what is yours: you may   70
Convey° your pleasures in a spacious plenty,
And yet seem cold, the time° you may so hoodwink.
We have willing dames enough. There cannot be
That vulture in you, to devour so many
As will to greatness dedicate themselves,   75
Finding it so inclined.

Malcolm.   With this there grows
In my most ill-composed affection° such

---

⁵¹*particulars* special kinds   ⁵¹*grafted* engrafted   ⁵²*opened* in bloom,
i.e., revealed   ⁵⁵*confineless harms* unbounded evils   ⁵⁸*Luxurious* lech-
erous   ⁵⁹*Sudden* violent   ⁶¹*voluptuousness* lust   ⁶⁴*continent* restraining
⁶⁷*In nature* in man's nature   ⁷¹*Convey* secretly manage   ⁷²*time* age,
i.e., people   ⁷⁷*ill-composed affection* evilly compounded character

A stanchless° avarice that, were I King,
I should cut off the nobles for their lands,
80   Desire his jewels and this other's house:
And my more-having would be as a sauce
To make me hunger more, that I should forge
Quarrels unjust against the good and loyal,
Destroying them for wealth.

Macduff.   This avarice
85   Sticks deeper, grows with more pernicious root
Than summer-seeming° lust, and it hath been
The sword of our slain kings.° Yet do not fear.
Scotland hath foisons to fill up your will
Of your mere own.° All these are portable,°
90   With other graces weighed.

Malcolm. But I have none: the king-becoming graces,
As justice, verity, temp'rance, stableness,
Bounty, perseverance, mercy, lowliness,
Devotion, patience, courage, fortitude,
95   I have no relish of° them, but abound
In the division of each several crime,°
Acting it many ways. Nay, had I pow'r, I should
Pour the sweet milk of concord into hell,
Uproar° the universal peace, confound
All unity on earth.

100 *Macduff.*   O Scotland, Scotland!

Malcolm. If such a one be fit to govern, speak:
I am as I have spoken.

Macduff.   Fit to govern!
No, not to live. O nation miserable!
With an untitled tyrant bloody-sceptered,
105   When shalt thou see thy wholesome days again,

---

78 *stanchless* never-ending   86 *summer-seeming* befitting summer, i.e.,
youthful (?) transitory (?)   87 *sword of our slain kings* i.e., the cause
of death to our kings   88-89 *foisons . . . own* enough abundance of
your own to satisfy your covetousness   89 *portable* bearable   95 *relish
of* taste for (?) trace of (?)   96 *division of each several crime* varia-
tions of each kind of crime   99 *Uproar* put into a tumult

Since that the truest issue of thy throne
By his own interdiction° stands accursed,
And does blaspheme his breed?° Thy royal father
Was a most sainted king: the queen that bore thee,
Oft'ner upon her knees than on her feet,   *110*
Died° every day she lived. Fare thee well!
These evils thou repeat'st upon thyself
Hath banished me from Scotland. O my breast,
Thy hope ends here!

Malcolm.   Macduff, this noble passion,
Child of integrity, hath from my soul   *115*
Wiped the black scruples,° reconciled my thoughts
To thy good truth and honor. Devilish Macbeth
By many of these trains° hath sought to win me
Into his power; and modest wisdom° plucks me
From over-credulous haste: but God above   *120*
Deal between thee and me! For even now
I put myself to° thy direction, and
Unspeak mine own detraction; here abjure
The taints and blames I laid upon myself,
For° strangers to my nature. I am yet   *125*
Unknown to woman, never was forsworn,
Scarcely have coveted what was mine own,
At no time broke my faith, would not betray
The devil to his fellow, and delight
No less in truth than life. My first false speaking   *130*
Was this upon myself. What I am truly,
Is thine and my poor country's to command:
Whither indeed, before thy here-approach,
Old Siward, with ten thousand warlike men,
Already at a point,° was setting forth.   *135*
Now we'll together, and the chance of goodness
Be like our warranted quarrel!° Why are you
    silent?

---

107 *interdiction* curse, exclusion   108 *breed* ancestry   111 *Died* i.e., prepared for heaven   116 *scruples* suspicions   118 *trains* plots   119 *modest
wisdom* i.e., prudence   122 *to* under   125 *For* as   135 *at a point* prepared
136-37 *the chance . . . quarrel* i.e., may our chance of success equal the
justice of our cause

Macduff. Such welcome and unwelcome things at once
    'Tis hard to reconcile.

Enter a Doctor.

Malcolm. Well, more anon. Comes the King forth, I
140   pray you?

Doctor. Ay, sir. There are a crew of wretched souls
    That stay° his cure: their malady convinces
    The great assay of art;° but at his touch,
    Such sanctity hath heaven given his hand,
    They presently amend.°

145 *Malcolm.*   I thank you, doctor.

Exit [Doctor].

Macduff. What's the disease he means?

Malcolm.   'Tis called the evil:°
    A most miraculous work in this good King,
    Which often since my here-remain in England
    I have seen him do. How he solicits heaven,
150   Himself best knows: but strangely-visited° people,
    All swoll'n and ulcerous, pitiful to the eye,
    The mere° despair of surgery, he cures,
    Hanging a golden stamp° about their necks,
    Put on with holy prayers: and 'tis spoken,
155   To the succeeding royalty he leaves
    The healing benediction. With this strange virtue°
    He hath a heavenly gift of prophecy,
    And sundry blessings hang about his throne
    That speak° him full of grace.

Enter Ross.

Macduff.   See, who comes here?

160 *Malcolm.* My countryman; but yet I know him not.

---

142 *stay* await   142-43 *convinces/The great assay of art* i.e., defies the
efforts of medical science   145 *presently amend* immediately recover
146 *evil* (scrofula, called "the king's evil" because it could allegedly be
cured by the king's touch)   150 *strangely-visited* oddly afflicted
152 *mere* utter   153 *stamp* coin   156 *virtue* power   159 *speak* proclaim

Macduff. My ever gentle° cousin, welcome hither.

Malcolm. I know him now: good God, betimes°
    remove
The means that makes us strangers!

Ross.   Sir, amen.

Macduff. Stands Scotland where it did?

Ross.   Alas, poor country!
Almost afraid to know itself! It cannot   165
Be called our mother but our grave, where nothing°
But who knows nothing is once seen to smile;
Where sighs and groans, and shrieks that rent the
    air,
Are made, not marked;° where violent sorrow seems
A modern ecstasy.° The dead man's knell   170
Is there scarce asked for who, and good men's lives
Expire before the flowers in their caps,
Dying or ere they sicken.

Macduff.   O, relation
Too nice,° and yet too true!

Malcolm.   What's the newest grief?

Ross. That of an hour's age doth hiss the speaker;°   175
Each minute teems° a new one.

Macduff.   How does my wife?

Ross. Why, well.

Macduff.   And all my children?

Ross.   Well too.

Macduff. The tyrant has not battered at their peace?

Ross. No; they were well at peace when I did leave
    'em.

---

161 *gentle* noble **162** *betimes* quickly **166** *nothing* no one **169** *marked*
noticed **170** *modern ecstasy* i.e., ordinary emotion **173-74** *relation/Too
nice* tale too accurate **175** *That . . . speaker* i.e., the report of the
grief of an hour ago is hissed as stale news **176** *teems* gives birth to

180 *Macduff.* Be not a niggard of your speech: how goes 't?

    Ross. When I came hither to transport the tidings,
        Which I have heavily° borne, there ran a rumor
        Of many worthy fellows that were out;°
        Which was to my belief witnessed° the rather,
185   For that I saw the tyrant's power° afoot.
        Now is the time of help. Your eye in Scotland
        Would create soldiers, make our women fight,
        To doff their dire distresses.

    Malcolm.   Be 't their comfort
        We are coming thither. Gracious England hath
190   Lent us good Siward and ten thousand men;
        An older and a better soldier none
        That Christendom gives out.°

    Ross.   Would I could answer
        This comfort with the like! But I have words
        That would° be howled out in the desert air,
        Where hearing should not latch° them.

195 *Macduff.*   What concern they?
        The general cause or is it a fee-grief
        Due to some single breast?°

    Ross.   No mind that's honest
        But in it shares some woe, though the main part
        Pertains to you alone.

    Macduff.   If it be mine,
200   Keep it not from me, quickly let me have it.

    Ross. Let not your ears despise my tongue for ever,
        Which shall possess them with the heaviest sound
        That ever yet they heard.

    Macduff.   Humh! I guess at it.

    Ross. Your castle is surprised;° your wife and babes

---

182 *heavily* sadly 183 *out* i.e., up in arms 184 *witnessed* attested
185 *power* army 192 *gives out* reports 194 *would* should 195 *latch*
catch 196-97 *fee-grief/Due to some single breast* i.e., a personal grief
belonging to an individual 204 *surprised* suddenly attacked

Savagely slaughtered. To relate the manner,   205
Were, on the quarry° of these murdered deer,
To add the death of you.

Malcolm.   Merciful heaven!
What, man! Ne'er pull your hat upon your brows;
Give sorrow words. The grief that does not speak
Whispers the o'er-fraught heart,° and bids it break.   210

Macduff. My children too?

Ross.   Wife, children, servants, all
That could be found.

Macduff.   And I must be from thence!
My wife killed too?

Ross.   I have said.

Malcolm.   Be comforted.
Let's make us med'cines of our great revenge,
To cure this deadly grief.   215

Macduff. He has no children. All my pretty ones?
Did you say all? O hell-kite!° All?
What, all my pretty chickens and their dam
At one fell swoop?

Malcolm. Dispute° it like a man.

Macduff.   I shall do so;   220
But I must also feel it as a man.
I cannot but remember such things were,
That were most precious to me. Did heaven look on,
And would not take their part? Sinful Macduff,
They were all struck for thee! Naught° that I am,   225
Not for their own demerits but for mine
Fell slaughter on their souls. Heaven rest them now!

Malcolm. Be this the whetstone of your sword. Let
    grief
Convert to anger; blunt not the heart, enrage it.

---

206 *quarry* heap of slaughtered game   210 *Whispers the o'er-fraught heart*
whispers to the overburdened heart   217 *hell-kite* hellish bird of prey
220 *Dispute* counter   225 *Naught* wicked

230 *Macduff.* O, I could play the woman with mine eyes,
       And braggart with my tongue! But, gentle heavens,
       Cut short all intermission;° front to front°
       Bring thou this fiend of Scotland and myself;
       Within my sword's length set him. If he 'scape,
       Heaven forgive him too!

235 *Malcolm.*   This time goes manly.
       Come, go we to the King. Our power is ready;
       Our lack is nothing but our leave.° Macbeth
       Is ripe for shaking, and the pow'rs above
       Put on their instruments.° Receive what cheer you
          may.
240   The night is long that never finds the day.   *Exeunt*

---

232 *intermission* interval   232 *front to front* forehead to forehead i.e.,
face to face   237 *Our lack is nothing but our leave* i.e., we need only
to take our leave   239 *Put on their instruments* arm themselves (?)
urge us, their agents, onward (?)

ACT V

Scene I. [*Dunsinane. In the castle.*]

*Enter a Doctor of Physic and a
Waiting-Gentlewoman.*

Doctor. I have two nights watched with you, but can
perceive no truth in your report. When was it she
last walked?

Gentlewoman. Since his Majesty went into the field, I
have seen her rise from her bed, throw her night- 5
gown upon her, unlock her closet,° take forth
paper, fold it, write upon 't, read it, afterwards seal
it, and again return to bed; yet all this while in a
most fast sleep.

Doctor. A great perturbation in nature, to receive at 10
once the benefit of sleep and do the effects of
watching!° In this slumb'ry agitation, besides her
walking and other actual performances,° what, at
any time, have you heard her say?

Gentlewoman. That, sir, which I will not report after 15
her.

Doctor. You may to me, and 'tis most meet° you
should.

Gentlewoman. Neither to you nor anyone, having no
witness to confirm my speech. 20

Enter Lady [Macbeth], with a taper.

V.i. 6 *closet* chest 11-12 *effects of watching* deeds of one awake
13 *actual performance* deeds 17 *meet* suitable

Lo you, here she comes! This is her very guise,°
and, upon my life, fast asleep! Observe her; stand
close.°

Doctor. How came she by that light?

25 *Gentlewoman.* Why, it stood by her. She has light by
her continually. 'Tis her command.

Doctor. You see, her eyes are open.

Gentlewoman. Ay, but their sense° are shut.

Doctor. What is it she does now? Look, how she rubs
30 her hands.

Gentlewoman. It is an accustomed action with her, to
seem thus washing her hands: I have known her
continue in this a quarter of an hour.

Lady Macbeth. Yet here's a spot.

35 *Doctor.* Hark! she speaks. I will set down what comes
from her, to satisfy° my remembrance the more
strongly.

Lady Macbeth. Out, damned spot! Out, I say! One:
two: why, then 'tis time to do 't. Hell is murky.
40 Fie, my lord, fie! A soldier, and afeard? What need
we fear who knows it, when none can call our
pow'r to accompt?° Yet who would have thought
the old man to have had so much blood in him?

Doctor. Do you mark that?

45 *Lady Macbeth.* The Thane of Fife had a wife. Where is
she now? What, will these hands ne'er be clean? No
more o' that, my lord, no more o' that! You mar
all with this starting.

Doctor. Go to,° go to! You have known what you
50 should not.

Gentlewoman. She has spoke what she should not, I

---

21 *guise* custom   23 *close* hidden   28 *sense* i.e., powers of sight   36 *satis-*
fy confirm   42 *to accompt* into account   49 *Go to* (an exclamation)

He cannot buckle his distempered° cause   15
Within the belt of rule.°

Angus.   Now does he feel
His secret murders sticking on his hands;
Now minutely revolts upbraid° his faith-breach.
Those he commands move only in command,
Nothing in love. Now does he feel his title   20
Hang loose about him, like a giant's robe
Upon a dwarfish thief.

Menteith.   Who then shall blame
His pestered° senses to recoil and start,
When all that is within him does condemn
Itself for being there?

Caithness.   Well, march we on,   25
To give obedience where 'tis truly owed.
Meet we the med'cine° of the sickly weal,°
And with him pour we, in our country's purge,
Each drop of us.°

Lennox.   Or so much as it needs
To dew° the sovereign° flower and drown the
    weeds.   30
Make we our march towards Birnam.

                                   Exeunt, marching.

Scene III.   [*Dunsinane. In the castle.*]

Enter Macbeth, Doctor, and Attendants.

Macbeth. Bring me no more reports; let them fly all!
Till Birnam Wood remove to Dunsinane
I cannot taint° with fear. What's the boy Malcolm?

15 *distempered* swollen by dropsy   16 *rule* self-control   18 *minutely
revolts upbraid* rebellions every minute rebuke   23 *pestered* tormented
27 *med'cine* i.e., Malcolm   27 *weal* commonwealth   29 *Each drop of
us* i.e., every last drop of our blood (?)   30 *dew* bedew, water (and
thus make grow)   30 *sovereign* (1) royal (2) remedial   V.iii. 3 *taint*
become infected

Was he not born of woman? The spirits that know
All mortal consequences° have pronounced me
    thus:
"Fear not, Macbeth; no man that's born of woman
Shall e'er have power upon thee." Then fly, false
    thanes,
And mingle with the English epicures.
The mind I sway° by and the heart I bear
Shall never sag with doubt nor shake with fear.

Enter Servant.

The devil damn thee black, thou cream-faced loon!°
Where got'st thou that goose look?

Servant. There is ten thousand——

Macbeth.   Geese, villain?

Servant.   Soldiers, sir.

Macbeth. Go prick thy face and over-red° thy fear,
Thou lily-livered boy. What soldiers, patch?°
Death of° thy soul! Those linen° cheeks of thine
Are counselors to fear. What soldiers, whey-face?

Servant. The English force, so please you.

Macbeth. Take thy face hence.   *[Exit Servant.]*
                    Seyton!—I am sick at heart,
When I behold—Seyton, I say!—This push°
Will cheer me ever, or disseat° me now.
I have lived long enough. My way of life
Is fall'n into the sear,° the yellow leaf,
And that which should accompany old age,
As honor, love, obedience, troops of friends,
I must not look to have; but, in their stead,
Curses not loud but deep, mouth-honor, breath,
Which the poor heart would fain deny, and dare not.
Seyton!

---

5 *mortal consequences* future human events 9 *sway* move 11 *loon* fool 14 *over-red* cover with red 15 *patch* fool 16 *of* upon 16 *linen* i.e., pale 20 *push* effort 21 *disseat* i.e., unthrone (with wordplay on "cheer," pronounced "chair") 23 *sear* withered

Enter Seyton.

Seyton. What's your gracious pleasure?

Macbeth. What news more? **30**

Seyton. All is confirmed, my lord, which was reported.

Macbeth. I'll fight, till from my bones my flesh be
  hacked.
    Give me my armor.

Seyton. 'Tis not needed yet.

Macbeth. I'll put it on.
  Send out moe° horses, skirr° the country round. **85**
  Hang those that talk of fear. Give me mine armor.
  How does your patient, doctor?

Doctor. Not so sick, my lord,
  As she is troubled with thick-coming fancies
  That keep her from her rest.

Macbeth. Cure her of that.
  Canst thou not minister to a mind diseased, **40**
  Pluck from the memory a rooted sorrow,
  Raze out° the written troubles of the brain,
  And with some sweet oblivious° antidote
  Cleanse the stuffed bosom of that perilous stuff
  Which weighs upon the heart?

Doctor. Therein the patient **45**
  Must minister to himself.

Macbeth. Throw physic° to the dogs, I'll none of it.
  Come, put mine armor on. Give me my staff.
  Seyton, send out.——Doctor, the thanes fly from
  me.——
  Come, sir, dispatch.° If thou couldst, doctor, cast **50**
  The water° of my land, find her disease
  And purge it to a sound and pristine health,
  I would applaud thee to the very echo,

---

85 *moe* more **35** *skirr* scour **42** *Raze out* erase **43** *oblivious* causing
forgetfulness **47** *physic* medical science **50** *dispatch* hurry **50-51** *cast/
The water* analyze the urine

That should applaud again.—Pull 't off, I say.—
55 What rhubarb, senna, or what purgative drug,
    Would scour these English hence? Hear'st thou of
        them?

Doctor. Ay, my good lord; your royal preparation
    Makes us hear something.

Macbeth.   Bring it° after me.
    I will not be afraid of death and bane°
60 Till Birnam Forest come to Dunsinane.

Doctor. [Aside] Were I from Dunsinane away
        and clear,
    Profit again should hardly draw me here.   Exeunt.

Scene IV.   [Country near Birnam Wood.]

Drum and colors. Enter Malcolm, Siward, Macduff, Siward's Son, Menteith, Caithness, Angus,
and Soldiers, marching.

Malcolm. Cousins, I hope the days are near at hand
    That chambers will be safe.°

Menteith.   We doubt it nothing.°

Siward. What wood is this before us?

Menteith.   The Wood of Birnam.

Malcolm. Let every soldier hew him down a bough
5   And bear 't before him. Thereby shall we shadow
    The numbers of our host, and make discovery°
    Err in report of us.

Soldiers.   It shall be done.

---

58 it i.e., the armor 59 bane destruction V.v. 2 That chambers will
be safe i.e., that a man will be safe in his bedroom 2 nothing not at
all 6 discovery reconnaisance

Siward. We learn no other but° the confident tyrant
    Keeps still in Dunsinane, and will endure°
    Our setting down before 't.

Malcolm.   'Tis his main hope,   10
    For where there is advantage to be given°
    Both more and less° have given him the revolt,
    And none serve with him but constrainèd things
    Whose hearts are absent too.

Macduff.   Let our just censures
    Attend the true event,° and put we on   15
    Industrious soldiership.

Siward.   The time approaches,
    That will with due decision make us know
    What we shall say we have and what we owe.°
    Thoughts speculative their unsure hopes relate,
    But certain issue strokes must arbitrate:°   20
    Towards which advance the war.°

                        Exeunt, marching.

Scene V.   [*Dunsinane. Within the castle.*]

*Enter Macbeth, Seyton, and Soldiers, with drum
and colors.*

Macbeth. Hang out our banners on the outward walls.
    The cry is still "They come!" Our castle's strength
    Will laugh a siege to scorn. Here let them lie
    Till famine and the ague° eat them up.
    Were they not forced° with those that should be
       ours,   5

8 *no other but* nothing but that   9 *endure* allow   11 *advantage to be given* afforded an opportunity   12 *more and less* high and low   14-15 *just censures/Attend the true event* true judgment await the actual outcome   18 *owe* own (the contrast is between "what we shall say we have" and "what we shall really have")   20 *certain issue strokes must arbitrate* the definite outcome must be decided by battle   21 *war* army V.v. 4 *ague* fever   5 *forced* reinforced

We might have met them dareful,° beard to beard,
And beat them backward home.

A cry within of women.

What is that noise?

Seyton. It is the cry of women, my good lord. [*Exit.*]

Macbeth. I have almost forgot the taste of fears:
10 The time has been, my senses would have cooled
To hear a night-shriek, and my fell° of hair
Would at a dismal treatise° rouse and stir
As life were in 't. I have supped full with horrors.
Direness, familiar to my slaughterous thoughts,
Cannot once start° me.

[*Enter Seyton.*]

15 Wherefore was that cry?

Seyton. The Queen, my lord, is dead.

Macbeth. She should° have died hereafter;
There would have been a time for such a word.°
Tomorrow, and tomorrow, and tomorrow
20 Creeps in this petty pace from day to day,
To the last syllable of recorded time;
And all our yesterdays have lighted fools
The way to dusty death. Out, out, brief candle!
Life's but a walking shadow, a poor player
25 That struts and frets his hour upon the stage
And then is heard no more. It is a tale
Told by an idiot, full of sound and fury
Signifying nothing.

Enter a Messenger.

Thou com'st to use thy tongue; thy story quickly!

30 *Messenger.* Gracious my lord,
I should report that which I say I saw,
But know not how to do 't.

Macbeth. Well, say, sir.

---

6 *met them dareful* i.e., met them in the battlefield boldly 11 *fell* pelt
12 *treatise* story 15 *start* startle 17 *should* inevitably would (?)
18 *word* message

Messenger. As I did stand my watch upon the hill,
   I looked toward Birnam, and anon, methought,
   The wood began to move.

Macbeth.   Liar and slave!   35

Messenger. Let me endure your wrath, if 't be not so.
   Within this three mile may you see it coming;
   I say a moving grove.

Macbeth.   If thou speak'st false,
   Upon the next tree shalt thou hang alive,
   Till famine cling° thee. If thy speech be sooth,°   40
   I care not if thou dost for me as much.
   I pull in resolution,° and begin
   To doubt° th' equivocation of the fiend
   That lies like truth: "Fear not, till Birnam Wood
   Do come to Dunsinane!" And now a wood   45
   Comes toward Dunsinane. Arm, arm, and out!
   If this which he avouches° does appear,
   There is nor flying hence nor tarrying here.
   I 'gin to be aweary of the sun,
   And wish th' estate° o' th' world were now undone.   50
   Ring the alarum bell! Blow wind, come wrack!
   At least we'll die with harness° on our back.

                               Exeunt.

Scene VI.   [*Dunsinane. Before the castle.*]

*Drum and colors. Enter Malcolm, Siward,
Macduff, and their army, with boughs.*

Malcolm. Now near enough. Your leavy° screens
    throw down,
   And show like those you are. You, worthy uncle,

40 *cling* wither 40 *sooth* truth 42 *pull in resolution* restrain confidence
43 *doubt* suspect 47 *avouches* asserts 50 *th' estate* the orderly condition 52 *harness* armor V.vi. 1 *leavy* leafy

Shall, with my cousin, your right noble son,
Lead our first battle.° Worthy Macduff and we°
5　Shall take upon 's what else remains to do,
According to our order.°

Siward.　　　　　　　　　　Fare you well.
Do we° but find the tyrant's power° tonight,
Let us be beaten, if we cannot fight.

Macduff. Make all our trumpets speak; give them all
　　breath,
10　Those clamorous harbingers of blood and death.

　　　　　　　　　　　Exeunt. Alarums continued.

Scene VII.　　[*Another part of the field.*]

Enter Macbeth.

Macbeth. They have tied me to a stake; I cannot fly,
But bearlike I must fight the course.° What's he
That was not born of woman? Such a one
Am I to fear, or none.

　　　　　　　　　Enter Young Siward.

Young Siward. What is thy name?

5　*Macbeth.*　　　　　　　Thou'lt be afraid to hear it.

Young Siward. No; though thou call'st thyself a hotter
　　name
Than any is in hell.

Macbeth.　　　　　My name's Macbeth.

---

4 *battle* battalion　4 *we* (Malcolm uses the royal "we")　6 *order* plan
7 *Do we* if we do　7 *power* forces　V.vii. 2 *course* bout, round (he has
in mind an attack of dogs or men upon a bear chained to a stake)

Young Siward. The devil himself could not pronounce
　　a title
　　More hateful to mine ear.

Macbeth.　　　　　　　　No, nor more fearful.

Young Siward. Thou liest, abhorrèd tyrant; with my
　　sword　　　　　　　　　　　　　　　　　　10
　　I'll prove the lie thou speak'st.

Fight, and Young Siward slain.

Macbeth.　　　　　　　Thou wast born of woman.
　　But swords I smile at, weapons laugh to scorn,
　　Brandished by man that's of a woman born.

Exit.

Alarums. Enter Macduff.

Macduff. That way the noise is. Tyrant, show thy face!
　　If thou be'st slain and with no stroke of mine,　　15
　　My wife and children's ghosts will haunt me still.
　　I cannot strike at wretched kerns,° whose arms
　　Are hired to bear their staves.° Either thou,
　　　Macbeth,
　　Or else my sword, with an unbattered edge,
　　I sheathe again undeeded.° There thou shouldst
　　　be;　　　　　　　　　　　　　　　　　　20
　　By this great clatter, one of greatest note
　　Seems bruited.° Let me find him, Fortune!
　　And more I beg not.　　　　　*Exit. Alarums.*

Enter Malcolm and Siward.

Siward. This way, my lord. The castle's gently
　　rend'red:°
　　The tyrant's people on both sides do fight;　　25
　　The noble thanes do bravely in the war;
　　The day almost itself professes° yours,
　　And little is to do.

---

17 *kerns* foot soldiers (contemptuous)　18 *staves* spears　20 *undeeded*
i.e., having done nothing　22 *bruited* reported　24 *gently rend'red* surrendered without a struggle　27 *itself professes* declares itself

Malcolm.   We have met with foes
That strike beside us.°

Siward.   Enter, sir, the castle.

                                    Exeunt. Alarum.

[Scene VIII.   *Another part of the field.*]

Enter Macbeth.

Macbeth. Why should I play the Roman fool, and die
On mine own sword? Whiles I see lives,° the gashes
Do better upon them.

Enter Macduff.

Macduff.   Turn, hell-hound, turn!

Macbeth. Of all men else I have avoided thee.
5 But get thee back! My soul is too much charged°
With blood of thine already.

Macduff.   I have no words:
My voice is in my sword, thou bloodier villain
Than terms can give thee out!°

Fight. Alarum.

Macbeth.   Thou losest labor:
As easy mayst thou the intrenchant° air
10 With thy keen sword impress° as make me bleed:
Let fall thy blade on vulnerable crests;
I bear a charmèd life, which must not yield
To one of woman born.

---

29 *beside us* i.e., deliberately miss us (?) as our comrades (?) V.viii.
2 *Whiles I see lives* so long as I see living men 5 *charged* burdened
8 *terms can give thee out* words can describe you 9 *intrenchant*
incapable of being cut 10 *impress* make an impression on

Macduff.   Despair° thy charm,
   And let the angel° whom thou still hast served
   Tell thee, Macduff was from his mother's womb   *15*
   Untimely ripped.

Macbeth. Accursèd be that tongue that tells me so,
   For it hath cowed my better part of man!°
   And be these juggling fiends no more believed,
   That palter° with us in a double sense;   *20*
   That keep the word of promise to our ear,
   And break it to our hope. I'll not fight with thee.

Macduff. Then yield thee, coward,
   And live to be the show and gaze o' th' time:°
   We'll have thee, as our rarer monsters° are,   *25*
   Painted upon a pole,° and underwrit,
   "Here may you see the tyrant."

Macbeth.   I will not yield,
   To kiss the ground before young Malcolm's feet,
   And to be baited° with the rabble's curse.
   Though Birnam Wood be come to Dunsinane,   *30*
   And thou opposed, being of no woman born,
   Yet I will try the last. Before my body
   I throw my warlike shield. Lay on, Macduff;
   And damned be him that first cries "Hold,
      enough!"   *Exeunt, fighting. Alarums.*

*[Re-]enter fighting, and Macbeth slain. [Exit
Macduff, with Macbeth.] Retreat and flour-
ish.° Enter, with drum and colors, Malcolm,
Siward, Ross, Thanes, and Soldiers.*

Malcolm. I would the friends we miss were safe
      arrived.   *35*

Siward. Some must go off;° and yet, by these I see,
   So great a day as this is cheaply bought.

---

13 *Despair* despair of   14 *angel* i.e., fallen angel, fiend   18 *better part
of man* manly spirit   20 *palter* equivocate   24 *gaze o' th' time* spectacle
of the age   25 *monsters* freaks   26 *Painted upon a pole* i.e., pictured
on a banner set by a showman's booth   29 *baited* assailed (like a bear
by dogs)   34 s.d. *Retreat and flourish* trumpet call to withdraw, and
fanfare   36 *go off* die (theatrical metaphor)

Malcolm. Macduff is missing, and your noble son.

Ross. Your son, my lord, has paid a soldier's debt:
40   He only lived but till he was a man;
    The which no sooner had his prowess confirmed
    In the unshrinking station° where he fought,
    But like a man he died.

Siward.   Then he is dead?

Ross. Ay, and brought off the field. Your cause of
    sorrow
45   Must not be measured by his worth, for then
    It hath no end.

Siward.   Had he his hurts before?

Ross. Ay, on the front.

Siward.   Why then, God's soldier be he!
    Had I as many sons as I have hairs,
    I would not wish them to a fairer death:
    And so his knell is knolled.

50 *Malcolm.*   He's worth more sorrow,
    And that I'll spend for him.

Siward.   He's worth no more:
    They say he parted well and paid his score:°
    And so God be with him! Here comes newer
    comfort.

    Enter Macduff, with Macbeth's head.

Macduff. Hail, King! for so thou art: behold, where
    stands
55   Th' usurper's cursèd head. The time is free.°
    I see thee compassed° with thy kingdom's pearl,
    That speak my salutation in their minds,
    Whose voices I desire aloud with mine:
    Hail, King of Scotland!

All.   Hail, King of Scotland!

---

42 *unshrinking station* i.e., place at which he stood firmly   52 *parted well and paid his score* departed well and settled his account   55 *The time is free* the world is liberated   56 *compassed* surrounded

Flourish.

Malcolm. We shall not spend a large expense of time   60
    Before we reckon with your several loves,°
    And make us even with you. My thanes and
        kinsmen,
    Henceforth be earls, the first that ever Scotland
    In such an honor named. What's more to do,
    Which would be planted newly with the time°—   65
    As calling home our exiled friends abroad
    That fled the snares of watchful tyranny,
    Producing forth the cruel ministers°
    Of this dead butcher and his fiendlike queen,
    Who, as 'tis thought, by self and violent° hands   70
    Took off her life—this, and what needful else
    That calls upon us,° by the grace of Grace
    We will perform in measure, time, and place:°
    So thanks to all at once and to each one,
    Whom we invite to see us crowned at Scone.   75

Flourish. Exeunt Omnes.

FINIS

---

61 *reckon with your several loves* reward the devotion of each of you
64-65 *What's more . . . time* i.e., what else must be done which should
be newly established in this age   68 *ministers* agents   70 *self and violent* her own violent   72 *calls upon us* demands my attention   73 *in
measure, time and place* fittingly, at the appropriate time and place

Textual Note

Macbeth, never printed during Shakespeare's lifetime, was first printed in the Folio of 1623. The play is remarkably short, and it may be that there has been some cutting. That in I.v Lady Macbeth apparently proposes to kill Duncan, and that later in the play Macbeth kills him, is scarcely evidence that a scene had been lost, but the inconsistent stage directions concerning Macbeth's death (one calls for him to be slain on stage, another suggests he is both slain and decapitated off stage) indicate some sort of revision. Nevertheless, when one reads the account of Macbeth in Holinshed (Shakespeare's source) one does not feel that the play as it has come down to us omits anything of significance. If, as seems likely, the play was presented at court, its brevity may well be due to King James's known aversion to long plays. On the other hand, it is generally believed that Hecate is a non-Shakespearean addition to the play (she dominates III.v and has a few lines in IV.i), but the evidence is not conclusive, although the passages (along with IV.i.125-32) sound un-Shakespearean.

The present division into acts and scenes is that of the Folio except for V.viii, a division added by the Globe editors. The present edition silently modernizes spelling and punctuation, regularizes speech prefixes, and translates into English the Folio's Latin designations of act and scene. Other departures from the Folio are listed below. The reading of the present text is given first, in italics, and then the reading of the Folio (F) in roman.

I.i.9 *Second Witch . . . Anon* [F attributes to "All," as part of the ensuing speech]

I.ii.13 *gallowglasses* gallowgrosses   14 *quarrel* Quarry   26 *thunders break* Thunders   33-34 *Dismayed . . . Banquo* [one line in F]   33-35 *Dismayed . . . lion* [three lines in F, ending: Banquoh, Eagles, Lyon]   42 *But . . . faint* [F gives to previous line]   46 *So . . . look* [F gives to next line]   59 *Sweno . . . king* [F gives to previous line]

I.iii.5 *Give . . . I* [F prints as a separate line]

32 *weïrd* weyward [also at I.v.9; II.i.20; "weyard" at III.i.2; III.iv.134; IV.i.136]   39 *Forres* Soris   78 *Speak . . . you* [F prints as a separate line]   81-82 *Into . . . stayed* [three lines in F, ending: corporall, Winde, stay'd]   98 *Came* can   108 *why . . . me* [F gives to next line]   111-14 *Which . . . not* [five lines in F, ending: loose, Norway, helpe, labour'd, not]   131 *If ill* [F gives to next line]   140-42 *Shakes . . . not* [F's lines end: Man, surmise, not]   143 *If . . . crown me* [two lines in F, ending: King, crown me]   149-53 *Give . . . time* [seven lines in F, ending: fauour, forgotten, registred, Leafe, them, vpon, time]   156 *Till . . . friends* [two lines in F, ending: enough, friends]

I.iv.1 *Are not* Or not [given in F to next line]   2-8 *My . . . died* [seven lines in F, ending: back, die, hee, Pardon, Repentance, him, dy'de]   23-27 *In . . . honor* [six lines in F, ending: selfe, Duties, State, should, Loue, Honor]

I.v.23-24 *And yet . . . have it* [three lines in F, ending: winne, cryes, haue it]

I.vi.1 *the air* [F gives to next line]   4 *martlet* Barlet   9 *most must*   17-20 *Against . . . hermits* [F's lines end: broad, House, Dignities, Ermites]

I. vii.6 *shoal* Schoole [variant spelling]   47 *do* no   58 *as you* [F gives to next line]

II.i.4 *Hold . . . heaven* [two lines in F, ending: Sword, Heauen]   7-9 *And . . . repose* [F's endings: sleepe, thoughts, repose]   13-17 *He . . . content* [F's endings: Pleasure, Offices, withall, Hostesse, content]   25 *when 'tis* [F gives to next line]   55 *strides* sides   56 *sure* sowre   57 *way they* they may

II.ii.2-6 *What . . . possets* [6 lines in F, ending: fire, shriek'd, good-night, open, charge, Possets] 13 s.d. *Enter Macbeth* [F places after "die" in 1.8] 14 *I . . . noise* [two lines in F, ending: deed, noyse] 18-19 *Hark . . . chamber* [one line in F] 22-25 *There's . . . sleep* [F's endings: sleepe, other, Prayers, sleepe] 32 *Stuck . . . throat* [F gives to previous line] 64-65 *To wear . . . chamber* [three lines in F, ending: white, entry, Chamber] 68 *Hath . . . knocking* [two lines in F, ending: vnattended, knocking] 72-73 *To . . . couldst* [four lines in F, ending: deed, my selfe, knocking, could'st. The s.d. "Knock" appears after "deed"]

II.iii.25-27 *Faith . . . things* [two lines of verse in F, the second beginning "And"] 44 s.d. *Enter Macbeth* [F places after 1.43] 53-54 *I'll . . . service* [one line of prose in F] 56-63 *The night . . . shake* [10 lines in F, ending: vnruly, downe, Ayre, Death, terrible, Euents, time, Night, feuorous, shake] 66 *Tongue nor heart* [F gives to next line] 88-89 *O . . . murdered* [one line in F] 137-43 *What . . . bloody* [nine lines in F, ending: doe, them, Office, easie, England, I, safer, Smiles, bloody]

II.iv.14 *And . . . horses* [F prints as a separate line] 17 *make* [F gives to next line] 19 *They . . . so* [F prints as a separate line]

III.i.34-35 *Craving . . . with you* [three lines in F, ending: Horse, Night, you] 42-43 *The sweeter . . . you* [three lines in F, ending: welcome, alone, you] 72 *Who's there* [F prints as a separate line] 75-82 *Well . . . might* [ten lines in F, ending: then, speeches, past, fortune, selfe, conference, with you, crost, them, might] 85-91 *I . . . ever* [nine lines in F, ending: so, now, meeting, predominant, goe, man, hand, begger'd, euer] 111 *I do* [F gives to previous line] 114-15 *Both . . . enemy* [one line in F] 128 *Your . . . most* [two lines in F, ending: you, most]

III.ii.16 *But . . . suffer* [two lines in F, ending: dis-ioynt, suffer] 22 *Duncan . . . grave* [F prints as a separate line] 43 *there . . . done* [F gives to next line] 50 *and . . . crow* [F gives to next line]

III.iii.9 *The rest* [F gives to next line] 17 *O . . . fly, fly, fly* [two lines in F, the first ending: Trecherie] 21 *We . . . affair* [two lines in F, ending: lost, Affaire]

III.iv.21-22 *Most . . . perfect* [four lines in F, ending: Sir, scap'd, againe, perfect] 49 *Here . . . Highness* [two lines in F, ending: Lord, Highness] 110 *broke . . . meeting* [F gives to next line]

122 s.d. *Exeunt* Exit   123 *blood will have blood* [F prints as a separate line]   145 *in deed* indeed

III.v.36 *back again* [F prints as a separate line]

III.vi.1 *My . . . thoughts* [two lines in F, ending: Speeches, Thoughts]   24 *son* Sonnes   38 *the* their

IV.i.46-47 *Open . . . knocks* [one line in F]   59 *germens* Germaine   71 *Beware Macduff* [F prints as a separate line]   79 *Laugh to scorn* [F prints as a separate line]   86 *What is this* [F gives to next line]   93 *Dunsinane* Dunsmane   98 *Birnam* Byrnan [this F spelling, or with *i* for *y* or with a final *e*, occurs at V.ii.5, 31; V.iii.2, 60; V.iv.3; V.v.34, 44; V.viii.30]   119 *eighth* eight   133 *Let . . . hour* [F prints as a separate line]

IV.ii.27 *Fathered . . . fatherless* [two lines in F, ending: is, Father-lesse] IV.ii.34 *Poor bird* [F prints as a separate line]   36-43 *Why . . . for thee* [ten lines in F, ending: Mother, for, saying, is dead, Father, Husband, Market, againe, wit, thee]   48-49 *Every . . . hanged* [two lines of verse in F, ending: Traitor, hang'd]   57-58 [two lines of verse in F, ending: Monkie, Father]   77 *What . . . faces* [F prints as a separate line]

IV.iii.4 *down-fall'n* downfall   15 *deserve* discerne   25 *where . . . doubts* [F prints as a separate line]   102 *Fit to govern* [F gives to next line]   107 *accursed* accust   133 *thy* they   140 *I pray you* [F prints as a separate line]   173 *O relation* [F gives to next line]   211-12 *Wife . . . found* [one line in F]   212-13 *And . . . too* [one line in F]

V.iii.39 *Cure her* Cure   55 *senna* Cyme

V.vi.1 *Your . . . down* [F prints as a separate line]

V.viii.54 *behold . . . stands* [F prints as a separate line]

The Source of Macbeth

The selections given below, from the second edition (1587) of Raphael Holinshed's *Chronicles of England, Scotland, and Ireland,* are the materials that furnished Shakespeare his plot. A study of Holinshed's account of Macbeth's usurpation, and of Donwald's murder of King Duff (which Shakespeare in part transferred to the story of Macbeth), may help a reader to see Shakespeare's play more clearly, for what he added he must have felt necessary, and what he omitted he must have felt undesirable. Some of the changes are examined by E. E. Stoll in an essay printed in this volume, but, excellent as his essay is, he has not said the last word on the relation of the play to the historical account. It should be mentioned that scholars have occasionally suggested Shakespeare may have supplemented Holinshed with other accounts, but there is no evidence that he certainly did so. But of course other books gave him hints for phrases. For example, the Porter's comment on those who "go the primrose way to th' everlasting bonfire" (II.iii) is indebted to the Bible's mention of "the wide gate and broad way that leadeth to destruction; and many there be which go in thereat." But Holinshed alone seems to have provided Shakespeare with the raw material of the story of Macbeth. Presumably Shakespeare read Holinshed's narrative of Macbeth, and in browsing through the adjacent material he hit on the idea of revising this narrative in the light of Donwald's murder of King Duff. Relevant selections from these two portions of Holinshed's chronicle of Scotland are printed below, followed by a brief selection (relevant to V.viii.39-53) from the chronicle of England telling of Old Siward's response to the news of his son's death. The spelling, except for many proper nouns, has been modernized.

Selections from Raphael Holinshed
Chronicles of England, Scotland, and Ireland

[Donwald] conceived such an inward malice towards the king (though he showed it not outwardly at the first) that the same continued still boiling in his stomach, and ceased not, till through setting on of his wife, and in revenge of such unthankfulness, he found means to murder the king within the foresaid castle of Fores where he used to sojourn. For the king being in that country, was accustomed to lie most commonly within the same castle, having a special trust in Donwald, as a man whom he never suspected.

But Donwald, not forgetting the reproach which his lineage had sustained by the execution of those his kinsmen, whom the king for a spectacle to the people had caused to be hanged, could not but show manifest tokens of great grief at home amongst his family: which his wife perceiving, ceased not to travel with him, till she understood what the cause was of his displeasure. Which at length when she had learned by his own relation, she as one that bare no less malice in her heart towards the king, for the like cause on her behalf, than her husband did for his friends, counseled him (sith the king oftentimes used to lodge in his house without any guard about him, other than the garrison of the castle, which was wholly at his commandment) to make him away, and showed him the means whereby he might soonest accomplish it.

Donwald thus being the more kindled in wrath by the words of his wife, determined to follow her advice in the execution of so heinous an act. Whereupon devising with himself for a while, which way he might best accomplish his cursed intent, at length got opportunity, and sped his purpose as followeth. It chanced that the king upon the day before he purposed to depart forth of the castle, was long in his oratory at his prayers, and there continued till it was late in the night. At the last, coming forth, he called such afore him as had faithfully served him in pursuit and apprehension of the rebels, and giving them hearty thanks, he bestowed sundry honorable gifts amongst them, of the which number Donwald was one, as he that had been ever accounted a most faithful servant to the king.

At length, having talked with them a long time, he got him into his privy chamber, only with two of his chamberlains, who having brought him to bed, came forth again, and then fell to banqueting with Donwald and his wife, who had prepared diverse delicate dishes, and sundry sorts of drinks for their rear supper or collation, whereat they sat up so long, till they had charged their stomachs with such full gorges, that their heads were no sooner got to the pillow, but asleep they were so fast, that a man might have removed the chamber over them, sooner than to have awaked them out of their drunken sleep.

Then Donwald, though he abhorred the act greatly in heart, yet through instigation of his wife he called four of his servants unto him (whom he had made privy to his wicked intent before, and framed to his purpose with large gifts) and now declaring unto them, after what sort they should work the feat, they gladly obeyed his instructions, & speedily going about the murder, they enter the chamber (in which the king lay a little before cocks crow, where they secretly cut his throat as he lay sleeping, without any buskling at all: and immediately by a postern gate they carried forth the dead body into the fields. . . .

Donwald, about the time that the murder was in doing, got him amongst them that kept the watch, and so continued in company with them all the residue of the night. But in the morning when the noise was raised in the king's chamber how the king was slain, his body conveyed away, and the bed all berayed with blood; he with the watch ran thither, as though he had known nothing of the matter, and breaking into the chamber, and finding cakes of blood in the bed, and on the floor about the sides of it, he forthwith slew the chamberlains, as guilty of that heinous murder, and then like a mad man running to and fro, he ransacked every corner within the castle, as though it had been to have seen if he might have found either the body, or any of the murderers hid in any privy place: but at length coming to the postern gate, and finding it open, he burdened the chamberlains, whom he had slain, with all the fault, they having the keys of the gates committed to their keeping all the night, and therefore it could not be otherwise (said he) but that they were of counsel in the committing of that most detestable murder.

Finally, such was his overearnest diligence in the severe inquisition and trial of the offenders herein, that some of the lords began to mislike the matter, and to smell forth shrewd tokens, that he should not be altogether clear himself. But for so much as they were in that country, where he had the whole rule, what by reason of his friends and authority together, they doubted to utter what they thought, till time and place should better serve thereunto, and hereupon got them away every man to his home. For the space of six months together, after this heinous murder thus committed, there appeared no sun by day, nor moon by night in any part of the realm, but still was the sky covered with continual clouds, and sometimes such outrageous winds arose, with lightnings and tempests, that the people were in great fear of present destruction. . . .

Monstrous sights also that were seen within the Scottish

kingdom that year were these: horses in Louthian, being of singular beauty and swiftness, did eat their own flesh, and would in no wise taste any other meat. In Angus there was a gentlewoman brought forth a child without eyes, nose, hand, or foot. There was a sparhawk also strangled by an owl. Neither was it any less wonder that the sun, as before is said, was continually covered with clouds for six months' space. But all men understood that the abominable murder of King Duffe was the cause hereof. . . .

Thus might he seem happy to all men, having the love both of his lords and commons: but yet to himself he seemed most unhappy, as he that could not but still live in continual fear, lest his wicked practice concerning the death of Malcolme Duffe should come to light and knowledge of the world. For so cometh it to pass, that such as are pricked in conscience for any secret offense committed, have ever an unquiet mind. And (as the fame goeth) it chanced that a voice was heard as he was in bed in the night time to take his rest, uttering unto him these or the like words in effect: "Think not Kenneth that the wicked slaughter of Malcolme Duffe by thee contrived, is kept secret from the knowledge of the eternal God: thou art he that didst conspire the innocent's death, enterprising by traitorous means to do that to thy neighbor, which thou wouldst have revenged by cruel punishment in any of thy subjects, if it had been offered to thyself. It shall therefore come to pass, that both thou thyself, and thy issue, through the just vengeance of almighty God, shall suffer worthy punishment, to the infamy of thy house and family for evermore. For even at this present are there in hand secret practices to dispatch both thee and thy issue out of the way, that other may enjoy this kingdom which thou dost endeavor to assure unto thine issue."

The king, with this voice being stricken into great dread and terror, passed that night without any sleep coming in his eyes.

[*Macbeth's History*]

Doada was married unto Sinell the Thane of Glammis, by whom she had issue one Makbeth a valiant gentleman, and one that if he had not been somewhat cruel of nature, might have been thought most worthy the government of a realm. On the other part, Duncane was so soft and gentle of nature, that the people wished the inclinations and manners of these two cousins to have been so tempered and interchangeably bestowed betwixt them, that where the one had too much of clemency, and the other of cruelty, the mean virtue betwixt these two extremities might have reigned by indifferent partition in them both, so should Duncane have proved a worthy king, and Makbeth an excellent captain. The beginning of Duncane's reign was very quiet and peaceable, without any notable trouble; but after it was perceived how negligent he was in punishing offenders, many misruled persons took occasion thereof to trouble the peace and quiet state of the commonwealth, by seditious commotions which first had their beginnings in this wise.

Banquho the Thane of Lochquhaber, of whom the house of the Stewarts is descended, the which by order of lineage hath now for a long time enjoyed the crown of Scotland, even till these our days . . . gathered the finances due to the king. . . .

Then doubting not but for such contemptuous demeanor against the king's regal authority, they should be invaded with all the power the king could make, Makdowald one of great estimation among them, making first a confederacy with his nearest friends and kinsmen, took upon him to be chief captain of all such rebels as would stand against the king, in maintenance of their grievous offenses lately committed against him. . . . He used also such subtle persuasions and forged allurements, that in a small time he had gotten together a mighty power of men: for out of the western Isles there came unto him a great multitude of people . . . and out of Ireland . . . no small number of *Kerns and Galloglasses.* . . .

At length Makbeth speaking much against the king's softness, and overmuch slackness in punishing offenders, . . . he promised notwithstanding, if the charge were committed unto him and unto Banquho, so to order the matter, that the rebels should be shortly vanquished & quite put down, and that not so much as one of them should be found to make resistance within the country.

And even so it came to pass: for being sent forth with a new power, at his entering into Lochquhaber, the fame of his coming put the enemies in such fear, that a great number of them stole secretly away from their captain Makdowald, who nevertheless enforced thereto, gave battle unto Makbeth, with the residue which remained with him: but being overcome, and fleeing for refuge into a castle (within the which his wife & children were enclosed) at length when he saw how he could neither defend the hold any longer against his enemies, nor yet upon surrender be suffered to depart with life saved, he first slew his wife and children, and lastly himself, lest if he had yielded simply, he should have been executed in most cruel wise for an example to other. Makbeth entering into the castle by the gates, as then set open, found the carcass of Makdowald lying dead there amongst the residue of the slain bodies, which when he beheld, remitting no piece of his cruel nature with that pitiful sight, he caused the head to be cut off, and set upon a pole's end, and so sent it as present to the king, who as then lay at Bertha. The headless trunk he commanded to be hung up upon a high pair of gallows. . . . Thus was justice and law restored again to the old accustomed course, by the diligent means of Makbeth. Immediately whereupon word came that Sueno king of Norway was arrived in Fife with a puissant army, to subdue the whole realm of Scotland. . . . Makbeth and Banquho were sent with the king's authority, who having with them a convenient power, encountered the enemies, slew part of them, and chased the other to their ships. They that escaped and got once to their ships, obtained of Makbeth for a great sum of gold, that such of their friends as were slain at this last bickersuch as he had made privy to his enterprise, he caused himself to be proclaimed king, and forthwith went into Scone, where (by common consent) he received the investure of the kingdom according to the accustomed manner. The body of Duncane was first conveyed unto Elgine, & there buried in kingly wise; but afterwards it was removed and conveyed unto Colmekill, and there laid in a sepulcher amongst his predecessors, in the year after the birth of our Savior, 1046.

Malcolme Cammore and Donald Bane the sons of King Duncane, for fear of their lives (which they might well know that Mackbeth would seek to bring to end for his more sure confirmation in the estate) fled into Cumberland, where Malcolme remained, till time that Saint Edward the son of Ethelred recovered the dominion of England from the Danish power, the which Edward received Malcolme by way of most friendly entertainment: but Donald passed over into Ireland, where he was tenderly cherished by the king of that land. Mackbeth, after the departure thus of Duncane's sons, used great liberality towards the nobles of the realm, thereby to win their favor, and when he saw that no man went about to trouble him, he set his whole intention to maintain justice, and to punish all enormities and abuses, which had chanced through the feeble and slothful administration of Duncane. . . . He made many wholesome laws and statutes for the public weal of his subjects. [There follows a list of good laws.]

These and the like commendable laws Makbeth caused to be put as then in use, governing the realm for the space of ten years in equal justice. But this was but a counterfeit zeal of equity showed by him, partly against his natural inclination to purchase thereby the favor of the people. Shortly after, he began to show what he was, instead of equity practicing cruelty. For the prick of conscience (as it chanceth ever in tyrants, and such as attain to any estate by unrighteous means) caused him ever to fear, lest he should be served of the same cup, as he had ministered to his predecessor. The words also of the three weird sisters, would not out of his mind, which as they promised him the kingdom, so likewise did they promise it at the same time unto the posterity of Banquho. He willed therefore the same Banquho with his son named Fleance, to come to a supper that he had prepared for them, which was indeed, as he had devised, present death at the hands of certain murderers, whom he hired to execute that deed, appointing them to meet with the same Banquho and his son without the palace, as they returned to their lodgings, and there to slay them, so that he would not have his house slandered, but that in time to come he might clear himself, if anything were laid to his charge upon any suspicion that might arise.

It chanced yet by the benefit of the dark night, that though the father were slain, the son yet by the help of almighty God reserving him to better fortune, escaped that danger: and afterwards having some inkling (by the admonition of some friends which he had in the court) how his life was sought no less than his father's, who was slain not by chance-medley (as by the handling of the matter Makbeth would have had it to appear) but even upon a prepensed device: whereupon to avoid further peril he fled into Wales. . . .

But to return unto Makbeth, in continuing the history, and to begin where I left, ye shall understand that, after the contrived slaughter of Banquho, nothing prospered with the foresaid Makbeth: for in manner every man began to doubt his own life, and durst unneth appear in the king's presence; and even as there were many that stood in fear of him, so likewise stood he in fear of many, in such sort that he began to make those away by one surmised cavillation or other, whom he thought most able to work him any displeasure.

At length he found such sweetness by putting his nobles thus to death, that his earnest thirst after blood in this behalf might in no wise be satisfied: for ye must consider he won double profit (as he thought) hereby: for first they were rid out of the way whom he feared, and then again his coffers were enriched by their goods which were forfeited to his use, whereby he might better maintain a guard of armed men about him to defend his person from injury of them whom he had in any suspicion. Further, to the end he might the more cruelly oppress his subjects with all tyrantlike wrongs, he builded a strong castle on the top of a high hill called Dunsinane, situate in Gowrie, ten miles from Perth, on such a proud height, that, standing there aloft, a man might behold well near all the countries of Angus, Fife, Stermond, and Ernedale, as it were lying underneath him. This castle, then, being founded on the top of that high hill, put the realm to great charges before it was finished, for all the stuff necessary to the building could not be brought up without much toil and business. But Makbeth, being once determined to have the work go forward, caused the thanes of each shire within the realm, to come and help towards that building, each man his course about.

At the last, when the turn fell unto Makduffe, Thane of Fife, to build his part, he sent workmen with all needful provision, and commanded them to show such diligence in every behalf, that no occasion might be given for the king to find fault with him, in that he came not himself as other had done, which he refused to do, for doubt lest the king, bearing him (as he partly understood) no great good will, would lay violent hands upon him, as he had done upon diverse other. Shortly after, Makbeth coming to behold how the work went forward, and because he found not Makduffe there, he was sore offended, and said: "I perceive this man will never obey my commandments, till he be ridden with a snaffle; but I shall provide well enough for him." . . .

Neither could he afterwards abide to look upon the said Makduffe, either for that he thought his puissance overgreat; either else for that he had learned of certain wizards, in whose words he put great confidence (for that the prophecy had happened so right, which the three fairies or weird sisters had declared unto him) how that he ought to take heed of Makduffe, who in time to come should seek to destroy him.

And surely hereupon had he put Makduffe to death, but that a certain witch, whom he had in great trust, had told that he should never be slain with man born of any woman, nor vanquished till the wood of Bernane came to the castle of Dunsinane. By this prophecy Makbeth put all fear out of his heart, supposing he might do what he would, without any fear to be punished for the same, for by the one prophecy he believed it was unpossible for any man to vanquish him, and by the other unpossible to slay him. This vain hope caused him to do many outrageous things, to the grievous oppression of his subjects. At length Makduffe, to avoid peril of life, purposed with himself to pass into England, to procure Malcolme Cammore to claim the crown of Scotland. But this was not so secretly devised by Makduffe, but that Makbeth had knowledge given him thereof: for kings (as is said) have sharp sight like unto Lynx, and long ears like unto Midas. For Makbeth had in every nobleman's house one sly fellow or other in fee with him, to reveal all that was said or done within the same, by which sleight he oppressed the most part of the nobles of his realm.

Immediately then, being advertised whereabout Makduffe went, he came hastily with a great power into Fife, and forthwith besieged the castle where Makduffe dwelled, trusting to have found him therein. They that kept the house, without any resistance opened the gates, and suffered him to enter, mistrusting none evil. But nevertheless Makbeth most cruelly caused the wife and children of Makduffe, with all other whom he found in that castle, to be slain. Also he confiscated the goods of Makduffe, proclaimed him traitor, and confined him out of all the parts of his realm; but Makduffe was already escaped out of danger, and gotten into England unto Malcolme Cammore, to try what purchase he might make by means of his support, to revenge the slaughter so cruelly executed on his wife, his children, and other friends. At his coming unto Malcolme, he declared into what great misery the estate of Scotland was brought, by the detestable cruelties exercised by the tyrant Makbeth, having committed many horrible slaughters and murders, both as well of the nobles as commons, for the which he was hated right mortally of all his liege people, desiring nothing more than to be delivered of that intolerable and most heavy yoke of thralldom, which they sustained at such a caitiff's hands.

Malcome hearing Makduffe's words, which he uttered in very lamentable sort, for mere compassion and very ruth that pierced his sorrowful heart, bewailing the miserable state of his country, he fetched a deep sigh; which Makduffe perceiving, began to fall most earnestly in hand with him, to enterprise the delivering of the Scottish people out of the hands of so cruel and bloody a tyrant, as Makbeth by too many plain experiments did show himself to be: which was an easy matter for him to bring to pass, considering not only the good title he had, but also the earnest desire of the people to have some occasion ministered, whereby they might be revenged of those notable injuries, which they daily sustained by the outrageous cruelty of Makbeth's misgovernance. Though Malcolme was very sorrowful for the oppression of his countrymen the Scots, in manner as Makduffe had declared; yet doubting whether he were come as one that meant unfeignedly as he spoke, or else as sent from Makbeth to betray him, he thought to have some further trial, and thereupon dissembling his mind at the first, he answered as followeth.

"I am truly very sorry for the misery chanced to my country of Scotland, but though I have never so great affection to relieve the same, yet by reason of certain incurable vices, which reign in me, I am nothing meet thereto. First, such immoderate lust and voluptuous sensuality (the abominable fountain of all vices) followeth me, that if I were made king of Scots, I should seek to deflower your maids and matrons, in such wise that mine intemperancy should be more importable unto you than the bloody tyranny of Makbeth now is." Hereunto Makduffe answered: "This surely is a very evil fault, for many noble princes and kings have lost both lives and kingdoms for the same; nevertheless there are women enow in Scotland, and therefore follow my counsel. Make thyself king, and I shall convey the matter so wisely, that thou shalt be so satisfied at thy pleasure in such secret wise, that no man shall be aware thereof."

Then said Malcolme, "I am also the most avaricious creature on the earth, so that if I were king, I should seek so many ways to get lands and goods, that I would slay the most part of all the nobles of Scotland by surmised accusations, to the end I might enjoy their lands, goods, and possessions; and therefore to show you what mischief may ensue on you through mine unsatiable covetousness, I will rehearse unto you a fable. There was a fox having a sore place on him overset with a swarm of flies, that continually sucked out her blood: and when one that came by and saw this manner, demanded whether she would have the flies driven beside her, she answered no: for if these flies that are already full, and by reason thereof suck not very eagerly, should be chased away, other that are empty and fellie and hungered, should light in their places, and suck out the residue of my blood far more to my grievance than these, which now being satisfied do not much annoy me. Therefore," saith Malcolme, "suffer me to remain where I am, lest if I attain to the regiment of your realm, mine unquenchable avarice may prove such; that ye would think the displeasures which now grieve you, should seem easy in respect of the unmeasurable outrage, which might ensue through my coming amongst you."

Makduffe to this made answer, how it was a far worse fault than the other: "for avarice is the root of all mischief, and for that crime the most part of our kings have been slain and brought to their final end. Yet notwithstanding follow my counsel, and take upon thee the crown. There is gold and riches enough in Scotland to satisfy thy greedy desire." Then said Malcolme again, "I am furthermore inclined to dissimulation, telling of leasings, and all other kinds of deceit, so that I naturally rejoice in nothing so much, as to betray & deceive such as put any trust or confidence in my words. Then sith there is nothing that more becometh a prince than constancy, verity, truth, and justice, with the other laudable fellowship of those fair and noble virtues which are comprehended only in soothfastness, and that lying utterly overthroweth the same; you see how unable I am to govern any province or region: and therefore sith you have remedies to cloak and hide all the rest of my other vices, I pray you find shift to cloak this vice amongst the residue."

Then said Makduffe: "This yet is the worst of all, and there I leave thee, and therefore say: Oh ye unhappy and miserable Scottishmen, which are thus scourged with so many and sundry calamities, each one above other! Ye have one cursed and wicked tyrant that now reigneth over you, without any right or title, oppressing you with his most bloody cruelty. This other that hath the right to the crown, is so replete with the inconstant behavior and manifest vices of Englishmen, that he is nothing worthy to enjoy it: for by his own confession he is not only avaricious, and given to unsatiable lust, but so false a traitor withal, that no trust is to be had unto any word he speaketh. Adieu Scotland, for now I account myself a banished man forever, without comfort or consolation": and with those words the brackish tears trickled down his cheeks very abundantly.

At the last, when he was ready to depart, Malcolme took him by the sleeve, and said: "Be of good comfort Makduffe, for I have none of these vices before remembered, but have jested with thee in this manner, only to prove thy mind: for diverse times heretofore hath Makbeth sought by this manner of means to bring me into his hands, but the more slow I have showed myself to condescend to thy motion and request, the more diligence shall I use in accomplishing the same." Incontinently hereupon they embraced each other, and promising to be faithful the one to the other, they fell in consultation how they might best provide for all their business, to bring the same to good effect. Soon after, Makduffe repairing to the borders of Scotland, addressed his letters with secret dispatch unto the nobles of the realm, declaring how Malcolme was confederate with him, to come hastily into Scotland to claim the crown, and therefore he required them, sith he was right inheritor thereto, to assist him with their powers to recover the same out of the hands of the wrongful usurper.

In the meantime, Malcolme purchased such favor at King Edward's hands, that old Siward Earl of Northumberland was appointed with ten thousand men to go with him into Scotland, to support him in this enterprise, for recovery of his right. After these news were spread abroad in Scotland, the nobles drew into two several factions, the one taking part with Makbeth, and the other with Malcolme. Hereupon ensued oftentimes sundry bickerings, & diverse light skirmishes: for those that were of Malcolme's side, would not jeopard to join with their enemies in a pight field, till his coming out of England to their support. But after that Makbeth perceived his enemy's power to increase, by such aid as came to them forth of England with his adversary Malcolme, he recoiled back into Fife, there purposing to abide in camp fortified, at the castle of Dunsinane, and to fight with his enemies, if they meant to pursue him; howbeit some of his friends advised him, that it should be best for him, either to make some agreement with Malcolme, or else to flee with all speed into the Isles, and to take his treasure with him, to the end he might wage sundry great princes of the realm to take his part, & retain strangers, in whom he might better trust than in his own subjects, which stole daily from him: but he had such confidence in his prophecies, that he believed he should never be vanquished, till Birnane wood were brought to Dunsinane; nor yet to be slain with any man, that should be or was born of any woman.

Malcolme following hastily after Makbeth, came the night before the battle unto Birnane wood, and when his army had rested a while there to refresh them, he commanded every man to get a bough of some tree or other of that wood in his hand, as big as he might bear, and to march forth therewith in such wise, that on the next morrow they might come closely and without sight in this manner within view of his enemies. On the morrow when Makbeth beheld them coming in this sort, he first marveled what the matter meant, but in the end remembered himself that the prophecy which he had heard long before that time, of the coming of Birnane wood to Dunsinane castle, was likely to be now fulfilled. Nevertheless, he brought his men in order of battle, and exhorted them to do valiantly, howbeit his enemies had scarcely cast from them their boughs, when Makbeth perceiving their numbers, betook him straight to flight, whom Makduffe pursued with great hatred even till he came unto Lunfannaine, where Makbeth perceiving that Makduffe was hard at his back, leaped beside his horse, saying: "Thou traitor, what meaneth it that thou shouldest thus in vain follow me that am not appointed to be slain by any creature that is born of a woman, come on therefore, and receive thy reward which thou hast deserved for thy pains," and therewithal he lifted up his sword thinking to have slain him.

But Makduffe quickly avoiding from his horse, ere he came at him, answered (with his naked sword in his hand) saying: "It is true Makbeth, and now shall thine insatiable cruelty have an end, for I am even he that thy wizards have told thee of, who was never born of my mother, but ripped out of her womb": therewithal he stepped unto him, and slew him in the place. Then cutting his head from his shoulders, he set it upon a pole, and brought it unto Malcolme. This was the end of Makbeth, after he had reigned 17 years over the Scottishmen. In the beginning of his reign he accomplished many worthy acts, very profitable to the commonwealth (as ye have heard), but afterward by illusion of the devil, he defamed the same with most terrible cruelty. He was slain in the year of the incarnation 1057, and in the 16 year of King Edward's reign over the Englishmen.

Malcolme Cammore thus recovering the realm (as ye have heard) by support of King Edward, in the 16 year of the same Edward's reign, he was crowned at Scone, the 25 day of April, in the year of our Lord 1057. Immediately after his coronation he called a parliament at Forfair, in the which he rewarded them with lands and livings that had assisted him against Makbeth, advancing

them to fees and offices, as he saw cause, & commanded
that specially those, that bare the surname of any offices
or lands, should have and enjoy the same. He created
many'earls, lords, barons, and knights. Many of them,
that before were thanes, were at this time made earls,
as Fife, Menteth . . . Leuenox . . . Cathnes, Rosse, and
Angus. These were the first earls that have been heard
of amongst the Scottishmen as their histories do make
mention. Many new surnames were taken up at this time
amongst them, as Cauder . . . Seiton . . . with many
other that had possessions given them, which gave names
to the owners for the time. . . .

[Siward and his Son]

About the thirteenth year of King Edward his reign (as
some write) or rather about the nineteenth or twentieth
year, as should appear by the Scottish writers, Siward
the noble Earl of Northumberland with a great power of
horsemen went into Scotland, and in battle put to flight
Mackbeth that had usurped the crown of Scotland, and,
that done, placed Malcolme surnamed Camoir, the son
of Duncane, sometime king of Scotland, in the government of that realm, who afterward slew the said Mackbeth, and then reigned in quiet. . . .

It is recorded also, that, in the foresaid battle, in
which Earl Siward vanquished the Scots, one of Siward's
sons chanced to be slain, whereof although the father had
good cause to be sorrowful, yet, when he heard that he
died of a wound which he had received in fighting stoutly,
in the forepart of his body, and that with his face towards the enemy, he greatly rejoiced thereat, to hear
that he died so manfully. But here is to be noted, that not
now, but a little before (as *Henry Hunt* saith) that Earl
Siward went into Scotland himself in person, he sent his
son with an army to conquer the land, whose hap was
there to be slain: and when his father heard the news,
he demanded whether he received the wound whereof he
died, in the forepart of the body, or in the hinder part:

and when it was told him that he received it in the fore-part: "I rejoice (saith he) even with all my heart, for *I would not wish* either to my son nor to myself any other kind of *death.*"

Commentaries

Samuel Johnson

Macbeth

Most of the notes which the present editor has sub-
joined to this play were published by him in a small
pamphlet in 1745.

I.i. *"Enter three* Witches." In order to make a true
estimate of the abilities and merit of a writer, it is always necessary to examine the genius of his age and the
opinions of his contemporaries. A poet who should now
make the whole action of his tragedy depend upon enchantment and produce the chief events by the assistance
of supernatural agents, would be censured as transgress-
ing the bounds of probability, be banished from the
theater to the nursery, and condemned to write fairy
tales instead of tragedies; but a survey of the notions
that prevailed at the time when this play was written will
prove that Shakespeare was in no danger of such censures, since he only turned the system that was then

From *The Plays of William Shakespeare* (1765).

universally admitted to his advantage and was far from overburdening the credulity of his audience.

The reality of witchcraft or enchantment, which, though not strictly the same, are confounded in this play, has in all ages and countries been credited by the common people, and in most, by the learned themselves. These phantoms have indeed appeared more frequently in proportion as the darkness of ignorance has been more gross; but it cannot be shown that the brightest gleams of knowledge have at any time been sufficient to drive them out of the world. The time in which this kind of credulity was at its height seems to have been that of the holy war, in which the Christians imputed all their defeats to enchantments or diabolical opposition, as they ascribed their success to the assistance of their military saints; and the learned Dr. Warburton appears to believe (*Supplement to the Introduction to "Don Quixote"*) that the first accounts of enchantments were brought into this part of the world by those who returned from their eastern expeditions. But there is always some distance between the birth and maturity of folly as of wickedness; this opinion had long existed, though perhaps application of it had in no foregoing age been so frequent, nor the reception so general. Olympiodorus, in Photius's extracts, tells us of one Libanius, who practiced this kind of military magic and having promised χωρὶς ὁπλιτῶν κατὰ βαρβάρων ἐνεργεῖν, *to perform great things against the barbarians without soldiers,* was, at the instances of the empress Placidia, put to death, when he was about to have given proof of his abilities. The empress showed some kindness in her anger by cutting him off at a time so convenient for his reputation.

But a more remarkable proof of the antiquity of this notion may be found in St. Chrysostom's book *de Sacerdotio,* which exhibits a scene of enchantments not exceeded by any romance of the Middle Age: he supposes a spectator overlooking a field of battle attended by one that points out all the various objects of horror, the engines of destruction, and the arts of slaughter. Δεικνύτο δὲ ἔτι παρὰ τοῖς ἐναντίοις καὶ πετομένους ἵππους διά τινος μαγγανείας, καὶ ὁπλίτας δι᾽ ἀέρος φερομένους, καὶ πάσην γοητείας δύναμιν καὶ ἰδέαν. "Let him then proceed to show him in the opposite armies horses flying by enchantment, armed men transported through the air, and every tower and form of magic." Whether St. Chrysostom believed that such performances were really to be seen in a day of battle, or only endeavored to enliven his description by adopting the notions of the vulgar, it is equally certain that such notions were in his time received, and that therefore they were not imported from the Saracens in a later age; the wars with the Saracens, however, gave occasion to their propagation, not only as bigotry naturally discovers prodigies, but as the scene of action was removed to a great distance.

The Reformation did not immediately arrive at its meridian, and though day was gradually increasing upon us, the goblins of witchcraft still continued to hover in the twilight. In the time of Queen Elizabeth was the remarkable trial of the witches of Warbois, whose conviction is still commemorated in an annual sermon at Huntingdon. But in the reign of King James, in which this tragedy was written, many circumstances concurred to propagate and confirm this opinion. The king, who was much celebrated for his knowledge, had, before his arrival in England, not only examined in person a woman accused of witchcraft but had given a very formal account of the practices and illusions of evil spirits, the compacts of witches, the ceremonies used by them, the manner of detecting them, and the justice of punishing them, in his dialogues of *Daemonologie,* written in the Scottish dialect, and published at Edinburgh. This book was, soon after his accession, reprinted at London, and as the ready way to gain King James's favor was to flatter his speculations, the system of *Daemonologie* was immediately adopted by all who desired either to gain preferment or not to lose it. Thus the doctrine of witchcraft was very powerfully inculcated; and as the greatest part of mankind have no other reason for their opinions than that they are in fashion, it cannot be doubted but this persuasion made a rapid progress, since vanity and credulity cooperated in its favor. The infection soon reached the Parliament, who, in the first year of King James, made a law, by which it was enacted, Chapter XII: That "if any person shall use any invocation or conjuration of any evil or wicked spirit; 2. or shall consult, covenant with, entertain, employ, feed or reward any evil or cursed spirit to or for any intent or purpose; 3. or take up any dead man, woman or child out of the grave,—or the skin, bone, or any part of the dead person, to be employed or used in any manner of witchcraft, sorcery, charm, or enchantment; 4. or shall use, practice, or exercise any sort of witchcraft, sorcery, charm, or enchantment; 5. whereby any person shall be destroyed, killed, wasted, consumed, pined, or lamed in any part of the body; 6. that every such person being convicted shall suffer death." This law was repealed in our own time.

Thus, in the time of Shakespeare, was the doctrine of witchcraft at once established by law and by the fashion, and it became not only unpolite, but criminal, to doubt it; and as prodigies are always seen in proportion as they are expected, witches were every day discovered and multiplied so fast in some places that Bishop Hall mentions a village in Lancashire where their number was greater than that of the houses. The Jesuits and sectaries took advantage of this universal error and endeavored to promote the interest of their parties by pretended cures of persons afflicted by evil spirits; but they were detected and exposed by the clergy of the Established Church.

Upon this general infatuation Shakespeare might be easily allowed to found a play, especially since he has followed with great exactness such histories as were then thought true; nor can it be doubted that the scenes of enchantment, however they may now be ridiculed, were both by himself and his audience thought awful and affecting.

I.vii.28. "*Enter* Lady Macbeth." The arguments by which Lady Macbeth persuades her husband to commit the murder afford a proof of Shakespeare's knowledge of human nature. She urges the excellence and dignity of courage, a glittering idea which has dazzled mankind from

age to age and animated sometimes the housebreaker
and sometimes the conqueror; but this sophism Macbeth
has forever destroyed, by distinguishing true from false
fortitude, in a line and a half; of which it may almost be
said that they ought to bestow immortality on the author,
though all his other productions had been lost;

> I dare do all that may become a man,
> Who dares do more, is none.

This topic, which has been always employed with too
much success, is used in this scene with peculiar propriety, to a soldier by a woman. Courage is the distinguishing virtue of a soldier, and the reproach of cowardice cannot be borne by any man from a woman, without great impatience.

She then urges the oaths by which he had bound himself to murder Duncan, another art of sophistry by which
men have sometimes deluded their consciences and per-
suaded themselves that what would be criminal in others
is virtuous in them; this argument Shakespeare, whose
plan obliged him to make Macbeth yield, has not con-
futed, though he might easily have shown that a former
obligation could not be vacated by a latter; that obligations laid on us by a higher power could not be over-
ruled by obligations which we lay upon ourselves.

II.i.49. *"Macbeth.* Now o'er the one half-world / Nature seems dead." That is, *over our hemisphere all action
and motion seem to have ceased.* This image, which is
perhaps the most striking that poetry can produce, has
been adopted by Dryden in his *Conquest of Mexico:*

> All things are hush'd as Nature's self lay dead,
> The mountains seem to nod their drowsy head;
> The little birds in dreams their songs repeat,
> And sleeping flow'rs beneath the night dews sweat.
> Even lust and envy sleep!

These lines, though so well known, I have transcribed,
that the contrast between them and this passage of Shakespeare may be more accurately observed.

Night is described by two great poets, but one describes a night of quiet, the other of perturbation. In the night of Dryden, all the disturbers of the world are laid asleep; in that of Shakespeare, nothing but sorcery, lust, and murder is awake. He that reads Dryden finds himself lulled with serenity and disposed to solitude and contemplation. He that peruses Shakespeare looks round alarmed and starts to find himself alone. One is the night of a lover, the other, of a murderer.

II.ii.55. "*Lady Macbeth.* gild the faces of the grooms withal; / For it must seem their guilt." Could Shakespeare possibly mean to play upon the similitude of *gild* and *guilt?*

II.iii.113–14. "*Macbeth.* Here lay Duncan, / His silver skin lac'd with his golden blood." Mr. Pope has endeavored to improve one of these lines by substituting *gory blood* for *golden blood;* but it may easily be admitted that he who could on such occasion talk of *lacing the silver skin* would *lace it* with *golden blood*. No amendment can be made to this line, of which every word is equally faulty, but by a general blot.

It is not improbable that Shakespeare put these forced and unnatural metaphors into the mouth of Macbeth as a mark of artifice and dissimulation, to show the difference between the studied language of hypocrisy and the natural outcries of sudden passion. This whole speech so considered is a remarkable instance of judgment, as it consists entirely of antithesis and metaphor.

III.i.68–69. "Mine eternal jewel / Giv'n to the common enemy of man." It is always an entertainment to an inquisitive reader, to trace a sentiment to its original source, and therefore though the term "enemy of man," applied to the devil, is in itself natural and obvious, yet some may be pleased with being informed, that Shakespeare probably borrowed it from the first lines of the destruction of Troy, a book which he is known to have read.

That this remark may not appear too trivial, I shall take occasion from it to point out a beautiful passage of Milton evidently copied from a book of no greater authority, in describing the gates of hell. Book 2. v. 879. he says,

> . . . On a sudden open fly,
> With impetuous recoil and jarring sound,
> Th' infernal doors, and on their hinges grate
> Harsh thunder.

In the history of Don Bellianis, when one of the knights approaches, as I remember, the castle of Brandezar, the gates are said to open "grating harsh thunder upon their brazen hinges."

IV.i. As this is the chief scene of enchantment in the play, it is proper in this place to observe, with how much judgment Shakespeare has selected all the circumstances of his infernal ceremonies, and how exactly he has conformed to common opinions and traditions.

> Thrice the brinded cat hath mew'd.

The usual form in which familiar spirits are reported to converse with witches, is that of a cat. A witch, who was tried about half a century before the time of Shakespeare, had a cat named Rutterkin, as the spirit of one of those witches was Grimalkin; and when any mischief was to be done she used to bid Rutterkin "go and fly," but once when she would have sent Rutterkin to torment a daughter of the countess of Rutland, instead of "going" or "flying," he only cried "mew," from whence she discovered that the lady was out of his power, the power of witches not being universal, but limited, as Shakespeare has taken care to inculcate.

> Though his bark cannot be lost,
> Yet it shall be tempest tost.

The common afflictions which the malice of witches produced were melancholy, fits, and loss of flesh, which are threatened by one of Shakespeare's witches.

> Weary sev'n-nights, nine times nine,
> Shall he dwindle, peak and pine.

It was likewise their practice to destroy the cattle of
their neighbors, and the farmers have to this day many
ceremonies to secure their cows and other cattle from
witchcraft; but they seem to have been most suspected
of malice against swine. Shakespeare has accordingly
made one of his witches declare that she has been "killing swine," and Dr. Harsenet observes, that about that
time, "a sow could not be ill of the measles, nor a girl
of the sullens, but some old woman was charged with
witchcraft."

> Toad, that under the cold stone,
> Days and nights has, thirty-one,
> Swelter'd venom sleeping got;
> Boil thou first i' th' charmed pot.

Toads have likewise long lain under the reproach of being
by some means accessory to witchcraft, for which reason
Shakespeare, in the first scene of this play, calls one of
the spirits Padock or toad, and now takes care to put a
toad first into the pot. When Vaninus was seized at
Tholouse, there was found at his lodgings *ingens Bufo
Vitro inclusus, a great Toad shut in a Vial,* upon which
those that prosecuted him *Veneficium exprobrabant,
charged him,* I suppose, with witchcraft.

> Fillet of a fenny snake,
> In the cauldron boil and bake;
> Eye of newt, and toe of frog . . .
> For a charm, &c.

The propriety of these ingredients may be known by
consulting the books *de Viribus Animalium* and *de
Mirabilibus Mundi,* ascribed to Albertus Magnus, in
which the reader, who has time and credulity, may discover wonderful secrets.

> Finger of birth-strangled babes,
> Ditch-deliver'd by a drab. . . .

It has been already mentioned in the law against witches, that they are supposed to take up dead bodies to use in enchantments, which was confessed by the woman whom King James examined, and who had of a dead body that was divided in one of their assemblies, two fingers for her share. It is observable that Shakespeare, on this great occasion, which involves the fate of a king, multiplies all the circumstances of horror. The babe, whose finger is used, must be strangled in its birth; the grease must not only be human, but must have dropped from a gibbet, the gibbet of a murderer; and even the sow, whose blood is used, must have offended nature by devouring her own farrow. These are touches of judgment and genius.

> And now about the cauldron sing . . .
> Black spirits and white,
>   Blue spirits and grey,
> Mingle, mingle, mingle,
>   You that mingle may.

And in a former part,

> . . . weyward sisters, hand in hand, . . .
> Thus do go about, about,
> Thrice to thine, and thrice to mine,
> And thrice again to make up nine!

These two passages I have brought together, because they both seem subject to the objection of too much levity for the solemnity of enchantment, and may both be shown, by one quotation from Camden's account of Ireland, to be founded upon a practice really observed by the uncivilized natives of that country. "When any one gets a fall," says the informer of Camden, "he starts up, and *turning three times to the right* digs a hole in the earth; for they imagine that there is a spirit in the ground, and if he falls sick in two or three days, they send one of their women that is skilled in that way to the place, where she says, I call thee from the east, west, north and south, from the groves, the woods, the rivers, and the fens, from the *fairies red, black, white*." There was likewise a book written before the time of Shakespeare, describing, amongst other properties, the colors of spirits.

Many other circumstances might be particularized, in which Shakespeare has shown his judgment and his knowledge.

General Observation. This play is deservedly celebrated for the propriety of its fictions, and solemnity, grandeur, and variety of its action; but it has no nice discriminations of character, the events are too great to admit the influence of particular dispositions, and the course of the action necessarily determines the conduct of the agents.

The danger of ambition is well described; and I know not whether it may not be said in defense of some parts which now seem improbable, that, in Shakespeare's time, it was necessary to warn credulity against vain and illusive predictions.

The passions are directed to their true end. Lady Macbeth is merely detested; and though the courage of Macbeth preserves some esteem, yet every reader rejoices at his fall.

A. C. Bradley

From *Shakespearean Tragedy*

From this murky background stand out the two great terrible figures who dwarf all the remaining characters of the drama. Both are sublime, and both inspire, far more than the other tragic heroes, the feeling of awe. They are never detached in imagination from the atmosphere which surrounds them and adds to their grandeur and terror. It is, as it were, continued into their souls. For within them is all that we felt without—the darkness of night, lit with the flame of tempest and the hues of blood, and haunted by wild and direful shapes, "murdering ministers," spirits of remorse, and maddening visions of peace lost and judgment to come. The way to be untrue to Shakespeare here, as always, is to relax the tension of imagination, to conventionalize, to conceive Macbeth, for example, as a halfhearted cowardly criminal, and Lady Macbeth as a wholehearted fiend.

These two characters are fired by one and the same passion of ambition; and to a considerable extent they are alike. The disposition of each is high, proud, and commanding. They are born to rule, if not to reign. They are peremptory or contemptuous to their inferiors. They are not children of light, like Brutus and Hamlet; they are of the world. We observe in them no love of country, and no interest in the welfare of anyone outside their fam-

From *Shakespearean Tragedy* by A. C. Bradley. London: Macmillan & Company, Ltd., 1904. Reprinted by permission of Macmillan & Company, Ltd. (London), St Martin's Press, Inc. (New York), and The Macmillan Company of Canada, Ltd. (Toronto).

ily. Their habitual thoughts and aims are, and, we imagine, long have been, all of station and power. And though in both there is something, and in one much, of what is higher—honor, conscience, humanity—they do not live consciously in the light of these things or speak their language. Not that they are egoists, like Iago; or, if they are egoists, theirs is an *egoïsme à deux*. They have no separate ambitions.[1] They support and love one another. They suffer together. And if, as time goes on, they drift a little apart, they are not vulgar souls, to be alienated and recriminate when they experience the fruitlessness of their ambition. They remain to the end tragic, even grand.

So far there is much likeness between them. Otherwise they are contrasted, and the action is built upon this contrast. Their attitudes towards the projected murder of Duncan are quite different; and it produces in them equally different effects. In consequence, they appear in the earlier part of the play as of equal importance, if indeed Lady Macbeth does not overshadow her husband; but afterwards she retires more and more into the background, and he becomes unmistakably the leading figure. His is indeed far the more complex character: and I will speak of it first.

Macbeth, the cousin of a King mild, just, and beloved, but now too old to lead his army, is introduced to us as a general of extraordinary prowess, who has covered himself with glory in putting down a rebellion and repelling the invasion of a foreign army. In these conflicts he showed great personal courage, a quality which he continues to display throughout the drama in regard to all plain dangers. It is difficult to be sure of his customary demeanor, for in the play we see him either in what appears to be an exceptional relation to his wife, or else in the throes of remorse and desperation; but from his behavior during his journey home after the war, from his

[1] The assertion that Lady Macbeth sought a crown for herself, or sought anything for herself, apart from her husband, is absolutely unjustified by anything in the play. It is based on a sentence of Holinshed's which Shakespeare did *not* use.

later conversations with Lady Macbeth, and from his language to the murderers of Banquo and to others, we imagine him as a great warrior, somewhat masterful, rough, and abrupt, a man to inspire some fear and much admiration. He was thought "honest," or honorable; he was trusted, apparently, by everyone; Macduff, a man of the highest integrity, "loved him well." And there was, in fact, much good in him. We have no warrant, I think, for describing him, with many writers, as of a "noble" nature, like Hamlet or Othello;[2] but he had a keen sense both of honor and of the worth of a good name. The phrase, again, "too full of the milk of human kindness," is applied to him in impatience by his wife, who did not fully understand him; but certainly he was far from devoid of humanity and pity.

At the same time he was exceedingly ambitious. He must have been so by temper. The tendency must have been greatly strengthened by his marriage. When we see him, it has been further stimulated by his remarkable success and by the consciousness of exceptional powers and merit. It becomes a passion. The course of action suggested by it is extremely perilous: it sets his good name, his position, and even his life on the hazard. It is also abhorrent to his better feelings. Their defeat in the struggle with ambition leaves him utterly wretched, and would have kept him so, however complete had been his outward success and security. On the other hand, his passion for power and his instinct of self-assertion are so vehement that no inward misery could persuade him to relinquish the fruits of crime, or to advance from remorse to repentance.

In the character as so far sketched there is nothing very peculiar, though the strength of the forces contending in it is unusual. But there is in Macbeth one marked peculiarity, the true apprehension of which is the key to Shakespeare's conception.[3] This bold ambitious man of

[2] The word is used of him (I.ii.67), but not in a way that decides this question or even bears on it.

[3] This view, thus generally stated, is not original, but I cannot say who first stated it.

action has, within certain limits, the imagination of a poet
—an imagination on the one hand extremely sensitive to
impressions of a certain kind, and, on the other,
productive of violent disturbance both of mind and body.
Through it he is kept in contact with supernatural impressions and is liable to supernatural fears. And through
it, especially, come to him the intimations of conscience
and honor. Macbeth's better nature—to put the matter for
clearness' sake too broadly—instead of speaking to him
in the overt language of moral ideas, commands, and pro-
hibitions, incorporates itself in images which alarm and
horrify. His imagination is thus the best of him, something
usually deeper and higher than his conscious thoughts;
and if he had obeyed it he would have been safe. But his
wife quite misunderstands it, and he himself understands
it only in part. The terrifying images which deter him
from crime and follow its commission, and which are
really the protest of his deepest self, seem to his wife the
creations of mere nervous fear, and are sometimes referred by himself to the dread of vengeance or the restlessness of insecurity.[4] His conscious or reflective mind,
that is, moves chiefly among considerations of outward success and failure, while his inner being is con-
vulsed by conscience. And his inability to understand himself is repeated and exaggerated in the interpretations of
actors and critics, who represent him as a coward, cold-
blooded, calculating, and pitiless, who shrinks from crime
simply because it is dangerous, and suffers afterwards
simply because he is not safe. In reality his courage is
frightful. He strides from crime to crime, though his soul
never ceases to bar his advance with shapes of terror,
or to clamor in his ears that he is murdering his peace
and casting away his "eternal jewel."

It is of the first importance to realize the strength, and
also (what has not been so clearly recognized) the limits,
of Macbeth's imagination. It is not the universal meditative imagination of Hamlet. He came to see in man, as

---

[4] The latter, and more important, point was put quite clearly by
Coleridge.

Hamlet sometimes did, the "quintessence of dust"; but he must always have been incapable of Hamlet's reflections on man's noble reason and infinite faculty, or of seeing with Hamlet's eyes "this brave o'erhanging firmament, this majestical roof fretted with golden fire." Nor could he feel, like Othello, the romance of war or the infinity of love. He shows no sign of any unusual sensitiveness to the glory or beauty in the world or the soul; and it is partly for this reason that we have no inclination to love him, and that we regard him with more of awe than of pity. His imagination is excitable and intense, but narrow. That which stimulates it is, almost solely, that which thrills with sudden, startling, and often supernatural fear.[5] There is a famous passage late in the play (V.v.10) which is here very significant, because it refers to a time before his conscience was burdened, and so shows his native disposition:

> The time has been, my senses would have cool'd
> To hear a night-shriek; and my fell of hair
> Would at a dismal treatise rise and stir
> As life were in't.

This "time" must have been in his youth, or at least before we see him. And, in the drama, everything which terrifies him is of this character, only it has now a deeper and a moral significance. Palpable dangers leave him unmoved or fill him with fire. He does himself mere justice when he asserts he "dare do all that may become a man," or when he exclaims to Banquo's ghost,

> What man dare, I dare:
> Approach thou like the rugged Russian bear,
> The arm'd rhinoceros, or the Hyrcan tiger;
> Take any shape but that, and my firm nerves
> Shall never tremble.

---

[5] It is the consequent insistence on the idea of fear, and the frequent repetition of the word, that have principally led to misinterpretation.

What appalls him is always the image of his own guilty
heart or bloody deed, or some image which derives from
them its terror or gloom. These, when they arise, hold him
spellbound and possess him wholly, like a hypnotic
trance which is at the same time the ecstasy of a poet.
As the first "horrid image" of Duncan's murder—of himself murdering Duncan—rises from unconsciousness and
confronts him, his hair stands on end and the outward
scene vanishes from his eyes. Why? For fear of "consequences"? The idea is ridiculous. Or because the deed
is bloody? The man who with his "smoking" steel "carved
out his passage" to the rebel leader, and "unseam'd him
from the nave to the chaps," would hardly be frightened
by blood. How could fear of consequences make the dagger
he is to use hang suddenly glittering before him in the
air, and then as suddenly dash it with gouts of blood?
Even when he *talks* of consequences, and declares that if
he were safe against them he would "jump the life to
come," his imagination bears witness against him, and
shows us that what really holds him back is the hideous
vileness of the deed:

> He's here in double trust;
> First, as I am his kinsman and his subject,
> Strong both against the deed; then, as his host,
> Who should against his murderer shut the door,
> Not bear the knife myself. Besides, this Duncan
> Hath borne his faculties so meek, hath been
> So clear in his great office, that his virtues
> Will plead like angels, trumpet-tongued, against
> The deep damnation of his taking-off;
> And pity, like a naked new-born babe,
> Striding the blast, or heaven's cherubim, horsed
> Upon the sightless couriers of the air,
> Shall blow the horrid deed in every eye,
> That tears shall drown the wind.

It may be said that he is here thinking of the horror that
others will feel at the deed—thinking therefore of consequences. Yes, but could he realize thus how horrible

the deed would look to others if it were not equally horrible to himself?

It is the same when the murder is done. He is well-nigh mad with horror, but it is not the horror of detection. It is not he who thinks of washing his hands or getting his nightgown on. He has brought away the daggers he should have left on the pillows of the grooms, but what does he care for that? What *he* thinks of is that, when he heard one of the men awaked from sleep say "God bless us," he could not say "Amen"; for his imagination presents to him the parching of his throat as an immediate judgment from heaven. His wife heard the owl scream and the crickets cry; but what *he* heard was the voice that first cried "Macbeth doth murder sleep," and then, a minute later, with a change of tense, denounced on him, as if his three names gave him three personalities to suffer in, the doom of sleeplessness:

Glamis hath murdered sleep, and therefore Cawdor
Shall sleep no more, Macbeth shall sleep no more.

There comes a sound of knocking. It should be perfectly familiar to him; but he knows not whence, or from what world, it comes. He looks down at his hands, and starts violently: "What hands are here?" For they seem alive, they move, they mean to pluck out his eyes. He looks at one of them again; it does not move; but the blood upon it is enough to dye the whole ocean red. What has all this to do with fear of "consequences"? It is his soul speaking in the only shape in which it can speak freely, that of imagination.

So long as Macbeth's imagination is active, we watch him fascinated; we feel suspense, horror, awe; in which are latent, also, admiration and sympathy. But so soon as it is quiescent these feelings vanish. He is no longer "infirm of purpose": he becomes domineering, even brutal, or he becomes a cool pitiless hypocrite. He is generally said to be a very bad actor, but this is not wholly true. Whenever his imagination stirs, he acts badly. It so possesses him, and is so much stronger than his reason, that his face betrays him, and his voice utters the most improbable untruths[6] or the most artificial rhetoric.[7] But when it is asleep he is firm, self-controlled and practical, as in the conversation where he skillfully elicits from Banquo that information about his movements which is required for the successful arrangement of his murder.[8] Here he is hateful; and so he is in the conversation with the murderers, who are not professional cutthroats but old soldiers, and whom, without a vestige of remorse, he beguiles with calumnies against Banquo and with such appeals as his wife had used to him.[9] On the other hand, we feel much pity as well as anxiety in the scene (I.vii) where she overcomes his op-

---

[6] E.g., I.iii.149, where he excuses his abstraction by saying that his "dull brain was wrought with things forgotten," when nothing could be more natural than that he should be thinking of his new honor.

[7] E.g., in I.iv. This is so also in II.iii. 110 ff., though here there is some real imaginative excitement mingled with the rhetorical antitheses and balanced clauses and forced bombast.

[8] III.i. Lady Macbeth herself could not more naturally have introduced at intervals the questions "Ride you this afternoon?" (1. 19), "Is't far you ride?" (1. 23), "Goes Fleance with you?" (1. 35).

[9] We feel here, however, an underlying subdued frenzy which awakes some sympathy. There is an almost unendurable impatience expressed even in the rhythm of many of the lines; e.g.:

> Well then, now
> Have you consider'd of my speeches? Know
> That it was he in the times past which held you
> So under fortune, which you thought had been
> Our innocent self: this I made good to you
> In our last conference, pass'd in probation with you,
> How you were borne in hand, how cross'd, the instruments,
> Who wrought with them, and all things else that might
> To half a soul and to a notion crazed
> Say, "Thus did Banquo."

This effect is heard to the end of the play in Macbeth's less poetic speeches, and leaves the same impression of burning energy, though not of imaginative exaltation, as his great speeches. In these we find either violent, huge, sublime imagery, or a torrent of figurative expressions (as in the famous lines about "the innocent sleep"). Our impressions as to the diction of the play are largely derived from these speeches of the hero, but not wholly so. The writing almost throughout leaves an impression of intense, almost feverish, activity.

position to the murder; and we feel it (though his imagination is not specially active) because this scene shows
us how little he understands himself. This is his great mis-
fortune here. Not that he fails to realize in reflection the
baseness of the deed (the soliloquy with which the scene
opens shows that he does not). But he has never, to put it
pedantically, accepted as the principle of his conduct the
morality which takes shape in his imaginative fears. Had
he done so, and said plainly to his wife, "The thing is
vile, and, however much I have sworn to do it, I will
not," she would have been helpless; for all her arguments
proceed on the assumption that there is for them no
such point of view. Macbeth does approach this position
once, when, resenting the accusation of cowardice, he answers,

> I dare do all that may become a man;
> Who dares do more is none.

She feels in an instant that everything is at stake, and,
ignoring the point, overwhelms him with indignant and
contemptuous personal reproach. But he yields to it because he is himself half-ashamed of that answer of his,
and because, for want of habit, the simple idea which it
expresses has no hold on him comparable to the force
it acquires when it becomes incarnate in visionary fears
and warnings.

Yet these were so insistent, and they offered to his ambition a resistance so strong, that it is impossible to regard him as falling through the blindness or delusion of
passion. On the contrary, he himself feels with such intensity the enormity of his purpose that, it seems clear,
neither his ambition nor yet the prophecy of the Witches
would ever without the aid of Lady Macbeth have overcome this feeling. As it is, the deed is done in horror
and without the faintest desire or sense of glory—done,
one may almost say, as if it were an appalling duty;
and, the instant it is finished, its futility is revealed to
Macbeth as clearly as its vileness had been revealed be-

forehand. As he staggers from the scene he mutters in despair,

> Wake Duncan with thy knocking! I would thou could'st.

When, half an hour later, he returns with Lennox from the room of the murder, he breaks out:

> Had I but died an hour before this chance,
> I had lived a blessed time; for from this instant
> There's nothing serious in mortality:
> All is but toys: renown and grace is dead;
> The wine of life is drawn, and the mere lees
> Is left this vault to brag of.

This is no mere acting. The language here has none of the false rhetoric of his merely hypocritical speeches. It is meant to deceive, but it utters at the same time his profoundest feeling. And this he can henceforth never hide from himself for long. However he may try to drown it in further enormities, he hears it murmuring,

> Duncan is in his grave:
> After life's fitful fever he sleeps well:

or,

> better be with the dead:

or,

> I have lived long enough:

and it speaks its last words on the last day of his life:

> Out, out, brief candle!
> Life's but a walking shadow, a poor player
> That struts and frets his hour upon the stage
> And then is heard no more: it is a tale

Told by an idiot, full of sound and fury,
Signifying nothing.

How strange that this judgment on life, the despair of a
man who had knowingly made mortal war on his own
soul, should be frequently quoted as Shakespeare's own
judgment, and should even be adduced, in serious criticism, as a proof of his pessimism!

It remains to look a little more fully at the history of
Macbeth after the murder of Duncan. Unlike his first
struggle this history excites little suspense or anxiety
on his account: we have now no hope for him. But it is
an engrossing spectacle, and psychologically it is perhaps
the most remarkable exhibition of the *development* of a
character to be found in Shakespeare's tragedies.

That heartsickness which comes from Macbeth's perception of the futility of his crime, and which never leaves
him for long, is not, however, his habitual state. It could
not be so, for two reasons. In the first place the consciousness of guilt is stronger in him than the consciousness of failure; and it keeps him in a perpetual
agony of restlessness, and forbids him simply to droop
and pine. His mind is "full of scorpions." He cannot
sleep. He "keeps alone," moody and savage. "All that is
within him does condemn itself for being there." There is
a fever in his blood which urges him to ceaseless action
in the search for oblivion. And, in the second place, ambition, the love of power, the instinct of self-assertion,
are much too potent in Macbeth to permit him to resign,
even in spirit, the prize for which he has put rancors in
the vessel of his peace. The "will to live" is mighty in him.
The forces which impelled him to aim at the crown re-
assert themselves. He faces the world, and his own
conscience, desperate, but never dreaming of acknowl-
edging defeat. He will see "the frame of things disjoint"
first. He challenges fate into the lists.

The result is frightful. He speaks no more, as before
Duncan's murder, of honor or pity. That sleepless torture, he tells himself, is nothing but the sense of insecurity and the fear of retaliation. If only he were safe,

it would vanish. And he looks about for the cause of his fear; and his eye falls on Banquo. Banquo, who cannot fail to suspect him, has not fled or turned against him: Banquo has become his chief counselor. Why? Because, he answers, the kingdom was promised to Banquo's children. Banquo, then, is waiting to attack him, to make a way for them. The "bloody instructions" he himself taught when he murdered Duncan, are about to return, as he said they would, to plague the inventor. *This* then, he tells himself, is the fear that will not let him sleep; and it will die with Banquo. There is no hesitation now, and no remorse: he has nearly learned his lesson. He hastens feverishly, not to murder Banquo, but to procure his murder: some strange idea is in his mind that the thought of the dead man will not haunt him, like the memory of Duncan, if the deed is done by other hands.[10] The deed is done: but, instead of peace descending on him, from the depths of his nature his half-murdered conscience rises; his deed confronts him in the apparition of Banquo's Ghost, and the horror of the night of his first murder returns. But, alas, *it* has less power, and *he* has more will. Agonized and trembling, he still faces this rebel image, and it yields:

> Why, so: being gone,
> I am a man again.

Yes, but his secret is in the hands of the assembled lords. And, worse, this deed is as futile as the first. For, though Banquo is dead and even his Ghost is conquered, that inner torture is unassuaged. But he will not bear it. His guests have hardly left him when he turns roughly to his wife:

> How say'st thou, that Macduff denies his person
> At our great bidding?

[10] See his first words to the Ghost: "Thou canst not say I did it."

Macduff it is that spoils his sleep. He shall perish,—he and aught else that bars the road to peace.

> For mine own good
> All causes shall give way: I am in blood
> Stepp'd in so far that, should I wade no more,
> Returning were as tedious as go o'er:
> Strange things I have in head that will to hand,
> Which must be acted ere they may be scann'd.

She answers, sick at heart,

> You lack the season of all natures, sleep.

No doubt: but he has found the way to it now:

> Come, we'll to sleep. My strange and self abuse
> Is the initiate fear that wants hard use:
> We are yet but young in deed.

What a change from the man who thought of Duncan's virtues, and of pity like a naked newborn babe! What a frightful clearness of self-consciousness in this descent to hell, and yet what a furious force in the instinct of life and self-assertion that drives him on!

He goes to seek the Witches. He will know, by the worst means, the worst. He has no longer any awe of them.

> How now, you secret, black and midnight hags!

—so he greets them, and at once he demands and threatens. They tell him he is right to fear Macduff. They tell him to fear nothing, for none of woman born can harm him. He feels that the two statements are at variance; infatuated, suspects no double meaning; but, that he may "sleep in spite of thunder," determines not to spare Macduff. But his heart throbs to know one thing, and he forces from the Witches the vision of Banquo's children

crowned. The old intolerable thought returns, "for Banquo's issue have I filed my mind"; and with it, for all the
absolute security apparently promised him, there returns
that inward fever. Will nothing quiet it? Nothing but destruction. Macduff, one comes to tell him, has escaped
him; but that does not matter: he can still destroy: [11]

> And even now,
> To crown my thoughts with acts, be it thought and
>   done:
> The castle of Macduff I will surprise;
> Seize upon Fife; give to the edge o' the sword
> His wife, his babes, and all unfortunate souls
> That trace him in's line. No boasting like a fool;
> This deed I'll do before this purpose cool.
> But no more sights!

No, he need fear no more "sights." The Witches have
done their work, and after this purposeless butchery his
own imagination will trouble him no more.[12] He has dealt
his last blow at the conscience and pity which spoke
through it.

The whole flood of evil in his nature is now let loose.

[11]   For only in destroying I find ease
        To my relentless thoughts.—*Paradise Lost,* IX. 129.

Milton's portrait of Satan's misery here, and at the beginning of
Book IV., might well have been suggested by *Macbeth.* Coleridge,
after quoting Duncan's speech, I. iv. 35 ff., says: "It is a fancy;
but I can never read this, and the following speeches of Macbeth,
without involuntarily thinking of the Miltonic Messiah and Satan."
I doubt if it was a mere fancy. (It will be remembered that Milton thought at one time of writing a tragedy on Macbeth.)

[12] The immediate reference in "But no more sights" is doubtless
to the visions called up by the Witches; but one of these, the
"blood-bolter'd Banquo," recalls to him the vision of the preceding
night, of which he had said,

> You make me strange
> Even to the disposition that I owe,
> When now I think you can behold such *sights,*
> And keep the natural ruby of your cheeks,
> When mine is blanch'd with fear.

He becomes an open tyrant, dreaded by everyone about him, and a terror to his country. She "sinks beneath the yoke."

> Each new morn
> New widows howl, new orphans cry, new sorrows
> Strike heaven on the face.

She weeps, she bleeds, "and each new day a gash is added to her wounds." She is not the mother of her children, but their grave;

> where nothing,
> But who knows nothing, is once seen to smile:
> Where sighs and groans and shrieks that rend the air
> Are made, not mark'd.

For this wild rage and furious cruelty we are prepared; but vices of another kind start up as he plunges on his downward way.

> I grant him bloody,
> Luxurious, avaricious, false, deceitful,
> Sudden, malicious,

says Malcolm; and two of these epithets surprise us. Who would have expected avarice or lechery [13] in Macbeth? His ruin seems complete.

Yet it is never complete. To the end he never totally loses our sympathy; we never feel towards him as we do to those who appear the born children of darkness. There remains something sublime in the defiance with which, even when cheated of his last hope, he faces earth and hell and heaven. Nor would any soul to whom evil was congenial be capable of that heartsickness which over-

---

[13] "Luxurious" and "luxury" are used by Shakespeare only in this older sense. It must be remembered that these lines are spoken by Malcolm, but it seems likely that they are meant to be taken as true throughout.

comes him when he thinks of the "honor, love, obedience, troops of friends" which "he must not look to
have" (and which Iago would never have cared to have),
and contrasts with them

> Curses, not loud but deep, mouth-honor, breath,
> Which the poor heart would fain deny, and dare not,

(and which Iago would have accepted with indifference).
Neither can I agree with those who find in his reception
of the news of his wife's death proof of alienation or
utter carelessness. There is no proof of these in the words,

> She should have died hereafter;
> There would have been a time for such a word,

spoken as they are by a man already in some measure prepared for such news, and now transported by the
frenzy of his last fight for life. He has no time now to
feel.[14] Only, as he thinks of the morrow when time to
feel will come—if anything comes, the vanity of all hopes
and forward-lookings sinks deep into his soul with an
infinite weariness, and he murmurs,

> Tomorrow, and tomorrow, and tomorrow,
> Creeps in this petty pace from day to day
> To the last syllable of recorded time,
> And all our yesterdays have lighted fools
> The way to dusty death.

[14] I do not at all suggest that his love for his wife remains what
it was when he greeted her with the words "My dearest love,
Duncan comes here tonight." He has greatly changed; she has
ceased to help him, sunk in her own despair; and there is no
intensity of anxiety in the questions he puts to the doctor about
her. But his love for her was probably never unselfish, never the
love of Brutus, who, in somewhat similar circumstances, uses, on
the death of Cassius, words which remind us of Macbeth's:

> I shall find time, Cassius, I shall find time.

For the opposite strain of feeling cf. Sonnet 90:

> Then hate me if thou wilt; if ever, now,
> Now while the world is bent my deeds to cross.

In the very depths a gleam of his native love of goodness, and with it a touch of tragic grandeur, rests upon
him. The evil he has desperately embraced continues to
madden or to wither his inmost heart. No experience in
the world could bring him to glory in it or make his peace
with it, or to forget what he once was and Iago and
Goneril never were.

Elmer Edgar Stoll

Source and Motive in *Macbeth* and *Othello*

*The best tragedy—highest tragedy in short—is that
of the worthy encompassed by the inevitable.*
THOMAS HARDY

Shakespeare, of course, has, like the Greeks—unlike
the Bourbon French—no *règles,* neither rule nor
formula. But for all that, why in *Othello* and *Macbeth,*
two of the great tragedies that are not histories and that
apparently are not in any measure *rifacimenti* of previous
plays, does he, in the matter of motivation, deviate so
widely and so similarly from his source?

I

What in *Macbeth* he has omitted and what substituted
Sir Arthur Quiller-Couch has made admirably clear, but
has not considered the reasons for this or the similarity
of procedure in *Othello.* In Holinshed's Chronicle there
is the suggestion that, cut off by the nomination of Malcolm as successor to the throne from his own expectations, Macbeth had for his usurpation "a juste quarell so
to do (as he tooke the matter)." The crown was then not
strictly hereditary, and "by the old lawes of the realme,
if he that should succeed were not of able age to take
the charge upon himselfe, he that was next of blood

From *From Shakespeare to Joyce* by Elmer Edgar Stoll. New York:
Doubleday and Company, Inc., 1944. Copyright 1944 by Elmer Edgar
Stoll. Reprinted by permission of Doubleday and Company, Inc.

should be admitted." [1] "Did Shakespeare use that one hint, enlarge that loophole?" asks Sir Arthur. "He did not."

> Instead of using a paltry chance to condone Macbeth's guilt, he seized on it and plunged it threefold deeper . . .
>
> He made this man, a sworn soldier, murder Duncan, his liege-lord.
>
> He made this man, a host, murder Duncan, a guest within his gates.
>
> He made this man, strong and hale, murder Duncan, old, weak, asleep and defenceless.
>
> He made this man commit murder for nothing but his own advancement.
>
> He made this man murder Duncan, who had steadily advanced him hitherto, who had never been aught but trustful, and who (that no detail of reproach might be wanting) had that very night, as he retired, sent, in most kindly thought, the gift of a diamond to his hostess.
>
> To sum up: instead of extenuating Macbeth's criminality, Shakespeare doubles and redoubles it. (*Shakespeare's Workmanship* [Holt, N. Y., 1930], pp. 19–20.)

And yet Macbeth is the protagonist, the hero, with whom as such, for the right tragic effect, there must, naturally, be some large measure of sympathy. So, having thus put him much farther beyond the reach of our sympathy than in the original, what does the dramatist then do but (indirectly) bring him back within it—in general, by the power of poetry, in particular, by the exhibition of the hero's bravery and virtue at the beginning, by emphasizing the influence of the supernatural

---

[1] *Boswell-Stone's Holinshed* (1896), p. 25. Sir Arthur's quotation, preceding, is curtailed: "for that Duncane did what in him lay to defraud him of all maner of title and claime, which he might, in time to come, pretend unto the crowne."

presented, and of his wife's inordinate ambition distinctly mentioned, in the source.

There are additional devices which Sir Arthur dwells upon, such as the flattening of the other characters—that the hero and heroine may stand out in high relief, to absorb our interest and (presumably on the principle considered in the preceding chapter) our sympathy also; and such as the keeping of the murders, as the ancients do, in the background, off the stage. "There is some deep law in imaginative illusion," says Watts-Dunton,[2] "whereby the identification of the spectator's personality is with the active character in most dramatic actions rather than the passive." We share the emotions, the perturbations, of Macbeth and his Lady, as even of Clytemnestra and Phaedra, because they are the impassioned doers and speakers, constantly in the foreground; and it is with their ears that we hear the owl and the cricket, the voices in the castle and the knocking at the gate. And still more clearly than in the veiling of the horrors the method is that of the ancients. The central complication—the contrast—is that recommended by Aristotle,[3] the *good* man doing the dreadful deed, though not unwittingly, nor quite unwillingly either. As with the ancients, again, he is under the sway of fate; for the Weird Sisters and his Lady—"burning in unquenchable desire to beare the name of a queene" [4]—together amount to that.

This, of course, is not what we ordinarily call motivation, not psychology. For both—the narrative or external motivation and the internal—there was, positively and negatively, better provision in Holinshed—not only the "juste quarell (as he tooke the matter)" but also "the feeble and slouthfull administration of Duncane," [5] no treachery or violation of the laws of hospitality in the killing, and the just and efficient rule (for ten years) in

2 *Harper's* (November, 1906), p. 818.

3 *Poetics, cap.* 13, 14.

4 *Boswell-Stone's Holinshed* (1896), p. 25.

5 *Ibid.,* p. 32. Cf. p. 20: "At length, Macbeth speaking much against the kings softnes and overmuch slacknesse in punishing offenders." . . .

the sequel.[6] *La carrière ouverte aux talents,* and Macbeth had the justification of Napoleon, of Cromwell. But not Shakespeare's Macbeth.

Nor is this what we call drama, either, as it is ordinarily practiced today. It is as in Aristotle,—situation first and motivation or psychology afterwards, if at all. The effect is emotional, with which psychology or even simple narrative coherence often considerably interferes. To Schiller's neglect of careful motivation, and in a day of psychology and philosophy both, Goethe even attributes his superiority on the stage.[7] Shakespeare sometimes neglects it because it can be counted upon as familiar; sometimes, as with Hamlet's feigning of lunacy and Lear's dividing of the kingdom, because, the motive in the old play not being a good one, it is better that it should be omitted or only hinted at; but in Macbeth the omission is for a positive purpose, and the contravention of psychological probability is so as well. Here, as generally in Shakespeare, *Coriolanus* being only a partial exception, character is not its own destiny, the action is not exclusively derived from it. For Shakespeare "a human being" is *not,* as in Galsworthy's words or as in his own and his fellows' practice, "the best plot there is." To his minor characters the words better apply. The hero's conduct, at the heart of the action, is often not in keeping with his essential nature but in contrast with it.

Manifestly, and, if not forthwith, certainly upon a moment's consideration, by all the motives prompting or circumstances attending the murder of Duncan that have been omitted, the big, sharply outlined, highly emotional contrast in the situation of a good man doing the deed of horror would be broken or obscured. If Macbeth had been thwarted or (to use Holinshed's word) "defrauded," as having, at this juncture, a better title to the throne than Malcolm, or had thought himself better fitted to rule; or, again, if Duncan had not borne his faculties so

---

[6] *Ibid.,* p. 32: "he set his whole intention to maintaine justice and to punish all enormities and abuses which had chanced," etc.; "made manie holesome laws and statutes for the publike weale."
[7] Eckermann (Castle), I,400.

meek and been so clear in his great office, as in the tragedy but not the chronicle he is; why, then, Macbeth's conduct in killing him would have been more reasonable and more psychological in keeping, to be sure, but less terrible, less truly tragic. Even if Duncan had been less affectionate and generous, less admiring and confiding, still the hero's conduct would have been less truly tragic! There is positive need of "the deep damnation of his taking off." For the tragedy is of the brave and honorable man suddenly and squarely—fatally, too—turned against the moral order. Sir Arthur compares him to Satan about to engage in the temptation: "Evil, be thou my good." Or "Fair is foul and foul is fair," as the Weird Sisters have it, which Macbeth on his first appearance echoes—

> So foul and fair a day I have not seen.

And that situation, no question, is a contrast big and sharp enough.

Sir Arthur does not, indeed, pause to take notice how unpsychological the change here is. Others besides fallen archangels have so turned about, but evil they do not continue to call evil. Macbeth so does. He has scarcely a word of ambition beforehand, not a word of delight in the power when attained. As Mr. Firkins and even Mr. Bradley have noticed, it is the deterrents that he dwells upon, not the incentives; it is the spectral bloody dagger that he sees, not a glittering crown; it is "withered murder" that he follows to the chamber, not the call to sovereign sway and masterdom. In horror he commits the crime, even as he is to remember it. There is no satisfaction but only torment in the thought of it. The conscience in him, before and after, is that of a good man, not that of the man who can do such wickedness; first the voice of God, then either that or else—"accuser of mankind"!—the devil's. It is Macbeth himself that considers the "deep damnation," and neither before nor after does he deceive himself, as the good turning to wickedness necessarily do. But the contrast is kept clear and distinct; and the emotional effect—that the whole world has acknowledged.

If, on the other hand, Shakespeare had kept to history, to reality and psychology! If he had followed Holinshed—made more of Macbeth's grievances, dilated on Duncan's unfitness and his own fitness to rule, without bringing on his head the blood of an old man, asleep, his benefactor and guest! If he had dwelt on reasons for committing instead of not committing the crime! And if afterwards he had expressed the psychologically natural or appropriate opinions upon his own conduct, excusing or palliating it, perhaps even justifying it! If in short Macbeth (and his Lady, too, who invokes the powers of evil at the outset and is tormented by conscience at the end) had acted more like the human beings we know of; why, then we should have had decidedly less of contrast and excitement, of imaginative and emotional power generated and discharged, of poetry and drama.

II

The treatment of the material in *Othello*, probably an earlier play, is somewhat the same. In Cinthio there is no warrant for introducing the supernatural; but in Shakespeare's hands the villain takes the place of Fate—of the Weird Sisters and the Lady—and more completely than is usual in the tragedy of the Renaissance. He is a devil in the flesh, as Booth played him, as Coleridge and Lamb implied, and George Woodberry, J. J. Chapman, Lytton Strachey, John Palmer, not to mention others, have put it explicitly.[8] Iago himself practically acknowledges it in the soliloquies—"Hell and night," "Divinity of hell! when devils will the blackest sins put on"—and on that point apparently he and Othello at the end are agreed:

> If that thou beest a devil, I cannot kill thee . . .
>
> [*wounds Iago*]
>
> I bleed, sir, but not kill'd.

[8] For their opinions see my *Shakespeare and Other Masters*, pp. 233, 238, 243–44.

Before that, to be sure, the Ancient is misapprehended by everybody; yet as Fate, as master of the show, he is holding nearly all the strings of the action in hand, and leading both heroine and hero to destruction. In the victim now, not the victimizer, is the great change; but from good to evil only under a complete delusion—"be thou my good" he neither says nor thinks, and the prince of villains himself has no need to say it. For again, as in *Macbeth,* the motives are dispensed with. The Ensign of the *novella* is deprived of the internal incentives to his wickedness, and the Moor relieved of the traits which might have provoked or somewhat warranted it.

As Professor Wolfgang Keller notices, the villainy is "better motived" in the source. That is, more plausibly, more realistically. Not a devil in the flesh, a "black angel," as Mr. Chapman calls him, Cinthio's Ensign is still of "the most depraved nature in the world" (*della più scelerata natura che mai fosse huomo del mondo*). But as such he has provocation enough. He is a rejected suitor, and really suspects the Captain (Shakespeare's Cassio) of being the favored one. Against both him and the lady he has a grudge; his love for her is turned to the "bitterest hate"; whereas in the tragedy his love for Desdemona and her intrigue with Cassio are, like Cassio's and Othello's with Emilia, pretexts and afterthoughts. There he has need of these. His genuine reason for resentment is against Othello, but only for promoting Cassio above him, and against Cassio (incidentally) for being promoted. In soliloquy, as always in drama, the truth will out. "I hate the Moor," he mutters,

> *And it is thought* abroad that 'twixt my sheets
> He has done my office.

And the next moment the pretext is made still plainer: "I know not if't be true, but I for mere suspicion in that kind will do as if for surety." [9]

---

[9] Cf. *Shakespeare and Other Masters,* pp. 236–38, for the way that his suspicions become convictions.

So the Ensign is deprived of his motive as much as the Thane of Glamis—as much as Richard III of his, which was ambition, or as Goneril and Regan of theirs, which was envy,[10]—but without an external Fate to relieve him of the burden of his iniquity. He carries it indeed, like the Weird Sisters, lightly enough; and the Aristotelian contrast of the good man doing the deed of horror is presented in his victim, who, however, unlike Macbeth, is guilty only of a mistake in judgment—the *hamartia*—and is far from uttering Satan's cry. Othello never loses our sympathy, as Macbeth, despite the poignant presentation of his sufferings, cannot but in some measure do.

What is almost quite as important to the emotional effect—to the steep tragic contrast—as the apparently unmitigated wickedness of Iago, is, as in the Caledonian tragedy, the nature of the victim and the circumstances of the crime. As we have seen, Shakespeare's Moor has changed places with his wife in the villain's enmity. Love turned to hatred is too ambiguous and appealing a passion—it is that, moreover, into which the Moor himself is precipitated, and, as Strachey observes, the villain's must not be anything of a parallel. For the contrast, again, it must not be. Moreover, though Cinthio's Moor is given some noble and attractive traits, especially at the outset, Shakespeare's is both there and throughout on a far higher level of intelligence and feeling. He is not a stupid dupe or a vulgarly vindictive cuckold. He is not the man to call the informer in to do the killing, or the concealing of it afterwards. For his own safety, Shakespeare's, unlike Cinthio's Moor, shows no concern. Nor is there, for that matter, the slightest evidence in his conduct or his utterance, nor in the woman's either, of the love Iago suspects between him and Emilia—no more than there is in Iago's own conduct or utterance, indeed, of his own love for Desdemona—though of late there has been a

---

[10] In the old *King Leir*, envy of Cordelia's beauty, cf. E. E. Kellett, *Suggestions* (1923), p. 38. For Richard, cf. Brandl, *Shakespeare* (1937), p. 120.

fairly prominent critic to say there is.[11] That would be like thinking, with some Germans, that Hamlet had betrayed Ophelia, for which, to be sure, there is a little evidence, though far from enough; or with some Frenchmen, that Lady Macbeth as, re-enacting in memory the deed of blood, she whispers, "to bed, to bed! there's knocking at the gate . . . to bed, to bed, to bed," she, having enticed her husband, is now for rewarding him. On the contrary, the black man is made the grandest and noblest of Shakespeare's lovers; and it is only through Iago's overwhelming reputation for honesty and sagacity, the impenetrableness of his mask together with the potency of his seductive arts, that he is led astray and succumbs. For the highest tragic effect it is the great and good man that succumbs. Like other supreme artists, Shakespeare has here created his own world, which holds together. Like Corneille (*les grands sujets de la tragédie doivent toujours aller au delà du vraisemblable*) Goethe holds that *in den höheren Regionen des künstlerischen Verfahrens, hat der Künstler ein freieres Spiel, und er darf sogar zu Fiktionen schreiten.*[12] This Shakespeare boldly does. No one else sees through Iago, including his own wife; so Othello, for not seeing, is no gull or dupe. In the matter of the Ancient's cleverness in maneuver and also of his success in hypocrisy the English is a little indebted to the Italian writer; but the Ensign's wife does see through him and only for fear of him holds her tongue.

---

[11] It is of course not enough to urge the probabilities upon us— that a healthy and vigorous soldier of the time would lead "a *man's* life," and that Emilia was none too good for taking up with him. As I have repeatedly reminded my readers, no character in fiction has a private life, beyond the reach of the writer, which a character in a biography or history, on the other hand, has, not being the writer's own creation. And in Shakespearean drama, as in the ancient or the classical French, none has the "past" or the "love life" that is more readily expected, and so more easily suggested, today.

[12] Eckermann, April 18, 1827.—I hope Corneille here does not go beyond the endurable.

III

In both *Macbeth* and *Othello,* then, it is the whole situation that is mainly important, not the character; it is the reciprocal matter of motivation (whether present or missing), of defects or qualities in both victim and victimizer together. Here lies the chief point of the present discussion. What if Shakespeare's Macbeth and Duncan had been like Holinshed's, or like Henry IV and Richard II, or like Cromwell and Charles I? And as I have elsewhere said, "How the scope and stature of Iago's wickedness (and of Othello's virtue) would be limited by any adequate grudge!" [18] How they would be also by a credulous or suspicious nature—a predisposition or a psychology—in the hero! Against that Shakespeare has guarded not only by Iago's impregnable reputation and by his all-prevailing arts but also by Othello's own reputation for capability and for virtue. (A world of reputation and circumstance here, not of motive!) Before the temptation begins, as in *Macbeth,* but much more fully and felicitously, the Moor has not only in his own right but through the admiration of everybody (and here even of the villain) been firmly established in our good opinion and our sympathies. So with Desdemona, too, and she is not deceitful or supersubtle as Mr. Shaw would have her, not enough so "to strengthen the case for Othello's jealousy"; the dramatic preparations are emotional, not analytical and psychological, primarily for the situation, not the character. And both women, Emilia at the last and Desdemona once the action is well started, are shocked at the discoveries they make in their husbands. But she is justified, when hers gives signs of jealousy, in being unable to believe it; "not easily jealous" he himself says (where a Shakespearean hero, or his best friend, is expected to know and everything comes to light) at the end. Even Iago, hearing that Othello is angry, exclaims,

---

[18] *Shakespeare and Other Masters,* p. 245.

> and is he angry?
> Something of moment, then. I will go meet him.
> There's matter in't indeed, if he be angry.

And in the fourth act, when the jealous rage is fully upon
him, Lodovico, newly come from Venice, is moved to
wonder and to grief.

> Is this the nature
> Whom passion could not shake? whose solid virtue
> The shot of accident nor dart of chance
> Could neither graze nor pierce?

"He is much chang'd," Iago coolly, and still not super-
fluously, replies. So he is, until, in the last scene, by
Emilia's disclosures and Iago's self-betraying resentment,
he recovers something of his old stately and generous
self.

Macbeth too is changed, but for once and all. Othello
had suffered from an overpowering delusion, and has
just now, he thinks, performed an act of justice. Macbeth,
not deluded, has come under the dominion of evil, his
"eternal jewel given to the common enemy of man."
Neither change is probable. In neither is there much of
what can be called psychology. In life neither person
would really have done what he did. In both tragedy
and comedy, however, that is not exactly what is to be
expected: for a Henry IV, a Cromwell, we should turn
to history, not the stage. What is expected is what from
life we do not get—enlargement, excitement, another
world, not a copy of this. And that airy edifice, an imaginative structure, is the emotionally consistent story or
situation as a whole—the conduct of characters both active and passive, perhaps also a motiving both external
and internal, but in any case an interplay of relations or
circumstances as important as the motives themselves;
not to mention the apportionment of emphasis or relief
whether in the framework or the expression, the poetry
that informs both, and the individuality of the speech,
which, real, though poetical, leads one to accept and de-

light in the improbable things said or done. "It is when their minds (those of the audience) are preoccupied with his personality," says Dr. Bridges of Macbeth, "that the actions follow as unquestionable realities." [14] Not merely, that is, when the actions proceed from the character; and the convincing quality of the speech is only a participating element in the consistent overpowering imaginative and emotional effect of the whole.

IV

"In tragedy and comedy both," I have said elsewhere, "life must be, as it has ever been, piled on life, or we have visited the theater in vain." It is not primarily to present characters in their convincing reality that Shakespeare and the Greeks have written, nor in an action strictly and wholly of their doing, but to set them in a state of high commotion, and thus to move and elevate the audience in turn. And here I fall back upon the authority of Mr. Santayana, a philosopher (but also a poet and critic) who, without my knowledge until of late,[15] expressed, though from a different point of view, similar opinions before me:

> Aristotle was justified in making the plot the chief element in fiction; for it is by virtue of the plot that the characters live, or, rather, that we live in them, and by virtue of the plot accordingly that our soul rises to the imaginative activity by which we tend at once to escape from the personal life and to realise its ideal. . . .

And as the eminent critic proceeds, he maintains that poetry is not

---

[14] *The Influence of the Audience on Shakespeare's Drama.*
[15] *Poetry and Religion* (1900). Cf. my *Shakespeare and Other Masters,* p. 369. The passage here quoted is as in the *Works* (Scribner, N. Y., 1936) ii. Cf. my "Plot and Character," to appear.

at its best when it depicts a further possible experience, but when it initiates us, by feigning something which as an experience is impossible, into the meaning of the experience which we have actually had.

And that is partly because "in the theater," as the producer Mr. Robert Edmond Jones has assured us, "the actual thing is never the exciting thing. Unless life is turned into art on the stage it stops being alive and goes dead." [16] It is by the excitement that the meaning is brought home to us. And that is true . . . even without a stage or without poetry, as in Dickens, who, according to Chesterton, "could only make his characters probable if he was allowed to make them impossible."

Cleanth Brooks

The Naked Babe and the Cloak of Manliness

The debate about the proper limits of metaphor has perhaps never been carried on in so spirited a fashion as it has been within the last twenty-five years. The tendency has been to argue for a much wider extension of those limits than critics like Dr. Johnson, say, were willing to allow—one wider even than the Romantic poets were willing to allow. Indeed, some alarm has been expressed of late, in one quarter or another, lest John Donne's characteristic treatment of metaphor be taken as the type and norm, measured against which other poets must, of necessity, come off badly. Yet, on the whole, I think that it must be conceded that the debate on metaphor has been stimulating and illuminating—and not least so with reference to those poets who lie quite outside the tradition of metaphysical wit.

Since the "new criticism," so called, has tended to center around the rehabilitation of Donne, and the Donne tradition, the latter point, I believe, needs to be emphasized. Actually, it would be a poor rehabilitation which, if exalting Donne above all his fellow poets, in fact succeeded in leaving him quite as much isolated from the rest of them as he was before. What the new awareness of the importance of metaphor—if it is actually new, and if its character is really that of a freshened awareness— what this new awareness of metaphor results in when ap-

From *The Well Wrought Urn* by Cleanth Brooks. New York: Harcourt, Brace & Co, Inc., 1947; London: Dennis Dobson, Ltd., 1949. Copyright 1947, by Cleanth Brooks. Reprinted by permission of Harcourt, Brace & World, Inc.

plied to poets other than Donne and his followers is therefore a matter of first importance. Shakespeare provides, of course, the supremely interesting case.

But there are some misapprehensions to be avoided at the outset. We tend to associate Donne with the self-conscious and witty figure—his comparison of the souls of the lovers to the two legs of the compass is the obvious example. Shakespeare's extended figures are elaborated in another fashion. They are, we are inclined to feel, spontaneous comparisons struck out in the heat of composition, and not carefully articulated, self-conscious conceits at all. Indeed, for the average reader the connection between spontaneity and seriously imaginative poetry is so strong that he will probably reject as preposterous any account of Shakespeare's poetry which sees an elaborate pattern in the imagery. He will reject it because to accept it means for him the assumption that the writer was not a fervent poet but a preternaturally cold and self-conscious monster.

Poems are certainly not made by formula and blueprint. One rightly holds suspect a critical interpretation that implies that they are. Shakespeare, we may be sure, was no such monster of calculation. But neither, for that matter, was Donne. Even in Donne's poetry, the elaborated and logically developed comparisons are outnumbered by the abrupt and succinct comparisons—by what T. S. Eliot has called the "telescoped conceits." Moreover, the extended comparisons themselves are frequently knit together in the sudden and apparently uncalculated fashion of the telescoped images; and if one examines the way in which the famous compass comparison is related to the rest of the poem in which it occurs, he may feel that even this elaborately "logical" figure was probably the result of a happy accident.

The truth of the matter is that we know very little of the various poets' methods of composition, and that what may seem to us the product of deliberate choice may well have been as "spontaneous" as anything else in the poem. Certainly, the general vigor of metaphor in the Elizabethan period—as testified to by pamphlets, sermons, and plays—should warn us against putting the literature of that period at the mercy of our own personal theories of poetic composition. In any case, we shall probably speculate to better advantage—if speculate we must—on the possible significant interrelations of image with image rather than on the possible amount of pen-biting which the interrelations may have cost the author.

I do not intend, however, to beg the case by oversimplifying the relation between Shakespeare's intricate figures and Donne's. There are most important differences; and, indeed, Shakespeare's very similarities to the witty poets will, for many readers, tell against the thesis proposed here. For those instances in which Shakespeare most obviously resembles the witty poets occur in the earlier plays or in *Venus and Adonis* and *The Rape of Lucrece;* and these we are inclined to dismiss as early experiments—trial pieces from the Shakespearean workshop. We demand, quite properly, instances from the great style of the later plays.

Still, we will do well not to forget the witty examples in the poems and earlier plays. They indicate that Shakespeare is in the beginning not too far removed from Donne, and that, for certain effects at least, he was willing to play with the witty comparison. Dr. Johnson, in teasing the metaphysical poets for their fanciful conceits on the subject of tears, might well have added instances from Shakespeare. One remembers, for example, from *Venus and Adonis:*

> O, how her eyes and tears did lend and borrow!
> Her eyes seen in her tears, tears in her eye;
> Both crystals, where they view'd each other's
>   sorrow. . . .

Or, that more exquisite instance which Shakespeare, perhaps half-smiling, provided for the King in *Love's Labor's Lost:*

> So sweet a kiss the golden sun gives not

To those fresh morning drops upon the rose,
As thy eye-beams, when their fresh rays have smote
The night of dew that on my cheeks down flows:
Nor shines the silver moon one half so bright
Through the transparent bosom of the deep,
As does thy face through tears of mine give light:
Thou shin'st in every tear that I do weep,
No drop but as a coach doth carry thee:
So ridest thou triumphing in my woe.
Do but behold the tears that swell in me,
And they thy glory through my grief will show:
But do not love thyself—then thou wilt keep
My tears for glasses, and still make me weep.

But Berowne, we know, at the end of the play, foreswears all such

> Taffeta phrases, silken terms precise,
> Three-piled hyperboles, spruce affectation,
> Figures pedantical. . . .

in favor of "russet yeas and honest kersey noes." It is sometimes assumed that Shakespeare did the same thing in his later dramas, and certainly the epithet "taffeta phrases" does not describe the great style of *Macbeth* and *Lear*. Theirs is assuredly of a tougher fabric. But "russet" and "honest kersey" do not describe it either. The weaving was not so simple as that.

The weaving was very intricate indeed—if anything, *more* rather than *less* intricate than that of *Venus and Adonis,* though obviously the pattern was fashioned in accordance with other designs, and yielded other kinds of poetry. But in suggesting that there is a real continuity between the imagery of *Venus and Adonis,* say, and that of a play like *Macbeth,* I am glad to be able to avail myself of Coleridge's support. I refer to the remarkable fifteenth chapter of the *Biographia.*

There Coleridge stresses not the beautiful tapestry work—the purely visual effect—of the images, but quite another quality. He suggests that Shakespeare was prompted by a secret dramatic instinct to realize, in the imagery itself, that "constant intervention and running comment by tone, look and gesture" ordinarily provided by the actor, and that Shakespeare's imagery becomes under this prompting "a series and never broken chain . . . always vivid and, because unbroken, often minute. . . ." Coleridge goes on, a few sentences later, to emphasize further "the perpetual activity of attention required on the part of the reader, . . . the rapid flow, the quick change, and the playful nature of the thoughts and images."

These characteristics, Coleridge hastens to say, are not in themselves enough to make superlative poetry. "They become proofs of original genius only as far as they are modified by a predominant passion; or by associated thoughts or images awakened by that passion; or when they have the effect of reducing multitude to unity, or succession to an instant; or lastly, when a human and intellectual life is transferred to them from the poet's own spirit."

Of the intellectual vigor which Shakespeare possessed, Coleridge then proceeds to speak—perhaps extravagantly. But he goes on to say: "In Shakespeare's *poems,* the creative power and the intellectual energy wrestle as in a war embrace. Each in its excess of strength seems to threaten the extinction of the other."

I am tempted to gloss Coleridge's comment here, perhaps too heavily, with remarks taken from Chapter XIII where he discusses the distinction between the Imagination and the Fancy—the modifying and creative power, on the one hand, and on the other, that "mode of Memory" . . . "blended with, and modified by . . . Choice." But if in *Venus and Adonis* and *The Rape of Lucrece* the powers grapple "in a war embrace," Coleridge goes on to pronounce: "At length, in the *Drama* they were reconciled, and fought each with its shield before the breast of the other."

It is a noble metaphor. I believe that it is also an accurate one, and that it comprises one of the most bril-

liant insights ever made into the nature of the dramatic
poetry of Shakespeare's mature style. If it is accurate,
we shall expect to find, even in the mature poetry, the
"never broken chain" of images, "always vivid and, because unbroken, often minute," but we shall expect to
find the individual images, not mechanically linked together in the mode of Fancy, but organically related, modified by "a predominant passion," and mutually modifying
each other.

T. S. Eliot has remarked that "The difference between
imagination and fancy, in view of [the] poetry of wit, is
a very narrow one." If I have interpreted Coleridge cor-
rectly, he is saying that in Shakespeare's greatest work,
the distinction lapses altogether—or rather, that one is
caught up and merged in the other. As his latest champion, I. A. Richards, observes: "Coleridge often insisted
—and would have insisted still more often had he been a
better judge of his reader's capacity for misunderstanding—that Fancy and Imagination are not exclusive of, or
inimical to, one another."

I began by suggesting that our reading of Donne
might contribute something to our reading of Shakespeare, though I tried to make plain the fact that I had no
design of trying to turn Shakespeare into Donne, or—
what I regard as nonsense—of trying to exalt Donne
above Shakespeare. I have in mind specifically some such
matter as this: that since the *Songs and Sonets* of Donne,
no less than *Venus and Adonis,* requires a "perpetual
activity of attention . . . on the part of the reader from
the rapid flow, the quick change, and the playful nature of
the thoughts and images," the discipline gained from reading Donne may allow us to see more clearly the survival
of such qualities in the later style of Shakespeare. And,
again, I have in mind some such matter as this: that if a
reading of Donne has taught us that the "rapid flow, the
quick change, and the playful nature of the thoughts
and images"—qualities which we are all too prone to associate merely with the fancy—can, on occasion, take on
imaginative power, we may, thus taught, better appreciate
details in Shakespeare which we shall otherwise dismiss

as merely fanciful, or, what is more likely, which we shall simply ignore altogether.

With Donne, of course, the chains of imagery, "always vivid" and "often minute" are perfectly evident. For many readers they are all too evident. The difficulty is not to prove that they exist, but that, on occasion, they may subserve a more imaginative unity. With Shakespeare, the difficulty may well be to prove that the chains exist at all. In general, we may say, Shakespeare has made it relatively easy for his admirers to choose what they like and neglect what they like. What he gives on one or another level is usually so magnificent that the reader finds it easy to ignore other levels.

Yet there are passages not easy to ignore and on which even critics with the conventional interests have been forced to comment. One of these passages occurs in *Macbeth*, Act I, Scene vii, where Macbeth compares the pity for his victim-to-be, Duncan, to

> a naked new-born babe,
> Striding the blast, or heaven's cherubim, hors'd
> Upon the sightless couriers of the air . . .

The comparison is odd, to say the least. Is the babe natural or supernatural—an ordinary, helpless baby, who, as newborn, could not, of course, even toddle, much less stride the blast? Or is it some infant Hercules, quite capable of striding the blast, but, since it is powerful and not helpless, hardly the typical pitiable object?

Shakespeare seems bent upon having it both ways—and, if we read on through the passage—bent upon having the best of both worlds; for he proceeds to give us the option: pity is like the babe "or heaven's cherubim" who quite appropriately, of course, do ride the blast. Yet, even if we waive the question of the legitimacy of the alternative (of which Shakespeare so promptly avails himself), is the cherubim comparison really any more successful than is the babe comparison? Would not one of the great warrior archangels be more appropriate to the scene than the cherub? Does Shakespeare mean for pity or for fear of retribution to be dominant in Macbeth's mind?

Or is it possible that Shakespeare could not make up his own mind? Was he merely writing hastily and loosely, and letting the word "pity" suggest the typically pitiable object, the babe naked in the blast, and then, stirred by the vague notion that some threat to Macbeth should be hinted, using "heaven's cherubim"—already suggested by "babe"—to convey the hint? Is the passage vague or precise? Loosely or tightly organized? Comments upon the passage have ranged all the way from one critic's calling it "pure rant, and intended to be so" to another's laudation: "Either like a mortal babe, terrible in helplessness; or like heaven's angel-children, mighty in love and compassion. This magnificent passage . . ."

An even more interesting, and perhaps more disturbing passage in the play is that in which Macbeth describes his discovery of the murder:

> Here lay Duncan,
> His silver skin lac'd with his golden blood;
> And his gash'd stabs look'd like a breach in nature
> For ruin's wasteful entrance: there, the murderers,
> Steep'd in the colors of their trade, their daggers
> Unmannerly breech'd with gore. . . .

It is amusing to watch the textual critics, particularly those of the eighteenth century, fight a stubborn rearguard action against the acceptance of "breech'd." Warburton emended "breech'd" to "reech'd"; Johnson, to "drench'd"; Seward, to "hatch'd." Other critics argued that the *breeches* implied were really the handles of the daggers, and that, accordingly, "breech'd" actually here meant "sheathed." The Variorum page witnesses the desperate character of the defense, but the position has had to be yielded, after all. *The Shakespeare Glossary* defines "breech'd" as meaning "covered as with breeches," and thus leaves the poet committed to a reading which must still shock the average reader as much as it shocked that nineteenth-century critic who pronounced upon it as follows: "A metaphor must not be far-fetched nor dwell upon the details of a disgusting picture, as in these lines. There is little, and that far-fetched, similarity between *gold lace* and *blood,* or between *bloody daggers* and *breech'd legs.* The slightness of the similarity, recalling the greatness of the dissimilarity, disgusts us with the attempted comparison."

The two passages are not of the utmost importance, I dare say, though the speeches (of which each is a part) are put in Macbeth's mouth and come at moments of great dramatic tension in the play. Yet, in neither case is there any warrant for thinking that Shakespeare was not trying to write as well as he could. Moreover, whether we like it or not, the imagery is fairly typical of Shakespeare's mature style. Either passage ought to raise some qualms among those who retreat to Shakespeare's authority when they seek to urge the claims of "noble simplicity." They are hardly simple. Yet it is possible that such passages as these may illustrate another poetic resource, another type of imagery which, even in spite of its apparent violence and complication, Shakespeare could absorb into the total structure of his work.

Shakespeare, I repeat, is not Donne—is a much greater poet than Donne; yet the example of his typical handling of imagery will scarcely render support to the usual attacks on Donne's imagery—for, with regard to the two passages in question, the second one, at any rate, is about as strained as Donne is at his most extreme pitch.

Yet I think that Shakespeare's daggers attired in their bloody breeches can be defended as poetry, and as characteristically Shakespearean poetry. Furthermore, both this passage and that about the newborn babe, it seems to me, are far more than excrescences, mere extravagances of detail: each, it seems to me, contains a central symbol of the play, and symbols which we must understand if we are to understand either the detailed passage or the play as a whole.

If this be true, then more is at stake than the merit of the quoted lines taken as lines. (The lines as constituting mere details of a larger structure could, of course, be omitted in the acting of the play without seriously damaging the total effect of the tragedy—though this argument obviously cuts two ways. Whole scenes, and admittedly fine scenes, might also be omitted —have in fact *been* omitted—without quite destroying the massive structure of the tragedy.) What is at stake is the whole matter of the relation of Shakespeare's imagery to the total structures of the plays themselves.

I should like to use the passages as convenient points of entry into the larger symbols which dominate the play. They *are* convenient because, even if we judge them to be faulty, they demonstrate how obsessive for Shakespeare the symbols were—they demonstrate how far the conscious (or unconscious) symbolism could take him.

If we see how the passages are related to these symbols, and they to the tragedy as a whole, the main matter is achieved; and having seen this, if we still prefer "to wish the lines away," that, of course, is our privilege. In the meantime, we may have learned something about Shakespeare's methods—not merely of building metaphors—but of encompassing his larger meanings.

One of the most startling things which has come out of Miss Spurgeon's book on Shakespeare's imagery is her discovery of the "old clothes" imagery in *Macbeth*. As she points out: "The idea constantly recurs that Macbeth's new honours sit ill upon him, like a loose and badly fitting garment, belonging to someone else." And she goes on to quote passage after passage in which the idea is expressed. But, though we are all in Miss Spurgeon's debt for having pointed this out, one has to observe that Miss Spurgeon has hardly explored the full implications of her discovery. Perhaps her interest in classifying and cataloguing the imagery of the plays has obscured for her some of the larger and more important relationships. At any rate, for reasons to be given below, she has realized only a part of the potentialities of her discovery.

Her comment on the clothes imagery reaches its climax with the following paragraphs:

> And, at the end, when the tyrant is at bay at Dunsinane, and the English troops are advancing, the Scottish lords still have this image in their minds. Caithness sees him as a man vainly trying to fasten a large garment on him with too small a belt:

> > He cannot buckle his distemper'd cause
> > Within the belt of rule;

> while Angus, in a similar image, vividly sums up the essence of what they all have been thinking ever since Macbeth's accession to power:

> > > now does he feel his title
> > Hang loose about him, like a giant's robe
> > Upon a dwarfish thief.

This imaginative picture of a small, ignoble man encumbered and degraded by garments unsuited to him, should be put against the view emphasized by some critics (notably Coleridge and Bradley) of the likeness between Macbeth and Milton's Satan in grandeur and sublimity.

> Undoubtedly Macbeth . . . is great, magnificently great . . . But he could never be put beside, say, Hamlet or Othello, in nobility of nature; and there *is* an aspect in which he is but a poor, vain, cruel, treacherous creature, snatching ruthlessly over the dead bodies of kinsman and friend at place and power he is utterly unfitted to possess. It is worth remembering that it is thus that Shakespeare, with his unshrinking clarity of vision, repeatedly *sees* him.

But this is to make primary what is only one aspect of

the old-clothes imagery! And there is no warrant for interpreting the garment imagery as used by Macbeth's enemies, Caithness and Angus, to mean that *Shakespeare* sees Macbeth as a poor and somewhat comic figure.

The crucial point of the comparison, it seems to me, lies not in the smallness of the man and the largeness of the robes, but rather in the fact that—whether the man be large or small—these are not *his* garments; in Macbeth's case they are actually stolen garments. Macbeth is uncomfortable in them because he is continually conscious of the fact that they do not belong to him. There is a further point, and it is one of the utmost importance; the oldest symbol for the hypocrite is that of the man who cloaks his true nature under a disguise. Macbeth loathes playing the part of the hypocrite—and actually does not play it too well. If we keep this in mind as we look back at the instances of the garment images which Miss Spurgeon has collected for us, we shall see that the pattern of imagery becomes very rich indeed. Macbeth says in Act I:

> The Thane of Cawdor lives: why do you dress me
> In borrow'd robes?

Macbeth at this point wants no honors that are not honestly his. Banquo says in Act I:

> New honors come upon him,
> Like our strange garments, cleave not to their mold,
> But with the aid of use.

But Banquo's remark, one must observe, is not censorious. It is indeed a compliment to say of one that he wears new honors with some awkwardness. The observation becomes ironical only in terms of what is to occur later.

Macbeth says in Act I:

> He hath honor'd me of late; and I have bought
> Golden opinions from all sorts of people,

Which would be worn now in their newest gloss,
Not cast aside so soon.

Macbeth here is proud of his new clothes: he is
happy to wear what he has truly earned. It is the part of
simple good husbandry not to throw aside these new garments and replace them with robes stolen from Duncan.

But Macbeth has already been wearing Duncan's garments in anticipation, as his wife implies in the metaphor
with which she answers him:

> Was the hope drunk,
> Wherein you dress'd yourself?

(The metaphor may seem hopelessly mixed, and a full
and accurate analysis of such mixed metaphors in terms
of the premises of Shakespeare's style waits upon some
critic who will have to consider not only this passage but
many more like it in Shakespeare.) For our purposes
here, however, one may observe that the psychological
line, the line of the basic symbolism, runs on unbroken.
A man dressed in a drunken hope is garbed in strange
attire indeed—a ridiculous dress which accords thoroughly with the contemptuous picture that Lady Macbeth
wishes to evoke. Macbeth's earlier dream of glory has
been a drunken fantasy merely, if he flinches from action now.

But the series of garment metaphors which run through
the play is paralleled by a series of masking or cloaking
images which—if we free ourselves of Miss Spurgeon's
rather mechanical scheme of classification—show themselves to be merely variants of the garments which hide
none too well his disgraceful self. He is consciously hid-
ing that self throughout the play.

"False face must hide what the false heart doth know,"
he counsels Lady Macbeth before the murder of Duncan;
and later, just before the murder of Banquo, he invokes
night to "Scarf up the eye of pitiful day."

One of the most powerful of these cloaking images

is given to Lady Macbeth in the famous speech in Act I:

> Come, thick night,
> And pall thee in the dunnest smoke of hell,
> That my keen knife see not the wound it makes,
> Nor heaven peep through the blanket of the dark,
> To cry, "Hold, Hold!"

I suppose that it is natural to conceive the "keen knife" here as held in her own hand. Lady Macbeth is capable of wielding it. And in this interpretation, the imagery is thoroughly significant. Night is to be doubly black so that not even her knife may see the wound it makes. But I think that there is good warrant for regarding her "keen knife" as Macbeth himself. She has just, a few lines above, given her analysis of Macbeth's character as one who would "not play false,/ And yet [would] wrongly win." To bring him to the point of action, she will have to "chastise [him] with the valor of [her] tongue." There is good reason, then, for her to invoke night to become blacker still—to pall itself in the "dunnest smoke of hell." For night must not only screen the deed from the eye of heaven—conceal it at least until it is too late for heaven to call out to Macbeth "Hold, Hold!" Lady Macbeth would have night blanket the deed from the hesitant doer. The imagery thus repeats and reinforces the substance of Macbeth's anguished aside uttered in the preceding scene:

> Let not light see my black and deep desires;
> The eye wink at the hand; yet let that be
> Which the eye fears, when it is done, to see.

I do not know whether "blanket" and "pall" qualify as garment metaphors in Miss Spurgeon's classification: yet one is the clothing of sleep, and the other, the clothing of death—they are the appropriate garments of night; and they carry on an important aspect of the general clothes imagery. It is not necessary to attempt to give here an exhaustive list of instances of the garment metaphor; but one should say a word about the remarkable passage in II, iii.

Here, after the discovery of Duncan's murder, Banquo says

> And when we have our naked frailties hid,
> That suffer in exposure, let us meet,
> And question this most bloody piece of work—

that is, "When we have clothed ourselves against the chill morning air, let us meet to discuss this bloody piece of work." Macbeth answers, as if his subconscious mind were already taking Banquo's innocent phrase, "naked frailties," in a deeper, ironic sense:

> Let's briefly put on manly readiness. . . .

It is ironic; for the "manly readiness" which he urges the other lords to put on, is, in his own case, a hypocrite's garment: he can only pretend to be the loyal, grief-stricken liege who is almost unstrung by the horror of Duncan's murder.

But the word "manly" carries still a further ironic implication: earlier, Macbeth had told Lady Macbeth that he dared

> do all that may become a man;
> Who dares do more is none.

Under the weight of her reproaches of cowardice, however, he *has* dared do more, and has become less than a man, a beast. He has already laid aside, therefore, one kind of "manly readiness" and has assumed another: he has garbed himself in a sterner composure than that which he counsels to his fellows—the hard and inhuman "manly readiness" of the resolved murderer.

The clothes imagery, used sometimes with emphasis on one aspect of it, sometimes, on another, does pervade the play. And it should be evident that the daggers "breech'd with gore"—though Miss Spurgeon does not include the passage in her examples of clothes imagery —represent one more variant of this general symbol. Consider the passage once more:

> Here lay Duncan,
> His silver skin lac'd with his golden blood;
> And his gash'd stabs look'd like a breach in nature
> For ruin's wasteful entrance: there, the murderers,
> Steep'd in the colors of their trade, their daggers
> Unmannerly breech'd with gore. . . .

The clothes imagery runs throughout the passage; the body of the king is dressed in the most precious of garments, the blood royal itself; and the daggers too are dressed—in the same garment. The daggers, "naked" except for their lower parts which are reddened with blood, are like men in "unmannerly" dress—men, naked except for their red breeches, lying beside the red-handed grooms. The figure, though vivid, is fantastic; granted. But the basis for the comparison is *not* slight and adventitious. The metaphor fits the real situation on the deepest levels. As Macbeth and Lennox burst into the room, they find the daggers wearing, as Macbeth knows all too well, a horrible masquerade. They have been carefully "clothed" to play a part. They are not honest daggers, honorably naked in readiness to guard the king, or, "mannerly" clothed in their own sheaths. Yet the disguise which they wear will enable Macbeth to assume the robes of Duncan—robes to which he is no more entitled than are the daggers to the royal garments which they now wear, grotesquely.

The reader will, of course, make up his own mind as to the value of the passage. But the metaphor in question, in the light of the other garment imagery, cannot be dismissed as merely a strained ingenuity, irrelevant to the play. And the reader who *does* accept it as poetry will

probably be that reader who knows the play best, not
the reader who knows it slightly and regards Shakespeare's poetry as a rhetoric more or less loosely draped
over the "content" of the play.

And now what can be said of pity, the "naked newborn babe"? Though Miss Spurgeon does not note it
(since the governing scheme of her book would have
hardly allowed her to see it), there are, by the way, a
great many references to babes in this play—references
which occur on a number of levels. The babe appears
sometimes as a character, such as Macduff's child; sometimes as a symbol, like the crowned babe and the
bloody babe which are raised by the witches on the
occasion of Macbeth's visit to them; sometimes, in a
metaphor, as in the passage under discussion. The number of such references can hardly be accidental; and the
babe turns out to be, as a matter of fact, perhaps the most
powerful symbol in the tragedy.

But to see this fully, it will be necessary to review the
motivation of the play. The stimulus to Duncan's murder, as we know, was the prophecy of the Weird Sisters.
But Macbeth's subsequent career of bloodshed stems
from the same prophecy. Macbeth was to have the
crown, but the crown was to pass to Banquo's children.
The second part of the prophecy troubles Macbeth from
the start. It does not oppress him, however, until the
crown has been won. But from this point on, the effect
of the prophecy is to hurry Macbeth into action and more
action until he is finally precipitated into ruin.

We need not spend much time in speculating on whether
Macbeth, had he been content with Duncan's murder,
had he tempted fate no further, had he been willing to
court the favor of his nobles, might not have died peace-
ably in bed. We are dealing, not with history, but with a
play. Yet, even in history the usurper sometimes succeeds; and he sometimes succeeds on the stage. Shakespeare himself knew of, and wrote plays about, usurpers
who successfully maintained possession of the crown. But,
in any case, this much is plain: the train of murders into

which Macbeth launches aggravates suspicions of his
guilt and alienates the nobles.

Yet, a Macbeth who could act once, and then settle
down to enjoy the fruits of this one attempt to meddle
with the future would, of course, not be Macbeth. For
it is not merely his great imagination and his warrior
courage in defeat which redeem him for tragedy and
place him beside the other great tragic protagonists:
rather, it is his attempt to conquer the future, an attempt involving him, like Oedipus, in a desperate struggle
with fate itself. It is this which holds our imaginative
sympathy, even after he has degenerated into a bloody
tyrant and has become the slayer of Macduff's wife and
children.

To sum up, there can be no question that Macbeth
stands at the height of his power after his murder of
Duncan, and that the plan—as outlined by Lady Macbeth—has been relatively successful. The road turns toward disaster only when Macbeth decides to murder Banquo. Why does he make this decision? Shakespeare has
pointed up the basic motivation very carefully:

> Then prophet-like,
> They hail'd him father to a line of kings.
> Upon my head they plac'd a fruitless crown,
> And put a barren scepter in my gripe,
> Thence to be wrench'd with an unlineal hand,
> No son of mine succeeding. If't be so,
> For Banquo's issue have I fil'd my mind;
> For them the gracious Duncan have I murder'd;
> Put rancors in the vessel of my peace
> Only for them; and mine eternal jewel
> Given to the common enemy of man,
> To make them kings, the seed of Banquo kings!

Presumably, Macbeth had entered upon his course from
sheer personal ambition. Ironically, it is the more human
part of Macbeth—his desire to have more than a limited
personal satisfaction, his desire to found a line, his wish

to pass something on to later generations—which prompts him to dispose of Banquo. There is, of course, a resentment against Banquo, but that resentment is itself closely related to Macbeth's desire to found a dynasty. Banquo, who has risked nothing, who has remained upright, who has not defiled himself, will have kings for children; Macbeth, none. Again, ironically, the Weird Sisters who have given Macbeth, so he has thought, the priceless gift of knowledge of the future, have given the real future to Banquo.

So Banquo's murder is decided upon, and accomplished. But Banquo's son escapes, and once more, the future has eluded Macbeth. The murder of Banquo thus becomes almost meaningless. This general point may be obvious enough, but we shall do well to note some of the further ways in which Shakespeare has pointed up the significance of Macbeth's war with the future.

When Macbeth, at the beginning of Scene vii, Act I, contemplates Duncan's murder, it is the future over which he agonizes:

> If it were done, when 'tis done, then 'twere well
> It were done quickly; if the assassination
> Could trammel up the consequence, and catch
> With his surcease success; that but this blow
> Might be the be-all and the end-all here. . . .

But the continuum of time cannot be partitioned off; the future is implicit in the present. There is no net strong enough to trammel up the consequence—not even in this world.

Lady Macbeth, of course, has fewer qualms. When Macbeth hesitates to repudiate the duties which he owes Duncan—duties which, by some accident of imagery perhaps —I hesitate to press the significance—he has earlier actually called "children"—Lady Macbeth cries out that she is willing to crush her own child in order to gain the crown:

> I have given suck, and know
> How tender 'tis to love the babe that milks me;
> I would, while it was smiling in my face,
> Have pluck'd my nipple from his boneless gums
> And dash'd the brains out, had I so sworn as you
> Have done to this.

Robert Penn Warren has made the penetrating observation that all of Shakespeare's villains are rationalists. Lady Macbeth is certainly of their company. She knows what she wants; and she is ruthless in her consideration of means. She will always "catch the nearest way." This is not to say that she ignores the problem of scruples, or that she is ready to oversimplify psychological complexities. But scruples are to be used to entangle one's enemies. One is not to become tangled in the mesh of scruples himself. Even though she loves her husband and though her ambition for herself is a part of her ambition for him, still she seems willing to consider even Macbeth at times as pure instrument, playing upon his hopes and fears and pride.

Her rationalism is quite sincere. She is apparently thoroughly honest in declaring that

> The sleeping and the dead
> Are but as pictures; 'tis the eye of childhood
> That fears a painted devil. If he do bleed,
> I'll gild the faces of the grooms withal,
> For it must seem their guilt.

For her, there is no moral order: *guilt* is something like *gilt*—one can wash it off or paint it on. Her pun is not frivolous and it is deeply expressive.

Lady Macbeth abjures all pity; she is willing to unsex herself; and her continual taunt to Macbeth, when he falters, is that he is acting like a baby—not like a man. This "manhood" Macbeth tries to learn. He is a dogged pupil. For that reason he is almost pathetic when the shallow rationalism which his wife urges upon him fails. His tone is almost one of puzzled bewilderment at nature's unfairness in failing to play the game according to the rules—the rules which have applied to other murders:

> the time has been,
> That, when the brains were out, the man would die,
> And there an end; but now they rise again. . . .

Yet, after the harrowing scene, Macbeth can say, with a sort of dogged weariness:

> Come, we'll to sleep. My strange and self-abuse
> Is the initiate fear that wants hard use:
> We are yet but young in deed.

Ironically, Macbeth is still echoing the dominant metaphor of Lady Macbeth's reproach. He has not yet attained to "manhood"; that *must* be the explanation. He has not yet succeeded in hardening himself into something inhuman.

Tempted by the Weird Sisters and urged on by his wife, Macbeth is thus caught between the irrational and the rational. There is a sense, of course, in which every man is caught between them. Man must try to predict and plan and control his destiny. That is man's fate; and the struggle, if he is to realize himself as a man, cannot be avoided. The question, of course, which has always interested the tragic dramatist involves the terms on which the struggle is accepted and the protagonist's attitude toward fate and toward himself. Macbeth in his general concern for the future is typical—is Every Man. He becomes the typical tragic protagonist when he yields to pride and *hybris*. The occasion for temptation is offered by the prophecy of the Weird Sisters. They offer him knowledge which cannot be arrived at rationally. They offer a key—if only a partial key—to what is otherwise unpredictable. Lady Macbeth, on the other hand, by employing a ruthless clarity of perception, by discounting all emotional claims, offers him the promise of bringing about the course of events which he desires.

Now, in the middle of the play, though he has not lost confidence and though, as he himself says, there can be no turning back, doubts have begun to arise; and he returns to the Weird Sisters to secure unambiguous answers to his fears. But, pathetically and ironically for Macbeth, in returning to the Weird Sisters, he is really trying to impose rationality on what sets itself forth plainly as irrational: that is, Macbeth would force a rigid control on a future which, by definition—by the very fact that the Weird Sisters already know it—stands beyond his manipulation.

It is because of his hopes for his own children and his fears of Banquo's that he has returned to the witches for counsel. It is altogether appropriate, therefore, that two of the apparitions by which their counsel is revealed should be babes, the crowned babe and the bloody babe.

For the babe signifies the future which Macbeth would control and cannot control. It is the unpredictable thing itself—as Yeats has put it magnificently, "The uncontrollable mystery on the bestial floor." It is the one thing that can justify, even in Macbeth's mind, the murders which he has committed. Earlier in the play, Macbeth had declared that if the deed could "trammel up the consequence," he would be willing to "jump the life to come." But he cannot jump the life to come. In his own terms he is betrayed. For it is idle to speak of jumping the life to come if one yearns to found a line of kings. It is the babe that betrays Macbeth—his own babes, most of all.

The logic of Macbeth's distraught mind, thus, forces him to make war on children, a war which in itself reflects his desperation and is a confession of weakness. Macbeth's ruffians, for example, break into Macduff's castle and kill his wife and children. The scene in which the innocent child prattles with his mother about his absent father, and then is murdered, is typical Shakespearean "fourth act" pathos. But the pathos is not adventitious; the scene ties into the inner symbolism of the play. For the child, in its helplessness, defies the murderers. Its defiance testifies to the force which threatens Macbeth and which Macbeth cannot destroy.

But we are not, of course, to placard the child as The Future in a rather stiff and mechanical allegory. *Macbeth* is no such allegory. Shakespeare's symbols are richer and more flexible than that. The babe signifies not only the future; it symbolizes all those enlarging purposes which make life meaningful, and it symbolizes, furthermore, all those emotional and—to Lady Macbeth—irrational ties which make man more than a machine—which render him human. It signifies pre-eminently the pity which Macbeth, under Lady Macbeth's tutelage, would wean himself of as something "unmanly." Lady Macbeth's great speeches early in the play become brilliantly ironical when we realize that Shakespeare is using the same symbol for the unpredictable future that he uses for human compassion. Lady Macbeth is willing to go to any length to grasp the future: she would willingly dash out the brains of her own child if it stood in her way to that future. But this is to repudiate the future, for the child is its symbol.

Shakespeare does not, of course, limit himself to the symbolism of the child: he makes use of other symbols of growth and development, notably that of the plant. And this plant symbolism patterns itself to reflect the development of the play. For example, Banquo says to the Weird Sisters, early in the play:

> If you can look into the seeds of time,
> And say which grain will grow and which will not,
> Speak then to me. . . .

A little later, on welcoming Macbeth, Duncan says to him:

> I have begun to plant thee, and will labor
> To make thee full of growing.

After the murder of Duncan, Macbeth falls into the same

metaphor when he comes to resolve on Banquo's death.
The Weird Sisters, he reflects, had hailed Banquo as

> ... father to a line of kings.
> Upon my head they placed a fruitless crown,
> And put a barren scepter in my gripe. . . .

Late in the play, Macbeth sees himself as the winter-
stricken tree:

> I have liv'd long enough: my way of life
> Is fall'n into the sear, the yellow leaf. . . .

The plant symbolism, then, supplements the child symbolism. At points it merges with it, as when Macbeth
ponders bitterly that he has damned himself

> To make them kings, the seed of Banquo kings!

And, in at least one brilliant example, the plant symbolism unites with the clothes symbolism. It is a crown-
ing irony that one of the Weird Sisters' prophecies on
which Macbeth has staked his hopes is fulfilled when
Birnam Wood comes to Dunsinane. For, in a sense, Macbeth is here hoist on his own petard. Macbeth, who has
invoked night to "Scarf up the tender eye of pitiful day,"
and who has, again and again, used the "false face" to
"hide what the false heart doth know," here has the trick
turned against him. But the garment which cloaks the
avengers is the living green of nature itself, and nature
seems, to the startled eyes of his sentinels, to be rising up
against him.

But it is the babe, the child, that dominates the symbolism. Most fittingly, the last of the prophecies in which
Macbeth has placed his confidence, concerns the child:
and Macbeth comes to know the final worst when Macduff declares to him that he was not "born of woman" but
was from his "mother's womb/ Untimely ripp'd." The
babe here has defied even the thing which one feels
may reasonably be predicted of him—his time of birth.

With Macduff's pronouncement, the unpredictable has broken through the last shred of the net of calculation. The future cannot be trammeled up. The naked babe confronts Macbeth to pronounce his doom.

The passage with which we began this essay, then, is an integral part of a larger context, and of a very rich context:

> And pity, like a naked new-born babe,
> Striding the blast, or heaven's cherubim, hors'd
> Upon the sightless couriers of the air,
> Shall blow the horrid deed in every eye,
> That tears shall drown the wind.

Pity is like the naked babe, the most sensitive and helpless thing; yet, almost as soon as the comparison is announced, the symbol of weakness begins to turn into a symbol of strength; for the babe, though newborn, is pictured as "Striding the blast" like an elemental force—like "heaven's cherubim, hors'd/ Upon the sightless couriers of the air." We can give an answer to the question put earlier: is Pity like the human and helpless babe, or powerful as the angel that rides the winds? It is both; and it is strong because of its very weakness. The paradox is inherent in the situation itself; and it is the paradox that will destroy the overbrittle rationalism on which Macbeth founds his career.

For what will it avail Macbeth to cover the deed with the blanket of the dark if the elemental forces that ride the winds will blow the horrid deed in every eye? And what will it avail Macbeth to clothe himself in "manliness"—to become bloody, bold, and resolute,—if he is to find himself again and again, viewing his bloody work through the "eye of childhood/ That fears a painted devil"? Certainly, the final and climactic appearance of the babe symbol merges all the contradictory elements of the symbol. For, with Macduff's statement about his birth, the naked babe rises before Macbeth as not only the future that eludes calculation but as avenging angel as well.

The clothed daggers and the naked babe—mechanism and life—instrument and end—death and birth—that which should be left bare and clean and that which should be clothed and warmed—these are facets of two of the great symbols which run throughout the play. They are not the only symbols, to be sure; they are not the most obvious symbols: darkness and blood appear more often. But with a flexibility which must amaze the reader, the image of the garment and the image of the babe are so used as to encompass an astonishingly large area of the total situation. And between them—the naked babe, essential humanity, humanity stripped down to the naked thing itself, and yet as various as the future—and the various garbs which humanity assumes, the robes of honor, the hypocrite's disguise, the inhuman "manliness" with which Macbeth endeavors to cover up his essential humanity—between them, they furnish Shakespeare with his most subtle and ironically telling instruments.

Oscar James Campbell

From "Shakespeare and the 'New' Critics"

One of the sanest of recent applications of the new critical method to a Shakespearean play is an essay on *Macbeth,* entitled "The Naked Babe and the Cloak of Manliness." [1] The article illustrates the virtues of the method but also exemplifies its dangers, even though it be applied by a critic of unusual sensitivity and insight. Mr. Brooks, discovering two principal chains of imagery in *Macbeth,* one composed of garments or "old clothes," the other of babes, undertakes to prove that each chain subserves a deep imaginative unity. Since he realizes that what is at stake in his investigation is the whole matter of the relation of Shakespeare's imagery to the structure of the play, he proceeds with caution and (if his premises be granted) with adequate logic.

Miss Spurgeon, in her study of the images in *Macbeth,* pointed out that "the idea constantly recurs that Macbeth's new honors sit ill upon him, like a loose and badly fitting garment belonging to someone else." [2] And she illustrates the point by showing how many times Shakespeare repeats and varies the clothes image in order to

From *Joseph Quincy Adams: Memorial Studies,* ed. James G. Mc-Manaway, Giles E. Dawson, and Edwin E. Willoughby. Copyright 1948 for the Folger Shakespeare Library by the Trustees of Amherst College. Reprinted by permission of the author, and the Folger Shakespeare Library.

[1] This essay appears in Cleanth Brooks' *The Well Wrought Urn* (1947), pp. 21–46.

[2] *Shakespeare's Imagery,* p. 324.

keep before our minds "this imaginative picture of a small ignoble man encumbered and degraded by garments unsuited to him." The poet's manipulation of this image, as described by Miss Spurgeon, is the reverse of metaphysical; it is direct and simple. The imaginative significance of Banquo's remark as he observes Macbeth ruminating over the "supernatural soliciting" of the witches—

> New honors come upon him,
> Like our strange garments, cleave not to their mold
> But with the aid of use (I.iii.144–46)—

is easily grasped without the intervention of a new critic. So is Angus's comment upon Macbeth's conduct after his accession to power:

> Now does he feel his title
> Hang loose about him, like a giant's robe
> Upon a dwarfish thief.

These two passages are typical of Shakespeare's use of the clothes metaphor as a descriptive tag to pin upon Macbeth.

Mr. Brooks, however, finds such simple employment of the figure merely an adumbration of its more subtle manifestations. After glancing with approval at Miss Spurgeon's analysis, he asserts that these undisguised appearances of the metaphor are paralleled by a series of cloaking or masking images, variants of garment figures. The purpose of those figures is to suggest that throughout the play Macbeth is seeking to hide his "disgraceful self" from his own eyes as well as from the eyes of others. Mr. Brooks seeks to prove that the cloaking images form a chain, in the manner of the metaphysicals new and old, to keep alive the ironical contrast between the wretched creature that Macbeth really is and the pompous disguises he assumes to conceal the fact.

In attempting to build a structure out of the clothes images Mr. Brooks is forced to distort the meaning of

more than one passage. This is evident in the variant interpretation he offers for Lady Macbeth's

> Come, thick night,
> And pall thee in the dunnest smoke of hell,
> That my keen knife sees not the wound it makes,
> Nor heaven peep through the blanket of the dark
> To cry, Hold, Hold!

Mr. Brooks admits that it is natural to think of the "keen
knife" as in Lady Macbeth's hand and that she is begging
the night to be so dark that even her knife, much less
herself, may not see the wound it makes. The interpretation is more than natural, considering the fact that the
image comes at the end of a speech in which she seeks
to suppress her woman's nature so that she can be capable
of the horrid deed.

But since the figure thus interpreted cannot serve as
a link in the chain the critic is forging, Mr. Brooks offers the over-ingenious suggestion that the "keen knife"
may be Macbeth himself. Thus interpreted, the figure can
be forced to serve as one more indication of the efforts
of the two murderers to hide from themselves what they
are and what they do. Lady Macbeth would then be invok-
ing the pall, the clothing of death, to blanket the horrid
deed from the reluctant doer. But such an interpretation
seems to this writer to be strained beyond the limits of
credulity.

It is obvious that *Macbeth* contains much clothes
imagery, but it is equally undeniable that Shakespeare
used it in his own characteristic fashion. Once having employed the figure as a swift and startling method of char-
acterizing his villain hero, the poet found the image and
the word so securely lodged in his mind that it arose
repeatedly while he was at work on his drama. And instead of discarding it every time it demanded expression,
he subtly varied its form and employed it on many occa-
sions to intensify crucial moments in the action. A striking example of putting the figure to an original use
occurs when, at the end of a highly mannered passage,

Macbeth describes the murderers' daggers as "unmannerly breeched with gore." Mr. Brooks properly characterizes this image as vivid and fantastic. But his efforts to make it play a part in developing the disguise motif seems as fantastic as the metaphor. The daggers, naked except for their red breeches, are not only "unmannerly" but have also been clothed, or so he believes, in a horrible masquerade in order to play in this disguise a villainous role. For their natural guise was honorable nakedness, the form in which they could have guarded the King. This interpretation quite ignores the value of the metaphor for the speech in which it occurs. There it flashes a sudden light upon Macbeth's state of mind at the moment when he utters it. Shakespeare has designed the series of extravagant images—of which the daggers "unmannerly breeched with gore" is the last—as a means of revealing Macbeth's neurotic embarrassment, which is here on the verge of betraying his guilt to Macduff, Malcolm, and Donalbain. In other words, the figure epitomizes the murderer's state of mind and nerves at one of the play's high emotional moments. Mr. Brooks' analysis of the various clothes images does not establish the facts he desires. But it has the unconscious merit of throwing into sharp relief the difference between Shakespeare's habitual use of figurative language and the methods of the metaphysical poets, which the new critics falsely assume Shakespeare to have adopted.

Mr. Brooks' analysis of Shakespeare's employment of the image of the babe is less free of bias than his treatment of the clothes figure and leads to a less valid conclusion. He begins with a brilliant interpretation of some lines which many commentators have stigmatized as pure fustian:

> And pity, like a naked new-born babe,
> Striding the blast, or heaven's cherubim, hors'd
> Upon the sightless couriers of the air,
> Shall blow the horrid deed in every eye,
> That tears shall drown the wind. (I.vii.21)

The poet means, so says Mr. Brooks, that the nature of pity is paradoxical. When first aroused it seems to be as helpless as a newborn babe. Yet when it is blown into the hearts and minds of multitudes of men, it becomes stronger than the blasts of tempestuous wind. That is, its strength lies in its very weakness.

Mr. Brooks' close attention to this passage has led him to note many other references to babes in *Macbeth*. "Sometimes," he writes, "it is a character such as Macduff's child" (who is not a babe at all); "sometimes a symbol, like the crowned babe and the bloody babe which are raised by the witches; . . . sometimes in a metaphor." This babe, the critic arbitrarily decides, "signifies the future which Macbeth would control and cannot control." Mr. Brooks makes this identification in spite of the fact that in the passage he has just analyzed the babe is a symbol of something quite different. But not satisfied with this concrete use of the symbol Mr. Brooks explains that "the babe signifies not only the future; it symbolizes all those enlarging purposes which make life meaningful, and it symbolizes, furthermore, all those emotional and—to Lady Macbeth—irrational ties which make man more than a machine—which render him human." By this time the hard concrete core of the symbol has developed so amorphous an aura that its "burning center" has been almost completely obscured. By interpreting the babe as a recurrent symbol of the future Mr. Brooks is able to discover that Macbeth's tragedy is that of man making futile efforts to control the future. But this erratic, neo-Hegelian judgment reduces the rich complexity of Macbeth's human nature to a bare general proposition. His tragedy lies not in a failure of his efforts to impose his will upon the future but in the multitudinous fears and superstitions that form the psychological punishment for his crime. Whatever the value of imagery as an objective correlative of emotion, it obviously must not be interpreted in such a way as to contradict directly the clear meaning of the plot.

If Mr. Brooks' conclusions be false, it is important to discover at what points his method has been at fault.

In general his errors of judgment result from efforts to force all the references to babes into one connected system of imagery to form a structural principle for the drama. For example, Macbeth's famous soliloquy ending

> If th' assassination
> Could trammel up the consequence, and catch
> With his surcease, success; that but this blow
> Might be the be-all and the end-all here,
> But here, upon this bank and shoal of time,
> We'd jump the life to come (I.vii.2–7)

to Mr. Brooks means that Macbeth is agonizing over the future. But Macbeth's case is hopeless, he proceeds, because "the continuum of time cannot be partitioned off, the future is implicit in the present." Such recourse to a philosophical generality is perverse. Macbeth, like all murderers in Elizabethan plays, is afraid, not of his inability to control the future, but of the knife in the hands of a human avenger. This fear he expresses in the lines:

> We but teach
> Bloody instructions, which, being taught, return
> To plague the inventor.

This expectation of inevitable revenge is the reason why his fears in Banquo stick deep—why, in spite of the witches' assurance that he need fear no man of woman born, he fears Macduff so greatly that he orders his death.

One reason for Mr. Brooks' misunderstanding of the above passage is his misinterpretation of the phrase "the life to come." In its context it clearly refers to life after death and not, as Mr. Brooks thinks, to the future of Macbeth and his line in this world. Can it be that the critic has taken "jump" to mean "leap over"—that is, "skip" —instead of the correct "risk"? His following statement suggests this as a distinct possibility. "It is idle," he says, "to speak of jumping the life to come if one yearns to found a line of kings."

Mr. Brooks forces other passages into distorted shapes in his valiant effort to forge a chain of imagery out of materials extracted from the poetry. For example, he gives a sophistical interpretation to one of Lady Macbeth's most revealing exclamations—her scornful cry that she would rather have torn her baby from her breast and dashed out its brains than be so cowardly as to fail to kill Duncan, as her husband had sworn to do. This, says the critic, means that she is willing to go to any lengths to grasp the future. But her cry, Mr. Brooks continues, is extremely ironical because "she will grasp the future by repudiating the future of which the child is the symbol." This over-ingenious reading obscures and enfeebles the stark simplicity of Lady Macbeth's utterance. What she says to her husband is this: Rather than be such an irresolute coward as you now are, I had rather be guilty of the most fiendishly unnatural deed of which a mother is capable.

More than once Brooks forces upon an image an interpretation which, by the wildest stretch of the imagination, it cannot be made to bear. For example, he insists that when Macduff's little boy defies the murderers the child, whom he persists in calling a babe, testifies to the strength of the future, the force that threatens Macbeth and which he cannot destroy. The child, whose real dramatic function, besides the evocation of pity, is to show the wild killer that Macbeth has become in his efforts to kill fear itself, in Mr. Brooks' view "ties into the inner symbolism of the play." The truth is that Shakespeare has not used the image of the babe any more in the manner of a metaphysical poet than he did that of the clothes image. The word and the image reappeared in the poet's mind, but each time he used it for an immediate imaginative purpose relevant only to a specific situation.

Mary McCarthy

General Macbeth

He is a general and has just won a battle; he enters the scene making a remark about the weather. "So fair and foul a day I have not seen." On this flat note Macbeth's character tone is set. "Terrible weather we're having." "The sun can't seem to make up its mind." "Is it hot/cold/wet enough for you?" A commonplace man who talks in commonplaces, a golfer, one might guess, on the Scottish fairways, Macbeth is the only Shakespeare hero who corresponds to a bourgeois type: a murderous Babbitt, let us say.

You might argue just the opposite, that Macbeth is over-imaginative, the prey of visions. It is true that he is impressionable. Banquo, when they come upon the witches, amuses himself at their expense, like a man of parts idly chaffing a fortune-teller. Macbeth, though, is deeply impressed. "Thane of Cawdor and King." He thinks this over aloud. "How can I be Thane of Cawdor when the Thane of Cawdor is alive?" When this mental stumbling block has been cleared away for him (the Thane of Cawdor has received a death sentence), he turns his thoughts *sotto voce* to the next question. "How can I be king when Duncan is alive?" The answer comes back, "Kill him." It does fleetingly occur to Macbeth, as it would to most people, to leave matters alone and let destiny work it out. "If chance will have me king, why,

From *Harper's Magazine* (June, 1962). Copyright © 1962 by Mary McCarthy. Reprinted by permission of Mary McCarthy.

chance may crown me, without my stir." But this goes against his grain. A reflective man might wonder how fate would spin her plot, as the Virgin Mary wondered after the Angel Gabriel's visit. But Macbeth does not trust to fate, that is, to the unknown, the mystery of things; he trusts only to a known quantity—himself—to put the prophecy into action. In short, he has no faith, which requires imagination. He is literal-minded; that, in a word, is his "tragedy" and his tragedy.

It was not *his* idea, he could plead in self-defense, but the witches', that he should have the throne. *They* said it first. But the witches only voiced a thought that was already in his mind; after all, he was Duncan's cousin and close to the crown. And once the thought has been put into *words,* he is in a scrambling hurry. He cannot wait to get home to tell his wife about the promise; in his excitement, he puts it in a letter, which he sends on ahead, like a businessman briefing an associate on a piece of good news for the firm.

Lady Macbeth—has this been noted?—takes very little stock in the witches. She never pesters her husband, as most wives would, with questions about the Weird Sisters: "What did they say, exactly?" "How did they look?" "Are you sure?" She is less interested in "fate and metaphysical aid" than in the business at hand—how to nerve her husband to do what he wants to do. And later, when Macbeth announces that he is going out to consult the Weird Sisters again, she refrains from comment. As though she were keeping her opinion—"O proper stuff!" —to herself. Lady Macbeth is not superstitious. Macbeth is. This makes her repeatedly impatient with him, for Macbeth, like many men of his sort, is an old story to his wife. A tale full of sound and fury signifying nothing. Her contempt for him perhaps extends even to his ambition. "Wouldst not play false, And yet wouldst wrongly win." As though to say, "All right, if that's what you want, have the courage to get it." Lady Macbeth does not so much give the impression of coveting the crown herself as of being weary of watching Macbeth covet it. Macbeth, by the way, is surely her second husband (she has "given suck" and Macbeth "has no children"), and either her first husband was a better man than he, which galls her, or he was just another general, another superstitious golfer, which would gall her too.

Superstition here is the opposite of reason on the one hand and of imagination on the other. Macbeth is credulous, in contrast to Lady Macbeth, to Banquo, and, later, to Malcolm, who sets the audience an example of the right way by mistrusting Macduff until he has submitted him to an empirical test. Believing and knowing are paired in Malcolm's mind; what he *knows* he believes. Macbeth's eagerness to believe is the companion of his lack of faith. If all works out right for him in this world, Macbeth says, he can skip the next ("We'd jump the life to come"). Superstition whispers when true religion has been silenced, and Macbeth becomes the butt of his own know-nothing materialism incarnate in the jeering witches on the heath.

As in his first interview with them he is too quick to act literally on a dark saying, in the second he is too easily reassured. He will not be conquered till "Great Birnam Wood to High Dunsinane shall come against him." "Why, that can never happen!" he cries out in immediate relief, his brow clearing.

It never enters his mind to examine the saying more closely, test it, so to speak, for a double bottom, as was common in those days (Banquo even points this out to him) with prophetic utterances, which were known to be ambiguous and tricky. Any child knew that a prophecy often meant the reverse of what it seemed to say, and any man of imagination would ask himself how Birnam Wood *might* come to Dunsinane and take measures to prevent it, as King Laius took measures to prevent his own death by arranging to have the baby Oedipus killed. If Macbeth had thought it out, he could have had Birnam Wood chopped down and burned on the spot and the ashes dumped into the sea. True, the prophecy might still have turned against him (since destiny cannot be avoided and the appointment will be kept at Samarra), but that would have been another story, another tragedy, the tragedy of a clever man not clever enough to circumvent fate. Macbeth is not clever; he is taken in by surfaces, by appearance. He cannot think beyond the usual course of things. As with "No man of woman born." All men, he says to himself, sagely, are born of women; Malcolm and Macduff are men; therefore I am safe. This logic leaves out of account the extraordinary: the man brought into the world by Caesarean section. In the same way, it leaves out of account the supernatural—the very forces he is trafficking with. He might be overcome by an angel or a demon, as well as by Macduff.

Yet this pedestrian general sees ghosts and imaginary daggers in the air. Lady Macbeth does not, and this tendency in her husband grates on her nerves; she is sick of his terrors and fancies. A practical woman, Lady Macbeth, more a partner than a wife, though Macbeth treats her with a trite domestic fondness—"Love," "Dearest love," "Dearest chuck," "Sweet remembrancer." These endearments, this middle-aged, middle-class cuddliness, as though he called her "Honeybunch" or "Sweetheart," as well as the obligatory "Dear," are a master stroke of Shakespeare's and perfectly in keeping with the prosing about the weather, the heavy credulousness.

Naturally Macbeth is dominated by his wife. He is old Iron Pants in the field (as she bitterly reminds him), but at home she has to wear the pants; she has to unsex herself. No "chucks" or "dearests" escape her tightened lips, and yet she is more feeling, more human at bottom than Macbeth. She thinks of her father when she sees the old King asleep, and this natural thought will not let her kill him. Macbeth has to do it, just as the quailing husband of any modern virago is sent down to the basement to kill a rat or drown a set of kittens. An image of her father, irrelevant to her purpose, softens this monster woman; sleepwalking, she thinks of Lady Macduff. "The Thane of Fife had a wife. Where is she now?" Stronger than Macbeth, less suggestible, she is nevertheless imaginative, where he is not. She does not see ghosts and daggers; when she sleepwalks, it is simple reality that haunts her—the crime relived. "Who would have thought the old man to have had so much blood in him?" Over and over, the details of the crime repeat themselves on the screen of her consciousness. This nightly reliving is not penitence but more terrible—remorse, the agenbite of the restless deed. Lady Macbeth's uncontrollable imagination drives her to put herself in the place of others—the wife of the Thane of Fife—and to recognize a kinship between all human kind: the pathos of old age in Duncan makes her think, "Why, he might be my father!" This sense of a natural bond among men opens her to contrition—sorrowing with. To ask whether, waking, she is "sorry" for what she has done is impertinent. She lives with it and it kills her.

Macbeth has absolutely no feeling for others, except envy, a common middle-class trait. He *envies* the murdered Duncan his rest, which is a strange way of looking at your victim. What he suffers on his own account after the crimes is simple panic. He is never contrite or remorseful; it is not the deed but a shadow of it, Banquo's spook, that appears to him. The "scruples" that agitate him before Duncan's murder are mere echoes of conventional opinion, of what might be *said* about his deed: that Duncan was his king, his cousin, and a guest under his roof. "I have bought golden opinions," he says to himself (note the verb), "from all sorts of people"; now these people may ask for their opinions back if they suspect him of the murder. It is like a business firm's being reluctant to part with its "good will"—an asset. The fact that Duncan was such a good king bothers him, and why? Because there will be universal grief at his death. But his chief "scruple" is even simpler. "If we should fail?" he says timidly to Lady Macbeth. Sweet chuck tells him that they will not. Yet once she has ceased to be effectual as a partner, Dearest love is an embarrassment. He has no time for her; she should have died hereafter. That is, when he was not so busy. Again the general is speaking.

The idea of Macbeth as a conscience-tormented man is a platitude as false as Macbeth himself. Macbeth has no conscience. His main concern throughout the play is that most selfish of all concerns: to get a good night's sleep.

His invocation to sleep, while heartfelt, is perfectly conventional; sleep builds you up, enables you to start the day fresh. Thus the virtue of having a good conscience is seen by him in terms of bodily hygiene, as if it were a Simmons mattress or an electric blanket. Lady Macbeth shares these preoccupations. When he tells her he is going to see the witches, she remarks that he needs sleep.

Her wifely concern is mechanical and far from real solicitude. She is aware of Macbeth; she *knows* him (he does not know her at all, apparently), but she regards him coldly as a thing, a tool that must be oiled and polished. His soul-states do not interest her; her attention is narrowed on his morale, his public conduct, the shifting expressions of his face. But in a sense she is right, for there is nothing to Macbeth but fear and ambition, both of which he tries to hide, except from her. This naturally gives her a poor opinion of the inner man.

Why is it, though, that Lady Macbeth seems to us a monster while Macbeth does not? Partly because she is a woman and has "unsexed" herself, which makes her a monster by definition. Also because the very prospect of murder quickens an hysterical excitement in her, like the discovery of some object in a shop—a set of emeralds or a sable stole—which Macbeth can give her and which will be an "outlet" for all the repressed desires he cannot satisfy. She behaves as though Macbeth, through his weakness, will deprive her of self-realization; the unimpeded exercise of her will is the voluptuous end she seeks. That is why she makes naught of scruples, as inner brakes on her throbbing engines. Unlike Macbeth, she does not pretend to harbor a conscience, though this, on her part, by a curious turn, *is* a pretense, as the sleep-walking scene reveals. After the first crime, her will subsides, spent; the devil has brought her to climax and left her.

Macbeth is not a monster, like Richard III or Iago or Iachimo, though in the catalogue he might go for one because of the blackness of his deeds. But his deeds are only the wishes and fears of the average, undistinguished man translated halfheartedly into action. Pure evil is a kind of transcendence that he does not aspire to. He only wants to be king and sleep the sleep of the just, undisturbed. He could never have been a good man, even if he had not met the witches; hence we cannot see him as a devil incarnate, for the devil is a fallen angel. Macbeth does not fall; if anything, he somewhat improves as the result of his career of crime. He throws off his dependency and thus achieves the "greatness" he mistakenly sought in worldly symbols.

The isolation of Macbeth, which is at once a punishment and a tragic dignity or honor, takes place by stages and by deliberate choice; it begins when he does not tell Lady Macbeth that he has decided to kill Banquo and reaches its height in the final action. Up to this time, though he has cut himself off from all human contacts, he is relying on the witches as a substitute. When he first hears the news that Macduff is not "of woman born," he is unmanned; everything he trusted (the literal word) has betrayed him, and he screams in terror, "I'll not fight with thee!" But Macduff's taunts make a man of him; he cannot die like this, shamed. His death is his first act of courage, though even here he has had to be pricked to it by mockery, Lady Macbeth's old spur. Nevertheless, weaned by his very crimes from dependency, nursed in a tyrant's solitude, he meets death on his own, without metaphysical aid. "Lay on, Macduff."

What is modern and bourgeois in Macbeth's character is his wholly *social* outlook. He has no feeling for others, and yet until the end he is a vicarious creature, existing in his own eyes through others, through what they may say of him, through what they tell him or promise him. This paradox is typical of the social being—at once a wolf out for himself and a sheep. Macbeth, moreover, is an expert buck-passer; he sees how others can be used. It is he, not Lady Macbeth, who thinks of smearing the drunken chamberlains with blood, so that they shall be caught "red-handed" the next morning when Duncan's murder is discovered. At this idea he brightens; suddenly, he sees his way clear. It is the moment when at last he decides. The eternal executive, ready to fix responsibility on a subordinate, has seen the deed finally take a *recognizable* form. Now he can do it. And the crackerjack thought of killing the grooms afterwards (dead men tell no tales—old adage) is again purely his own on-the-spot inspiration; no credit to Lady Macbeth.

It is the sort of thought that would have come to Claudius in *Hamlet,* another trepidant executive. Indeed, Macbeth is more like Claudius than like any other character in Shakespeare. Both are doting husbands; both rose to power by betraying their superior's trust; both are easily frightened and have difficulty saying their prayers. Macbeth's "Amen" sticks in his throat, he complains, and Claudius, on his knees, sighs that he cannot make what priests call a "good act of contrition." The desire to say his prayers like any pew-holder, quite regardless of his horrible crime, is merely a longing for respectability. Macbeth "repents" killing the grooms, but this is strictly for public consumption. "O, yet I do repent me of my fury, That I did kill them." In fact, it is the one deed he does *not* repent (i.e., doubt the wisdom of) either before or after. This hypocritical self-accusation, which is his sidelong way of announcing the embarrassing fact that he has just done away with the grooms, and his simulated grief at Duncan's murder ("All is but toys; renown and grace is dead; The wine of life is drawn," etc.) are his basest moments in the play, as well as his boldest; here is nearly a magnificent monster.

The dramatic effect, too, is one of great boldness on Shakespeare's part. Macbeth is speaking pure Shakespearean poetry, but in his mouth, since we know he is lying, it turns into facile verse, Shakespearean poetry parodied. The same with "Here lay Duncan, his silver skin lac'd with his golden blood. . . ." If the image were given to Macduff, it would be uncontaminated poetry; from Macbeth it is "proper stuff"—fustian. This opens the perilous question of sincerity in the arts: is a line of verse altered for us by the sincerity of the poet (or speaker)? In short, is poetry relative to the circumstances or absolute? Or, more particularly, are Macbeth's soliloquies poetry, which they sound like, or something

else? Did Shakespeare intend to make Macbeth a poet,
like Hamlet, Lear, and Othello? In that case, how can
Macbeth be an unimaginative mediocrity? My opinion is
that Macbeth's soliloquies are not poetry but rhetoric.
They are tirades. That is, they do not trace any pensive
motion of the soul or heart but are a volley of words
discharged. Macbeth is neither thinking nor feeling aloud;
he is declaiming. Like so many unfeeling men, he has a
facile emotionalism, which he turns on and off. Not that
his fear is insincere, but his loss of control provides
him with an excuse for histrionics.

These gibberings exasperate Lady Macbeth. "What do
you mean?" she says coldly after she has listened to a
short harangue on "Methought I heard a voice cry 'Sleep
no more.' " It is an allowable question—what *does* he
mean? And his funeral oration on *her,* if she could have
heard it, would have brought her back to life to protest.
"She should have died hereafter"—fine, that was the real
Macbeth. But then, as if conscious of the proprieties, he
at once begins on a series of bromides ("Tomorrow and
tomorrow . . .") that he seems to have had ready to hand
for the occasion like a black mourning suit. All Macbeth's soliloquies have that ready-to-hand, if not hand-
me-down, air, which is perhaps why they are given to
schoolchildren to memorize, often with the result of making them hate Shakespeare. What children resent in these
soliloquies is precisely their sententiousness—the sound
they have of being already memorized from a copybook.

Macbeth's speeches often recall the Player's speech in
Hamlet—Shakespeare's example of how-not-to-do-it. He
tears a passion to tatters. He has a rather Senecan
rhetoric, the fustian of the time; in the dagger speech,
for example, he works in Hecate, Tarquin, and the wolf
—recherché embellishment for a man who is about to
commit a real murder. His taste for hyperbole goes with
a habit of euphuism, as when he calls the sea "the green
one." And what of the remarkable line just preceding,
"the multitudinous seas incarnadine," with its onomat-
opoeia of the crested waves rising in the *t*'s and *d*'s of
"multitudinous" and subsiding in the long swell of the

verb? This is sometimes cited as an example of pure
poetry, which it would be in an anthology of isolated
lines, but in the context, dramatically, it is bombast, a
kind of stuffing or padding.

The play between poetry and rhetoric, the *conversion*
of poetry to rhetoric, is subtle and horrible in *Macbeth,*
being itself a subversive process or treasonous manipulation. The suggestion seems to be that poetry used for an
ulterior purpose (as Macbeth uses it) turns into rhetoric.
Macbeth is the perfect utilitarian. If an explanation is
needed, you might say he learned to *use* words through
long practice in haranguing his troops, whipping them
and himself into battle frenzy. Up to recent times a
fighting general, like a football coach, was an orator.

But it must be noted that it is not only Macbeth who
rants. Nor is it only Macbeth who talks about the weather.
The play is stormy with atmosphere—the screaming and
shrieking of owls, the howling of winds. Nature herself is
ranting, like the witches, and Night, black Hecate, is
queen of the scene. Bats are flitting about; ravens and
crows are hoarse; the house-martin's nests on the battlements of Macbeth's castle give a misleading promise of
peace and gentle domesticity. "It will be rain tonight,"
says Banquo simply, looking at the sky (note the difference between this and Macbeth's pompous generality),
and the First Murderer growls at him, striking, "Let it
come down." The disorder of Nature, as so often in
Shakespeare, presages and reflects the disorder of the
body politic. Guilty Macbeth cannot sleep, but the night
of Duncan's murder, the whole house, as if guilty too, is
restless; Malcolm and Donalbain talk and laugh in their
sleep; the drunken porter, roused, plays that he is gate-
keeper of hell.

Indeed, the whole action takes place in a kind of hell
and is pitched to the demons' shriek of hyperbole. This
would appear to be a peculiar setting for a study of the
commonplace. But only at first sight. The fact that an
ordinary philistine like Macbeth goes on the rampage and
commits a series of murders is a sign that human na-

ture, like Nature, is capable of any mischief if left to its "natural" self. The witches, unnatural beings, are Nature spirits, stirring their snake-filet and owl's wing, newt's eye and frog toe in a camp stew: earthy ingredients boil down to an unearthly broth. It is the same with the man Macbeth. Ordinary ambition, fear, and a kind of stupidity make a deadly combination. Macbeth, a self-made king, is not kingly, but simply the original Adam, the social animal, and Lady Macbeth is Mother Eve.

There is no play of Shakespeare's (I think) that contains the words *Nature* and *natural* so many times, and the word *Nature* within the same speech can mean first something good and then something evil, as though it were a pun. Nature is two-sided, double-talking, like the witches. "Fair is foul and foul is fair," they cry, and Macbeth enters the play unconsciously echoing them, for he is never original but chock-full of the "milk of human kindness," which does not mean kindness in the modern sense but simply human "nature," human kind. The play is about Nature, and its blind echo, human nature.

Macbeth, in short, shows life in the cave. Without religion, animism rules the outer world, and without faith, the human soul is beset by hobgoblins. This at any rate was Shakespeare's opinion, to which modern history, with the return of the irrational in the Fascist nightmare and its new specters of Communism, Socialism, etc., lends support. It is a troubling thought that Macbeth, of all Shakespeare's characters, should seem the most "modern," the only one you could transpose into contemporary battle dress or a sport shirt and slacks.

The contemporary Macbeth, a churchgoer, is indifferent to religion, to the categorical imperative or any group of principles that may be held to stand above and govern human behavior. Like the old Macbeth, he'd gladly skip the future life, not only for himself but for the rest of humanity. He listens to soothsayers and prophets and has been out on the heath and in the desert, interfering with Nature on a grand scale, lest his rivals for power get ahead of him and Banquo's stock, instead of his, inherit the earth—why this should have seemed such a catas-

trophe to the real Macbeth, who had no children, is a
mystery the scholars never mention. Unloosing the po-
tential destructiveness that was always there in Nature,
as Shakespeare understood, the contemporary Macbeth,
like the old one, is not even a monster, though he may
breed monsters, thanks to his activities on the heath; he
is timorous, unimaginative, and the prayer he would like
to say most fervently is simply "Amen."

Suggested References

The number of possible references is vast and grows alarmingly. (The *Shakespeare Quarterly* devotes a substantial part of one issue each year to a list of the previous year's work, and *Shakespeare Survey*—an annual publication—includes a substantial review of recent scholarship, as well as an occasional essay surveying a few decades of scholarship on a chosen topic.) Though no works are indispensable, those listed below have been found helpful.

1. Shakespeare's Times

Byrne, M. St. Clare. *Elizabethan Life in Town and Country*. Rev. ed. New York: Barnes & Noble, Inc., 1961. Chapters on manners, beliefs, education, etc., with illustrations.

Craig, Hardin. *The Enchanted Glass: the Elizabethan Mind in Literature*. New York and London: Oxford University Press, 1936. The Elizabethan intellectual climate.

Joseph, B. L. *Shakespeare's Eden: The Commonwealth of England 1558–1629*. New York: Barnes & Noble, Inc., 1971. An account of the social, political, economic, and cultural life of England.

Nicoll, Allardyce (ed.). *The Elizabethans*. London: Cambridge University Press, 1957. An anthology of Elizabethan writings, especially valuable for its illustrations from paintings, title pages, etc.

Shakespeare's England. 2 vols. Oxford: The Clarendon Press, 1916. A large collection of scholarly essays on a wide variety of topics (e.g., astrology, costume, gardening, horsemanship), with special attention to Shakespeare's references to these topics.

Tillyard, E. M. W. *The Elizabethan World Picture*. London: Chatto & Windus, 1943; New York: The Macmillan Company, 1944. A brief account of some Elizabethan ideas of the universe.

Wilson, John Dover (ed.), *Life in Shakespeare's England*. 2nd ed. New York: The Macmillan Company, 1913. An anthology of Elizabethan writings on the countryside, superstition, education, the court, etc.

2. Shakespeare

Barnet, Sylvan. *A Short Guide to Shakespeare.* New York: Harcourt Brace Jovanovich, Inc., 1974. An introduction to all of the works and to the traditions behind them.

Bentley, Gerald E. *Shakespeare: A Biographical Handbook*. New Haven, Conn.: Yale University Press, 1961. The facts about Shakespeare, with virtually no conjecture intermingled.

Bradby, Anne (ed.). *Shakespeare Criticism, 1919–1935*. London: Oxford University Press, 1936. A small anthology of excellent essays on the plays.

Bush, Geoffrey Douglas. *Shakespeare and the Natural Condition*. Cambridge, Mass.: Harvard University Press; London: Oxford University Press, 1956. A short, sensitive account of Shakespeare's view of "Nature," touching most of the works.

Chambers, E. K. *William Shakespeare: A Study of Facts and Problems*. 2 vols. London: Oxford University Press, 1930. An invaluable, detailed reference work; not for the casual reader.

Chute, Marchette. *Shakespeare of London*. New York: E. P. Dutton & Co., Inc., 1949. A readable biography fused with portraits of Stratford and London life.

Clemen, Wolfgang H. *The Development of Shakespeare's Imagery*. Cambridge, Mass.: Harvard University Press, 1951. (Originally published in German, 1936.) A temperate account of a subject often abused.

Craig, Hardin. *An Interpretation of Shakespeare*. Columbia, Missouri: Lucas Brothers, 1948. A scholar's book designed for the layman. Comments on all the works.

Dean, Leonard F. (ed.). *Shakespeare: Modern Essays in Criticism*. New York: Oxford University Press, 1957. Mostly mid-twentieth-century critical studies, covering Shakespeare's artistry.

Granville-Barker, Harley. *Prefaces to Shakespeare*. 2 vols. Princeton, N.J.: Princeton University Press, 1946–47. Essays on ten plays by a scholarly man of the theater.

Harbage, Alfred. *As They Liked It*. New York: The Macmillan Company, 1947. A sensitive, long essay on Shakespeare, morality, and the audience's expectations.

————. *William Shakespeare: A Reader's Guide*. New York: Farrar, Straus, 1963. Extensive comments, scene by scene, on fourteen plays.

Ridler, Anne Bradby (ed.). *Shakespeare Criticism, 1935–1960*. New York and London: Oxford University Press, 1963. An excellent continuation of the anthology edited earlier by Miss Bradby (see above).

Schoenbaum, S. *Shakespeare's Lives*. Oxford: Clarendon Press, 1970. A review of the evidence, and an examination of many biographies, including those by Baconians and other heretics.

———. *William Shakespeare: A Compact Documentary Life*. New York: Oxford University Press, 1977. A readable presentation of all that the documents tell us about Shakespeare.

Smith, D. Nichol (ed.). *Shakespeare Criticism*. New York: Oxford University Press, 1916. A selection of criticism from 1623 to 1840, ranging from Ben Jonson to Thomas Carlyle.

Spencer, Theodore: *Shakespeare and the Nature of Man*. New York: The Macmillan Company, 1942. Shakespeare's plays in relation to Elizabethan thought.

Stoll, Elmer Edgar. *Shakespeare and Other Masters*. Cambridge, Mass.: Harvard University Press; London: Oxford University Press, 1940. Essays on tragedy, comedy, and aspects of dramaturgy, with special reference to some of Shakespeare's plays.

Traversi, D. A. *An Approach to Shakespeare*. Rev. ed. New York: Doubleday & Co., Inc., 1956. An analysis of the plays, beginning with words, images, and themes, rather than with characters.

Van Doren, Mark. *Shakespeare*. New York: Henry Holt & Company, Inc., 1939. Brief, perceptive readings of all of the plays.

Whitaker, Virgil K. *Shakespeare's Use of Learning*. San Marino, Calif.: Huntington Library, 1953. A study of the relation of Shakespeare's reading to his development as a dramatist.

3. Shakespeare's Theater

Adams, John Cranford. *The Globe Playhouse*. Rev. ed. New York: Barnes & Noble, Inc., 1961. A detailed conjecture about the physical characteristics of the theater Shakespeare often wrote for.

Beckerman, Bernard. *Shakespeare at the Globe, 1599–1609*. New York: The Macmillan Company, 1962. On the playhouse and on Elizabethan dramaturgy, acting, and staging.

Chambers, E. K. *The Elizabethan Stage*. 4 vols. New York: Oxford University Press, 1923. Reprinted with corrections, 1945. A valuable reference work on theaters, theatrical companies, and staging at court.

Gurr, Andrew. *The Shakespearean Stage 1574–1642*. Cambridge: Cambridge University Press, 1970. On the acting companies, the actors, the playhouses, the stages, and the audiences.

Harbage, Alfred. *Shakespeare's Audience*. New York: Columbia University Press. London: Oxford University Press, 1941. A study of the size and nature of the theatrical public.

Hodges, C. Walter. *The Globe Restored*. London: Ernest Benn, Ltd., 1953; New York: Coward-McCann, Inc., 1954. A well-illustrated and readable attempt to reconstruct the Globe Theatre.

Kernodle George R. *From Art to Theatre: Form and Convention in the Renaissance*. Chicago: University of Chicago Press, 1944 Pioneering and stimulating work on the symbolic and cultural meanings of theater construction.

Nagler, A. M *Shakespeare's Stage* Tr. by Ralph Manheim. New Haven, Conn.: Yale University Press, 1958. An excellent brief introduction to the physical aspect of the playhouse.

Smith, Irwin. *Shakespeare's Globe Playhouse*. New York: Charles Scribner's Sons, 1957. Chiefly indebted to J. C. Adams' controversial book, with additional material and scale drawings for model-builders.

Venezky, Alice S. *Pageantry on the Shakespearean Stage*. New York: Twayne Publishers, Inc., 1951. An examination of spectacle in Elizabethan drama.

4. Miscellaneous Reference Works

Abbott, E. A. *A Shakespearean Grammar*. New Edition. New York The Macmillan Company 1877. An examination of differences between Elizabethan and modern grammar.

Berman, Ronald *A Reader's Guide to Shakespeare's Plays*, rev. ed. Glenview, Ill.: Scott, Foresman and Company, 1973. A short bibliography of the chief articles and books on each play.

Bullough. Geoffrey. *Narrative and Dramatic Sources of Shakespeare*. 8 vols New York: Columbia University Press; London: Routledge & Kegan Paul Ltd., 1957-1975. A collection of many of the books Shakespeare drew upon.

Campbell, Oscar James and Edward G Quinn *The Reader's Encyclopedia of Shakespeare* New York: Thomas Y. Crowell Co., 1966 More than 2,700 entries, from a few sentences to a few pages on everything related to Shakespeare.

Greg, W. W. *The Shakespeare First Folio* New York and London: Oxford University Press, 1955. A detailed yet readable history of the first collection (1623) of Shakespeare's plays.

Kökeritz, Helge *Shakespeare's Names*. New Haven, Conn.: Yale University Press 1959; London: Oxford University Press 1960 A guide to the pronunciation of some 1,800 names appearing in Shakespeare.

————. *Shakespeare's Pronunciation*. New Haven, Conn.: Yale University Press; London: Oxford University Press, 1953. Contains much information about puns and rhymes.

Linthicum, Marie C. *Costume in the Drama of Shakespeare and His Contemporaries.* New York and London: Oxford University Press, 1936. On the fabrics and dress of the age, and references to them in the plays.

Muir, Kenneth. *Shakespeare's Sources.* London: Methuen & Co., Ltd., 1957. The first volume, on the comedies and tragedies, attempts to ascertain what books were Shakespeare's sources, and what use he made of them.

Onions, C. T. *A Shakespeare Glossary.* London: Oxford University Press, 1911; 2nd ed. rev., with enlarged addenda, 1953. Definitions of words (or senses of words) now obsolete.

Partridge, Eric. *Shakespeare's Bawdy.* Rev. ed. New York: E. P. Dutton & Co., Inc.; London: Routledge & Kegan Paul, Ltd.; 1955. A glossary of bawdy words and phrases.

Shakespeare Quarterly. See headnote to Suggested References.

Shakespeare Survey. See headnote to Suggested References.

Smith, Gordon Ross. *A Classified Shakespeare Bibliography 1936–1958.* University Park, Pa.: Pennsylvania State University Press, 1963. A list of some 20,000 items on Shakespeare.

Spevack, Marvin. *The Harvard Concordance to Shakespeare.* Cambridge, Mass.: Harvard University Press, 1973. An index to Shakespeare's words.

Wells, Stanley, ed. *Shakespeare: Select Bibliographies.* London: Oxford University Press, 1973. Seventeen essays surveying scholarship and criticism of Shakespeare's life, work, and theater.

5. Macbeth

Blissett, William. "The Secret'st Man of Blood. A Study of Dramatic Irony in Macbeth," *Shakespeare Quarterly,* 10 (1959), 397–408.

Bradley, A. C. *Shakespearean Tragedy.* London: Macmillan & Company, Ltd., 1904. Part of the material in *Macbeth* is reprinted above.

Champion, Larry S. *Shakespeare's Tragic Perspective.* Athens, Georgia: University of Georgia Press, 1976.

Charlton, H. B. *Shakespearean Tragedy.* New York and London: Cambridge University Press, 1948.

Coleridge, Samuel Taylor. *Shakespearean Criticism,* ed. Thomas Middleton Raysor. New York: E. P. Dutton & Co., Inc., 1960; London: J. M. Dent & Sons, Ltd., 1961. 2 vols.

Driver, Tom. *The Sense of History in Greek and Shakespearean Drama.* New York: Columbia University Press, 1960.

Elliott, G. R. *Dramatic Providence in "Macbeth."* Princeton, N. J.: Princeton University Press, 1958.

Farnham, Willard, *Shakespeare's Tragic Frontier*. Berkeley, Calif.: University of California Press; London: Cambridge University Press, 1950.

Frye, Roland M. "Theological and Non-Theological Structures in Tragedy," *Shakespeare Studies 4,* ed. J. Leeds Barroll. Dubuque: Wm. C. Brown Co., 1972, pp. 132–48.

Honigmann, E. A. J. *Shakespeare: Seven Tragedies*. London: Macmillan, 1976.

Knights, L. C. *Some Shakespearean Themes*. Stanford, Calif.: Stanford University Press, 1960; London: Chatto & Windus, Ltd., 1959.

Mack, Maynard. "The Jacobean Shakespeare: Some Observations on the Construction of the Tragedies," *Stratford-upon-Avon Studies I: Jacobean Theatre*. London: Edward Arnold (Publishers) Ltd., 1960; New York: St. Martin's Press, Inc., 1961, pp. 11–41. Reprinted in the Signet Classic edition of *Othello*.

Mack, Maynard Jr. *Killing the King*. New Haven: Yale University Press, 1973.

Muir, Kenneth, ed. *Shakespeare Survey 19*. Cambridge: Cambridge University Press, 1966.

Paul, Henry N. *The Royal Play of Macbeth*. New York and London: The Macmillan Company, 1950, 1951.

Rosen, William. *Shakespeare and the Craft of Tragedy*. Cambridge, Mass.: Harvard University Press; London: Oxford University Press, 1960.

Stirling, Brents. *Unity in Shakespearian Tragedy*. New York: Columbia University Press; London: Oxford University Press, 1956.

Walker, Roy. *The Time Is Free*. New York: The Macmillan Company; London: Andrew Dakers, Ltd., 1949.

The SIGNET CLASSIC Shakespeare

(0451)

☐ **ALL'S WELL THAT ENDS WELL, Sylvan Barnet,** ed., Tufts University. (516575—$1.95)

☐ **ANTONY AND CLEOPATRA, Barbara Everett,** ed., Cambridge University. (517725—$2.25)

☐ **AS YOU LIKE IT, Albert Gilman,** ed., Boston University. (516672—$1.95)

☐ **THE COMEDY OF ERRORS, Harry Levin,** Harvard. (517423—$2.25)

☐ **CORIOLANUS, Reuben Brower,** ed., Harvard. (515765—$2.25)

☐ **CYMBELINE, Richard Hosley,** ed., University of Arizona. (512685—$1.50)

☐ **HAMLET, Edward Hubler,** ed., Princeton University. (517636—$1.95)

☐ **HENRY IV, Part I, Maynard Mack,** ed., Yale. (515358—$1.95)

☐ **HENRY IV, Part II, Norman H. Holland,** ed., M.I.T. (517229—$2.50)

☐ **HENRY V, John Russell Brown,** ed., University of Birmingham. (515757—$1.95)

☐ **HENRY VI, Part I, Lawrence V. Ryan,** ed., Stanford. (517059—$3.50)

☐ **HENRY VI, Part II, Arthur Freeman,** ed. (515234—$2.95)

☐ **HENRY VI, Part III, Milton Crane,** ed. (513231—$1.95)

☐ **HENRY VIII, Samuel Schoenbaum,** ed., Northwestern University. (512464—$1.50)

☐ **JULIUS CAESAR, William and Barbara Rosen,** eds., University of Connecticut. (514300—$1.75)

☐ **KING JOHN, William H. Matchett,** ed., University of Washington. (513991—$1.95)

☐ **KING LEAR, Russel Fraser,** ed., Princeton University. (517687—$2.25)

☐ **LOVE'S LABOR LOST, John Arthos,** ed., University of Michigan. (517733—$2.50)

Buy them at your local

bookstore or use coupon

on next page for ordering.

The SIGNET CLASSIC Shakespeare

(0451)

- ☐ **MEASURE FOR MEASURE, S. Nagarajan**, ed., University of Poona, India. (514432—$1.95)
- ☐ **MACBETH, Sylvan Barnet**, ed., Tufts University. (515544—$1.95)
- ☐ **THE MERCHANT OF VENICE, Kenneth Myrick**, ed., Tufts University. (516222—$1.95)
- ☐ **THE MERRY WIVES OF WINDSOR, William Green**, ed., Queens College. (515986—$2.25)
- ☐ **A MIDSUMMER NIGHT'S DREAM, Wolfgang Clemen**, ed., University of Munich. (516192—$1.75)
- ☐ **MUCH ADO ABOUT NOTHING, David Stevenson**, ed., Hunter College. (517385—$2.25)
- ☐ **OTHELLO, Alvan Kernan**, ed., Yale University. (517407—$2.95)
- ☐ **RICHARD II, Kenneth Muir**, ed., University of Liverpool. (515188—$1.95)
- ☐ **RICHARD III, Mark Eccles**, ed., University of Wisconsin. (517288—$2.50)
- ☐ **ROMEO AND JULIET, Joseph Bryant**, ed., University of North Carolina. (516354—$1.95)
- ☐ **THE TAMING OF THE SHREW, Robert Heilman**, ed., University of Washington. (516370—$2.25)
- ☐ **THE TEMPEST, Robert Langbaum**, ed., University of Virginia. (515625—$1.95)
- ☐ **THE TWO NOBLE KINSMEN, TITUS ANDRONICUS, PERICLES, Sylvan Barnet**, general ed., Tuffs. (516397—$3.95)
- ☐ **TROILUS AND CRESSIDA, Daniel Seltzer**, ed., Harvard. (516974—$2.25)
- ☐ **TWELFTH NIGHT, Herschel Clay Baker**, ed., Harvard. (517741—$2.25)
- ☐ **THE TWO GENTLEMEN OF VERONA, Bertrand Evans**, ed., University of California. (516494—$2.50)
- ☐ **THE WINTER'S TALE, Frank Kermode**, ed., University of Bristol. (517008—$2.50)
- ☐ **THE SONNETS, William Burto**, ed., Introduction by W. H. Auden. (516478—$2.25)
